Maybe Someday

ADRIAN J. SMITH

EREKA PRESS

Maybe Someday

Cover Design by Cath Grace Designs

CHAPTER

One

ETERNALLY DISSATISFIED WITH EVERYTHING,
especially myself.

The thought cycled through her mind on repeat as Chris pouted in the middle of the restaurant. What the hell was she doing with herself?

"Do you mind if we sit here?" The young brunette pointed at the two chairs next to Chris, her smile cute and her bright blue eyes wide.

Jarred from her deep thoughts, Chris glanced around her favorite restaurant in town. It was packed, and there was no other table in sight that was empty. Chris gripped her soda glass tightly, the cold seeping into her skin. She really probably shouldn't. She'd come there that night to think about her future, evaluate where she wanted to go with her life now that she'd wasted away her retirement and would have to work until she croaked. Morose didn't even begin to describe her mood.

But Chris was nice, and she couldn't break that exterior persona she'd given herself for years, so she nodded. "Sure. It's just me, so the rest of the table is open."

"Thanks." The young woman smiled and moved to sit on the far end of the six-person high top, the woman who was with the brunette mirrored her stance. "I didn't realize it'd be so busy in here."

Chris nodded toward the television screens. "It's Friday, and it's game night. This place fills up pretty quickly." She'd gone there specifically because it would be busy. The background noise was something she was used to, and she craved being around people instead of on her own, where bad things could happen.

"Lucky you for getting here so early." The woman smiled again, her eyes light as if the world of darkness hadn't ever touched her soul. What might that feel like?

Chris wouldn't call it luck getting a table. She'd come immediately from her AA meeting, refusing to go home because she needed to think, and thinking alone could lead to dangerous choices, especially with the mood she was in.

Taking the chance, since she was now stuck with new dinner companions, Chris extended her hand. "I'm Chris."

"I'm Ash. This is my sister, Char."

"Good to meet you." A shiver ran through Chris at the touch of skin to skin. What was that? She hadn't felt that in years. Not this intensely. When her hand slipped away, she missed the touch. No, that was stupid. How could she miss the touch of a stranger?

"You too! And thank you again for letting us sit here. I just moved to town, and we haven't eaten since breakfast. We're starving and need something after unpacking all day."

"I need beer!" Char chimed in with a bit of an obnoxious giggle.

A waitress must have heard them because she came right over to take their drink orders. Ash didn't get an alcoholic drink, which intrigued Chris. She'd never met a young person who was opposed to drinking, but there had to be a few out there.

"Where did you move from?" Chris asked, trying to make polite conversation. That and the opportunity for distraction from her dark thoughts was more than welcome.

"Seattle," Ash answered, sending Chris an appraising look. Her gaze flittered all around Chris' face and down to her chest before back to her eyes. "I wanted to be closer to family."

Where Chris would expect Ash to look at her sister, she didn't. She kept her gaze on Chris the entire time, a deep intensity behind those bright blue eyes. Did Ash just check her out? Refusing to tear her gaze away, Chris turned full bodied toward Ash. This woman, and her intensity, deserved some kind of attention. Something niggled in the back of Chris' mind, something that pulled at the strings of her memories, but it never went beyond that. Still, it bugged her that she couldn't place what that mental tugging was from.

"Sounds reasonable." Chris had wanted to move here for the exact same reason. Her parents lived here, but now that her daughter was grown and out of the house, she'd been debating whether or not to move, to give herself some more space from her ex-wife and start fresh where she didn't have the history of being an alcoholic. That, and her parents had moved to a warmer climate.

"Yeah. I missed you, too!" Char wrinkled her nose as she took a sip of her beer. "You were too holed up by yourself in Seattle. It wasn't good for you."

Well, that was the biggest reason for Chris not moving away. The thought of being alone with no friends around and without her support system scared the living shit out of her.

Ash frowned but said nothing as she took a sip of her soda. There was an awkward pause in the conversation while Char and Ash refused to say whatever the elephant was in the room. Chris wanted to prod it, but that was her protective instincts kicking in, and they didn't have a place here.

"So what's good to eat here?" Ash's voice wobbled when she spoke, a sure sign that there was something deeper going on.

"Everything on the menu is good." Chris shifted in her seat uncomfortably. What was that feeling in the pit of her stomach? She wished belatedly that she'd invited her best friend, Mel, to come along. Chris needed a buffer between them because the things she was feeling she definitely shouldn't be feeling.

"That's good to know." Ash flashed Chris a grin, and Chris nearly melted into it.

Was Ash flirting? No, Chris was reading way too much into this one interaction. There was nothing going on between them, nothing more than two, well three—couldn't forget Char—strangers sharing a table. Chris played with her napkin.

"I think this is the first time I've eaten out without my kids in years." Ash seemed almost wistful.

"Probably," Char commented. "We can fix that, though. There's lots of single ladies in town."

Chris perked up at that. Maybe she hadn't mistaken Ash's attention. Then again, no one would want to date or be with her. She'd been lucky enough to catch someone like her ex-wife, and while they'd been married seventeen years, eventually Andry had left her as well. Chris was too screwed up for love and relationships. But one night stands? That she could manage.

"Char..." Ash answered, her voice tense. "I'm not ready to date anyone just yet."

"But you will be eventually." Char winked. "In which case, I'll be the best wing woman around."

Ash snorted a laugh, shaking her head. Then she turned to Chris, that intense gaze back. "Do you have anyone like this?"

Chris couldn't deny the question. "I do, actually. My best friend, Mel. Ever since she fell in love, she's been harping on me to join her on that train. I'd much rather avoid anything to do with relationships."

"Sounds like a woman after my own heart." Ash's lips pulled upward, curling perfectly.

Char choked on her beer. Ash shot her a dirty look.

Just what is going on here?

Ash was coming on pretty strong for someone who had just moved to town. Maybe she just enjoyed flirting. Chris had met plenty of people like that. Her ex-wife's new fiancée was one of them. And while it took some adjusting to get used to it, they had seemed to find a nice balance of working together. Considering Chris had hired the fiancée to save Andry from getting in trouble for dating her employee, she was happy they all seemed to get along.

But whatever was happening tonight had to be something else. The food they'd ordered arrived together, which shouldn't have surprised Chris. She always got the special treatment when she came here. She had taught the owner when he was in high school all those years ago. It was scary to think that some of the kids she'd taught had grown up and were already parents. It wouldn't be long before she started to see her students' kids in her current school, would it? She was surprised it hadn't happened yet.

Her depressed mood deepened. She was old, broken, and had nothing to show for it. She was in the same spot she'd been when she started out teaching, for the most part. Single. Broke. Struggling. The only difference was she'd become a drunk and now she was sober. Oh, and that divorce in there, too.

Wrinkling her nose, Chris dug into her dinner.

She had screwed up her life so much that she'd spend the next twenty years just putting everything back together. If she was lucky enough to even accomplish that.

"Ash is ready to get a new start on life." Char was already ordering a second drink. "She needs a break."

"Shut up, Char," Ash hissed.

Chris' lips quirked up, a chuckle nearly bursting from her. "Aren't sisters the best?"

"Do you have any?"

"One sister and one brother." Chris winked. "I'm the middle child."

Ash shook her head slowly. "I'm glad to be the youngest."

"But the more responsible one?" Chris pointed at the drinks to make her point. She was genuinely curious why Ash wasn't drinking, but she hadn't gotten up the courage to ask.

Ash's full lips parted before she finally looked Chris in the eye. "Some days, but not every day." The wink at the end was what took the cake.

Chris' heart went into overdrive, fluttering away at the blatant flirting. She would accept the flirting. It felt good to have attention on her even though she knew in the end she wasn't worth it. That was the whole purpose of non-committed relationships. No one ever had to know that she was shattered into a million pieces that could never be put back together again.

Chris grinned, relaxing even more into the conversation. "Being responsible is boring sometimes."

"True, but it keeps me out of trouble." Ash reached over and set her hand on Chris' briefly before moving back to her own space.

"Hey! I'm not trouble!" Char pouted, but she was about to break into a smile.

Ash shook her head, lips curled upward. "Sure you're not. That's why we're eating dinner at nine at night with a stranger because you just had to deal with the yard before unpacking the house. Which also means that I have a whole lot more work to do tomorrow with the girls around."

Chris chuckled. "My ex-wife would accuse me of the same thing. Always wanting to get the fun stuff done first."

"That'd be Char," Ash commented.

"And what about you? Do you always focus on the important things first?" Chris was fully engaged in the conversation now, forgetting why she'd originally gone out tonight.

"When I can." Ash pressed her lips together thinly, her entire focus on Chris. Her blue eyes contained a depth that Chris knew she was only dipping her toe into.

Did that mean something? Ash reached out, a hand on Chris' gently before retreating. That was the second time that happened. Chris flicked her gaze down to her fingers, still tingling from the touch.

"Are you a risk taker?" Ash asked, her tone light, but Chris could tell there was hidden meaning in the words.

"Some would call me that." Chris was enjoying this a little too much, but having the attention of a younger woman on her felt so damn good. Maybe she was worth something, even if it was a tryst for a night. Not that a night together would ever happen. Ash hadn't made any overt comments about anything like that.

"I can be, too." Ash winked, moving her hand back to Chris'. This time, it stayed there.

Chris had to bite back a moan at the sensations floating through her. She would take whatever Ash was willing to give her tonight. The distraction, the flirting, the attention was everything she needed to avoid the intense life choices she was contemplating.

"Hey Chris."

Chris shot her chin up, staring directly into the dark brown eyes of her ex-wife. Andry's fiancée, Isla, clung to her arm, hands folded together, a subtle cringe on her face as if she really didn't want to be here either.

"Andry," Chris' voice wavered. "Date night?"

"I see we were thinking the same thing." Andry glanced toward Ash, curiously, and the assumption Andry had made didn't go over Chris' head. Did Andry really think that she was on a date tonight? "We have a table over there, but I just thought we'd say hi."

Andry would do that, keep the tension and the awkwardness out of everything. She was so damn good at that. Chris envied it because she had been so weird around Andry since they'd separated. It had taken her years to figure out how to have a simple conversation that didn't revolve around money or their daughter. But they had managed it recently, and Chris applauded herself for that. Maybe they could eventually become friends again without all the pain and hurt coming up.

"Enjoy your dinner," Chris said, but her voice was tighter

than she expected it to be, the pit of unease burrowing its way into her chest.

"You too." Andry gave a broad smile as she turned.

Isla nodded her head toward Chris. "See you Monday."

"See you, Isla."

When Chris looked back at Ash, she realized belatedly that Ash hadn't taken her hand off Chris' during that entire interaction. "You okay?"

"Yeah," Chris squeaked out. "Andry is my ex-wife. We've been divorced about three years now. We're all good."

"I'm so sorry."

Shaking her head, Chris reached across to Ash's hand on hers and squeezed Ash's fingers with her free hand. "Don't be. It wasn't that messy, and we're both happier for it."

"I guess that's good."

"How long were you married?" Char chimed in, her second beer already gone as she flagged down a waiter for another.

"Seventeen years," Chris mumbled, dropping her gaze to Ash's still clasped hand. She reluctantly released her, and while Ash let go of Chris' fingers, she dropped her warm palm to Chris' thigh.

"That's a long time," Ash stated.

"Yeah. We got married young. Actually we got married a week after I finished my bachelor's degree."

"Higher education is so sexy on a woman." Ash's cheeks burned pink.

Chris' jaw dropped. That was definitely flirting. Covering Ash's hand with her own, Chris laughed. "Wait until you find out that I got my masters and then my doctorate about ten years later."

Ash's lips parted, her eyebrows raised slightly as she looked directly into Chris' eyes. "Are you trying to make something of this?"

"Only if you are."

Char snorted and then cheered as another drink was brought to her.

"I think your sister is getting drunk."

"She told me she would," Ash whispered.

"Is that why you're not drinking tonight?" There. Chris had finally asked the question. But when had she lowered her voice so it would be hard for Char to hear the conversation? And when had she leaned in like she was going to kiss Ash?

"It's one of the reasons." Ash moved in slightly.

Chris sucked in a sharp breath and pulled back. She was way in over her head. But the tingles running through her body, the warmth in her crotch, and the flutters in her belly told her that the attention Ash was giving her was exactly what she wanted.

Still, that niggling voice in the back of her head told her there was something she was missing throughout this entire interaction. It irked her that she couldn't remember it, but that was an issue with her because of her alcoholism. She just couldn't remember things the way she used to. But she really didn't want to bring up those painful emotions when Ash's hand was still on her thigh and inching higher.

"I think we're about done," Chris announced, waving the waitress down. "Can we have the check?"

"Are you splitting it?"

Ash looked down at her empty plate and then at Char who was halfway through her beer and her dinner was completely gone. Chris glanced at her. "Are you done?"

"Yes," Ash answered confidently.

"One check, please."

"You don't have to do that."

"You just moved here. It's my housewarming gift to you." Chris couldn't help but see Andry's gaze on her from across the room. What on earth was going on with her tonight? She'd been handed a golden opportunity for distraction, and she'd taken it. But just how far could she make this distraction go?

"Are you sure?"

"Yes." Chris smiled, covering Ash's hand on her leg and curling their fingers together. She doubted it would go past this, but it was nice to think that someone might want to touch her again. Maybe she wasn't as obviously screwed up as she thought. But when people got to know her, there was no denying it.

Once she had paid, and the three of them stood up, Chris gripped onto the back of the chair. What was she thinking? There was no way a woman years younger than her would be interested in her. Ash was merely trying to comfort her. She must be an empath or something.

Ash stepped close to Chris, but it was probably by accident. Sucking in a deep breath, Chris pushed in her chair and stopped short when she turned to find Andry standing right in front of her. Isla remained at the table, eyeing both of them.

"Chris." Andry stood up and stepped in close. She grabbed Chris' elbow, holding her in place. "Hold on a minute."

Chris stayed still, confused. "What?"

Andry moved her mouth close to Chris' ear, the heat from her breath fluttering across Chris' neck. "I just want you to be happy. Please know that."

The words echoed from what Chris had told her over a year ago, when Chris had agreed to hire Isla, when she'd finally let the water go under the bridge and stopped holding onto old grudges.

"Don't hold yourself back from happiness." Andry squeezed Chris' arm and let go. "Give yourself permission to enjoy life again."

Stunned. Chris stared into her ex-wife's eyes completely surprised. "Uh, yeah."

"Good." Andry leaned in and kissed her cheek. "I'll see you around, Chris."

Chris nearly stumbled as she stepped backward and out of Andry's reach. She waited until Andry sat back down with Isla, a knowing look on her face. Was the whole world out to get her into a relationship? First Mel and now her ex-wife? What was this? Especially considering she'd just met Ash that night—though Andry wouldn't know that, would she?

Ash wrapped her arm around Chris, and they started for the parking lot. Chris had parked up close since she had gotten there early enough. Ash snagged Chris' hand and held her back. "Thank you so much for letting us sit with you tonight."

"You're welcome."

"I hope we didn't ruin your night."

"Hardly." Chris couldn't stop staring down into Ash's eyes. "You honestly added to it. So thank you for joining me."

"Will I see you around?"

"If you want, that'd be nice."

Ash squeezed her hand and then let go, snagging her phone. "Give me your number."

Chris furrowed her brow but put her number into Ash's phone. This pretty much sealed the deal that there wouldn't be one-night of fuckery going on. Ash was probably looking for more of a relationship than Chris was, which meant this wouldn't work out in the end for either of them.

"I'll text you," Ash said, looking down into Chris' eyes.

"Yeah. Sure." Chris shoved her hands in her pockets. "See you around."

Ash snagged Char's arm and dragged her toward the back of the parking lot. Chris pursed her lips and rocked back on her heels. She was attracted to Ash, that was for sure. No doubts about that. But she had doubts about everything else between them. Still, she was allowed to look at attractive single women. There was nothing holding her back from that, and Ash's little glance over her shoulder as she walked away was the perfect reminder of that.

CHAPTER
Two

ASH SAT in the driver's seat of her car, turning the key, and hearing nothing. The engine didn't spark to life. The battery didn't click. The radio didn't even hum. All she had was the sound of dead silence. She closed her eyes, a pit in her stomach opening up and sinking. Of all things to continue to go awry. Everything had gone haywire since she'd decided to move to Cheyenne.

"What's wrong?" Char chimed from the passenger seat, her voice slurred from the amount of alcohol she'd had.

"No clue. I'll need a tow if Dad can't fix it." Ash fingered her phone, not wanting to call him. It wasn't in her nature to ask for help, even when she knew her parents would freely offer it. They'd given her the chance to live with them until she found a house she liked, but she'd bought one as soon as she could to avoid that.

"We can call him for a ride." Char would think it was okay. She'd always been daddy's little girl. Ash had been the independent one.

"I guess." She knew Char could probably barely hear her, but the sinking feeling in her stomach increased. Dinner had been so nice. Chris had been lovely, and Ash hadn't willingly thrown herself into flirting since—she couldn't think about that. Not now. If she did, she'd break down and cry.

Frustrated, Ash grabbed her phone and got out of the car, needing space. Cold air bit at her cheeks in the late January winter, but she couldn't be bothered with it. Was she even supposed to move here? Because it seemed like the universe was telling her this was a bad idea the moment the decision had been made. Even her girls had struggled with it. Hell, Avonlee still was, and Ash knew it was going to be a hell of a year.

A car stopped in the middle of the parking lot, blocking her vehicle in. Panic swelled in her chest, but she had to remind herself that she was in Cheyenne, not Seattle. No one was going to kidnap her here. At least she hoped not.

The driver's window rolled down, and she was greeted with Chris' confused and concerned face. She was adorable. There was something about her that had just put Ash at ease in a way she hadn't been in so very long. Being childless that night had made the decision to break down some of her usual walls easy. And Chris had warmed to her in an instant.

"Everything okay?" Chris stayed still, looking around at the car.

Ash shook her head before she could stop herself. "My car won't start."

"Shit." Chris shoved the car into park, shifting in her seat. "Is the battery dead?"

Ash frowned. "Don't think so. I was going to call my dad for a ride. Unless you know something about cars...?" She trailed off, hoping Chris would know everything about vehicles. Wasn't that a thing? Lesbians could fix cars? Butches? But was Chris really a butch? She didn't quite fit that definition, not that Ash liked labels.

"Not a clue about anything under the hood. Well, that hood." Chris' cheeks lit up a bright red in the parking lot lights.

Cursing her lack of luck, Ash straightened her shoulders. "Oh, well, thanks."

"Do you want to sit in my car while you wait? It's cold outside."

Ash dragged in a deep breath, looking through the driver's window. She put her hands against the sill, pulling herself up just to be closer to Chris. "Are you sure?"

"Yeah, I don't mind." Chris touched Ash's cold fingers. "It's still warming up, but it's better than being out in the wind."

"Let me get Char." Flipping around the back end of her car, Ash went to the passenger side to drag Char with her. Ash was so thankful to be sitting inside Chris' SUV warming up. They settled while Chris found a parking spot as close as possible to Ash's dead car. That fix was going to be expensive, which was the last thing she needed that month. At least the car had made it to Cheyenne. That was the silver lining, she supposed.

Blowing out a breath, Ash glanced at her phone, noting the time. It was close to ten-thirty at night. Her parents were likely sound asleep, and she really didn't want to wake them up for something as benign as this.

Char glanced at Ash's hands with the phone and Dad's number pulled up. Then Char locked her eyes on Ash's. Leaning forward, Char mumbled, "You can thank me later."

"What?"

"Do you think you could just drive us home? I don't want to inconvenience you, but it's late and we'd have to wake our dad up to get him out here."

"Oh." Chris turned around in her seat, her arm brushing Ash's in between the front seats as she looked back at Char. "Yeah, that's not a problem."

"Thanks." Char sat back, with her arms crossed, and a pleased look on her face.

They gave over their addresses, and Chris backed out of the parking spot. By the time they reached the main road, the heat was on full blast, and Ash's fingers were warming up instead of feeling like they were going to fall off. She had forgotten how cold the Rocky Mountains could be in winter.

"Char, you're the first one since it's the closest."

"Righteo, ma'am." Char chuckled.

Ash resisted rolling her eyes, but barely. Char was good and drunk, and she would have the hangover of a lifetime tomorrow when they unpacked even more of her house. Which meant she would be in charge of something away from everyone else and not keeping the girls out of Ash's hair while Ash set up their room. They still had to build the beds and find all their clothes, but their room was Ash's first priority.

Chris reached over and touched Ash's hand as she drove down the street. This was the comfort Ash had found, and it was so odd that it was with a complete stranger. Then again, something about Chris seemed so familiar, like a name on the tip of her tongue that she just couldn't manage to form the syllables of. Looking out the front windshield, Ash noted that everything was darker here than in Seattle. Fewer lights because of fewer people. It suited Ash's mood for the last two years. She'd been unable to get out of the funk since her wife had died, not that she was looking to fully get out of it either. She'd found she liked being the broken widow.

Leaning back in the seat, Chris drove, and silence permeated the car. Ash had no idea what to say to get the conversation going, but she didn't really want to either. She enjoyed the quiet, which was a rare occurrence when she was stuck at home with her two girls and no one else. Their fighting had been reaching an all time high lately. It took everything in her to keep from losing her temper, and she failed at that most times.

If only Mari was still there with her. She had the patience of Job. Ash found herself gripping Chris' hand tightly, and she pushed all thoughts of her late wife from her mind. Mari was gone and had been for two years. And it had been two years since Ash had allowed another woman to touch her. So what was it about Chris that made her think about this?

"Oh! This is me!" Char bubbled from the back seat. Chris

pulled up at the apartment building and parked. "Call me in the morning, Ash."

"Yeah, will do." But Ash wasn't looking at her sister. Instead she found herself looking into Chris' deep brown eyes, the tight curls of her hair as it fell over her shoulders and curved right along with her breasts. Ash's heart raced. Was she really considering this?

It would only be one night—that was for sure. Because she had already found the love of her life. She didn't need to find it again. Mari had been her perfect match, and she wasn't going to let that go ever.

"Where do you live?"

"Sun Valley."

"I know that area well. My best friend lives there." Chris still hadn't put the car back into drive. They were still looking at each other. Chris reached up, her fingers hesitating before she brushed a strand of Ash's hair behind her ear. "I hope that's okay."

Ash smiled, genuine happiness filling her chest. When was the last time that had happened? She nearly cried, feeling as though she should dig back down into the pit of grieving where she belonged. "It's welcome."

"Good." The lines in Chris' face softened, her smile fully blooming. "I'd hoped I wasn't misreading things."

"Char's *you'll thank me later* wasn't enough of a tell?"

"I never like to assume." Chris' thumb brushed along Ash's cheek.

The tender touch moved tingles through Ash's body, over her breasts, and hardened her nipples. Her breathing increased, and she leaned into it. One night. Physical touch. That's all this would ever be. "Are you going to take me home?"

"Do you want me to?" Chris' thumb moved to Ash's lips. "We can go anywhere you want."

"My house is a disaster. Boxes everywhere. No sheets on the bed." The excuses were already piling up, but Ash shoved them back down. Just because she'd found the love of her life didn't mean she couldn't also enjoy the physical side of being with someone. Right?

"Where would you be more comfortable?" Chris trailed her thumb down the hollow of Ash's neck, curling her fingers around the back, her thumb pressed right to the center.

It was possessive, but in a gentle way, a taste and promise of what Ash hoped was about to come. Ash wrinkled her nose at the unintentional but perfect pun. She loved that Chris was asking this. No one ever had before. With Mari, their first time had been in a random hotel room while they'd been on a work trip. Ash bit her lip, raising her gaze to meet Chris' and pulled herself out of her thoughts again.

"I'll be comfortable anywhere."

"Want to go to my place? It's messy, but I do have sheets on the bed. I may even have a blanket if we get cold." Chris winked, and it sank any excuses Ash had left. Not that she was looking very hard for them.

"What did your ex-wife say to you before we left?" Ash leaned in closer, the pressure of Chris' thumb on her throat tantalizing.

"She told me that she wanted me to be happy." Chris dashed her tongue across her lips. "She told me that I should allow myself to be happy."

"Do you hold back?"

"Not from this." Chris' voice was husky, full of deep desire. "Never from this."

"And what is this?"

"A night of happiness."

Ash could get on board with that. Leaning in closer, she nearly pressed their mouths together, but again, something held her back. Ash locked their gazes, her breathing shallow as Chris kept her grip on the side of Ash's neck firm. "Why do I feel like I've known you for years?"

"No idea." Chris' voice was soft, merely a breath of words.

"Are you sure you want this? We can always stop. I can drop you off at home, and that can be it."

Ash couldn't look away. Her body screamed *Yes, touch me!* Still, something lingered in her brain that there was more going on than merely sex. It was her first time since Mari. The first occasion she'd allowed herself to be this free with someone.

"Take me home, Chris. A night of happiness is what you promised me, and I'm cashing in on that."

Chris' grin was gorgeous. Ash's lips tingled, desperation pulling at her to just act already. But Chris didn't kiss her. Not yet. They would do this quickly, in the right time, when they were just there for fucking. Or was Chris one of those women who wouldn't kiss her at all? Ash would hate that, but she would go along with it if it was what Chris wanted.

With the car in drive, Chris pulled out of Char's apartment complex. Ash didn't want to lose the connection they'd found, so she rested her hand on Chris' thigh, trailing slow circles against the inside of her leg.

"Keep doing that, and we might not make it home."

Ash gave a short grunt. "I've had sex in a car before."

"Recently?" Chris shot her a glance before focusing back on the road.

"No. Not since I was in my early twenties."

"I'm a bit old for car sex, I think. Unless it's in the bed of a truck with an air-mattress."

"Not too difficult to arrange." Ash slid her hand up, pressing the edge of her pinky against the crease in Chris' leg. "Too much?"

"No," Chris squeaked. "Feel free to go farther."

"My kind of woman. Knows what she wants."

"When it comes to sex, I've never been accused of being timid."

Ash flicked her fingers between Chris' legs, over her crotch, against the heat pouring from between her legs and through her jeans. "You already feel amazing."

Chris grunted, her fingers tightening on the steering wheel, but she widened her knees enough for Ash to get a better angle and apply more pressure. "I can't wait to touch you."

"You'll have to. This is the bonus of not being the driver." Ash pressed three fingers hard against Chris.

Chris wiggled, and it brought a smile to Ash's lips. She still had it. Two years of no sex meant nothing. This was like riding a bike.

"Do you like it when I touch you like this?"

Turning to fully look Ash in the eyes, Chris winked. "You can touch me however you want."

"Perfect," Ash purred. "Because if we're only going to do this for one night, I want to make the most of it."

When had she become so confident? Ash was loving this side of herself. Something in Chris pulled it out of her in a way that she was adoring right now. In any other situation, she probably would hate it.

"Oh yes," Chris crooned. "Yes, let's make the most of it."

"That's all I can ask for." Because Ash didn't want anything else. "To our night of happiness."

CHAPTER
Three

"WE'RE HERE."

Chris pulled up outside her rental and put the car in park. Now what? Ash still had her fingers against her crotch, a slow deliberate pattern playing against her clit which made her anticipate what was to come more and more by the minute. But this still felt so awkward, somewhat stilted. Chris wasn't good with words. She wasn't good with controlling these kinds of situations despite what she'd implied earlier. Suddenly, she was nervous. That's what this was.

"Good." Ash leaned over, increasing the pressure between Chris' legs.

Chris groaned, rolling her shoulders back into the seat and closing her eyes as she finally let the full brunt of the sensations Ash caused to flow through her. She missed someone else touching her like this. Her own hand was useful, but having someone else interested, someone else who directed was gold. Chris bit the inside of her cheek.

"Keep doing that, Ash, and we're not going to make it inside."

"Definitely wouldn't want to miss that."

With a thundering heart, Chris forced her eyes open. Ash

looked so damn pleased with herself, her eyes bright and wide, her cheeks flushed. Chris blew out a breath and cupped Ash's chin, pulling her forward so their mouths could touch. The kiss was quick, and when Chris dove back in for a second one, Ash surged forward, and their teeth gnashed. Ash hissed and pulled back, rubbing her fingers over her lips.

"Sorry," Chris murmured. She wasn't good at this anymore.

Ash giggled and moved in swiftly with a peck of a kiss. "Don't stop now."

Chris pulled herself together, gathering what self-esteem she still had and dragged Ash's mouth back to hers. This time was so much better. They went slowly, a gentle push of lips against lips. Ash's hand was still pressed between Chris' legs, and as soon as Chris dashed her tongue against Ash's lips, Ash moved her fingers in a mimicking swipe.

Holy crap, she knows what she's doing.

Moaning, Chris opened her mouth and accepted Ash's tongue. Their embrace deepened. Heat rose in Chris' cheeks, sending shivers down her body, through her veins as the anticipation of what was happening ramped up again. Ash moved her fingers fully now, *press in, release, press in, release.* Chris was going to lose her mind without even making it inside.

She pulled back, rapid breaths leaving her lips. "We need to go inside."

"Yes, yes we do." Ash sounded as harried as Chris felt.

Without waiting, Chris opened the door and got out. She knew Ash would follow. They both wanted this immediately. Chris glanced over her shoulder as she opened the front door. Ash was right there. Flutters flew through her chest with anticipation and excitement. She needed this more than she cared to fully admit.

Snagging Ash's hand, Chris tugged Ash to her and pushed Ash against the door while she flipped the locks in place. Their mouths met in a feverish kiss. Chris sucked in a breath, her fingers finding their way back to Ash's neck and holding on while her other hand slid down the side of Ash's body, finally getting the full feel of her curves.

"You're gorgeous," Chris said before diving back in for another kiss.

Ash whined, her nails digging into Chris' back as she pulled Chris closer. Chris rocked her hips against Ash's body, having to tilt her chin up while they continued to kiss. Sinking into this feeling was exactly what she'd needed, the perfect distraction, the best kind actually. Andry used to distract her like this when they'd first started dating all those years ago. Chris pulled Ash's lower lip into her mouth and sucked.

Grinning, Ash dug her fingers under Chris' shirt and pulled it upward. This woman was fire. Chris had thought she was timid at first, but nothing about this exchange was hesitant. Chris kissed her fully again and moved to pull her shirt over her head, dropping it to the floor. While Chris knew she had good tits, that was about it. The rest of her body left a whole lot to be desired from her rectangular shape and narrow hips to her aging face and broad shoulders. Ash rested her shoulders against the door and ran her fingers smoothly across Chris' shoulders, her collar bone, and down between her breasts before bursting into a broad smile.

"I knew you were stunning under all of this."

"This?" Chris asked.

Ash leaned forward and deftly flicked the clasp of Chris' bra to unhook it. Both her hands covered Chris' breasts in an instant, massaging gently as she looked right into Chris' eyes. This was sexy as hell. Chris shook her head slowly and let out one chuckle before she reached for Ash's pants and pulled at her belt and the button.

Chris had her hand sliding down the front of Ash's pants in a second. "Please let me touch you."

"Oh my god, yes." Ash spread her legs, her shoulders once again resting on the door. "Touch me."

Nuzzling her nose into Ash's neck, Chris found her warm and

waiting. She wasn't quite soaking wet yet, but they had time for that. Chris started with a soft tease against Ash's clit, just a slow circle with the pads of her fingers. "So good."

Ash moaned, rocking her hips into Chris' fingers. "Why do you seem so familiar?"

Chris nearly faltered in her touch. But she managed to keep her pace. Moving away slightly, she looked up into Ash's face. Ash had her eyes closed, her lips slightly parted. Chris had thought the same thing, but she'd brushed it aside as nothing more than her brain being weird after years of drinking, but maybe there was more to it than this.

"Kismet?" Chris answered, not quite sure what else to say. Ash did seem familiar, but she couldn't place from where or what. And it wasn't like Chris had a wild life outside of school and her daughter.

"Yeah, that sounds about right." Ash's words were a breath of a whisper. "Keep that up and I'm going to come already."

Chris laughed. "Did you think I'd only get you off once tonight?"

"Fuck me," Ash muttered.

"Plan to," Chris responded, increasing the pressure of her fingers.

Ash's breath caught in her throat. She wrapped her arms around Chris' back and held her close. Chris moved her fingers lower, testing now to see if she could figure out where Ash was, and sure enough, wet heat pooled between Ash's legs. Chris slid her fingers through Ash's slit, gathering the moisture and moving right back to her clit.

"Fuck yes," Ash said, louder this time.

That had been exactly what they'd needed. Lubrication. Chris stopped the circles and instead started a back-and-forth pattern that sent shudders through Ash. She loved being able to see Ash's reactions to everything she was doing. She nipped at Ash's neck, biting slightly but not enough to leave a mark since they hadn't talked about that yet.

Ash tilted her head to the side, as if asking for more, so Chris did it again and again. Chris pushed Ash's shirt up over her breasts and pressed wet kisses to the soft skin she revealed. If she'd had her head on straight, she would have stripped Ash down first before she'd started this, but she'd had one goal in mind—give Ash as much pleasure as possible—and she certainly wasn't going to give in on that one. Not ever.

"Faster," Ash groaned the word.

Chris dipped back down for more moisture and picked up speed as commanded. She was willing to do anything Ash wanted her to do.

"Bite me."

Swirling her tongue against Ash's pillowy skin, Chris then sucked. She scraped her teeth. Teasing, she waited to bite, wanting to drag this out even longer, but it seemed as if Ash was looking for something specific that night.

"Bite me," Ash ground out, her jaw clenched.

Doing as she was told, Chris bit into the tender flesh at the top of Ash's breast. She sucked, knowing there would be a mark left on her skin. That thought sent a thrill through her. One night of happiness that would be a vivid memory for days. Chris bit again, harder this time, as it seemed to spur Ash on.

"God yes." Ash's voice was getting louder.

If they weren't careful, Chris' neighbors would make snarky comments in the morning. They were nosey old biddies. Still, Chris couldn't bring herself to care, not tonight, not with Ash hot against her fingers, rutting into her hand.

Ash clenched hard against Chris' back, her entire body jerking with a start. A smile lit up her face, her eyes still clenched, and her head thrown back against the door. Her cry of pleasure careened through the living room and was pure satisfaction to Chris. She had done something right for once, and while it was an easy thing, it was still something.

Without warning, Ash cupped Chris' cheeks and kissed her deeply. She straightened up and pushed Chris backward. Chris' butt hit her couch, and Ash knocked her over the arm of it. She gripped wildly at the back cushion to catch herself so she didn't fall, staring up into Ash's clouded eyes. Ash moved toward the door and hit the light switch, making it so Chris could see her full face.

"Your turn," Ash cooed. "Pull your pants down."

Chris hummed, but she righted her feet on the correct side of the couch and undid the button and zipper on her jeans, shimmying them and her underwear down to her knees. Ash knelt before her, sliding her palms up and down her thighs. Chris bent down kissing Ash fully.

"Mouth?" Ash asked.

"Yes." Chris pecked her lips again.

Ash pulled Chris' Chucks off and tossed them behind her, then pulled her pants all the way off. She stared, eyes wide, hands smoothly moving, but Ash stayed still for the most part. Chris' heart rate ramped up, a deep understanding of what Ash was looking at. Her ugly body. Her weirdly shaped chicken legs and definitely unshaved legs—because she hadn't expected this when she'd gone out tonight.

"Gorgeous," Ash whispered, breaking Chris' train of thought.

"What?" Chris barked.

"I said you're gorgeous."

Chris snorted lightly, but Ash didn't hear her. She was already pressing kisses against the tops of Chris' thighs and toward her knees, then back up again. Chris clenched her jaw as she waited for Ash's mouth to be right where she wanted it.

Ash didn't hold back. Chris' toes pressed into the floor as she lifted her hips up to meet Ash's intense licking and sucking. Chris bit back a moan and scrunched her nose. She was so much closer than she'd originally thought. All that teasing in the car, getting Ash off so quickly, Chris was ready for this.

"You taste so good," Ash murmured before diving back in.

"Yeah," was all Chris could manage to say, but she had no idea why she was saying it. She was at a complete loss for coherent words, something that was actually quite hard to achieve for her. Her fingers dug into the fabric on the back couch cushion, her nails hurt from how tightly she held onto it.

Ash dug her arms up under Chris' thighs, curling her hands around to hold on tightly and direct the movement. Chris loved that Ash was taking control now because while Chris liked giving all the attention, she wasn't sure that she could focus enough to do anything right now.

In an instant, it was like Ash was everywhere, surrounding Chris. Her mouth, fingers, scent. Everything was about this woman with her face buried between Chris' legs. Chris reached down and gripped the top of Ash's head as she crashed through her orgasm hard. The hardest one she'd had in years. She gasped for breath, her stomach heaving as she tried to breathe through the pleasure that consumed every inch of her body and washed all thoughts from her mind.

Ash pressed wet kisses to her legs, her stomach, her breasts, pulling Chris' nipples between her lips and teasing with the tip of her tongue. If Chris hadn't just had the best orgasm she'd experienced in the last decade, she'd be able to pay more attention to it. Instead, her mind swirled as she tried to focus on anything happening.

"Want another one?" Ash asked, her high-pitched, over-curious tone.

"I want that every day for the rest of my life." Chris laughed, the sound rolling through her freely. She was so relaxed, so carefree and purely herself in a way that she hadn't allowed in so long. She couldn't even remember the last time. Ash nipped just above Chris' hip, emitting a squeak from her.

"One night of happiness."

"Yeah, one night." Chris pushed up, moving into a sitting position, and the loudest queef left her, the air pushing through her swollen folds with a tickle. She looked directly into Ash's surprised gaze and burst out laughing. The joy emulated through her, filling all the gaps that had been left in the wake of her alcoholism, her divorce, her fuck ups. It was pure, simple, and perfect.

She landed on her back, the laughs rolling through her until tears streamed out of the corner of her eyes. Ash chuckled right along with her, climbing onto the couch with Chris. Ash's elbows pressed into the cushion on either side of Chris' head as Ash stared down at her, her lips parted as the rumbles of joy moved through her too.

"Holy crap." Chris laughed again. "I love laughing during sex."

"Me too." Ash bent down and kissed Chris loudly. "I'm so glad we managed to do that."

"Yes." Chris threaded her fingers through Ash's deep brown hair and pulled her in for another kiss. This one lingered. "Laughing feels so good."

"Happiness," Ash whispered.

"Yeah, happiness." Chris flittered her fingers over Ash's lips. "We're not done, are we?"

"I hope not."

"Good." Chris pulled at Ash's shirt and then her bra. "Do I have you all night?"

"If you want. Sleeping alone in my house is unappealing."

"Then stay here." Chris looked up at Ash, the seriousness of Ash's comment burrowing deep within her heart. There was an undertone to the words that Chris was missing. Then again, they were only there for one night, which meant she shouldn't be diving too deeply into what could be considered relationship territory.

"Are you sure?"

"Absolutely. It gives me more time to have my way with you."

"I wish I had your stamina." Ash laughed as she laid down fully on top of Chris, finally skin to skin.

"Oh, that feels good."

"It sure does." Ash kissed Chris' cheek, then her forehead,

then she moved toward Chris' ear, pulling her lobe between her teeth. "I would love you to make me come again."

"I plan on it. The night is still young." Even if she wasn't. Chris could stand to lose one night of sleep for this. Because one night was all she deserved, and she'd take it. "Take your pants off and sit on me."

"With pleasure."

"THANKS FOR THE NIGHT OF HAPPINESS." Ash winked as she leaned over the center console bright and early Saturday morning. She pressed her mouth to Chris' in one last lingering moment of joy before she pulled away. Ash only had an hour, if she was lucky, before her family showed up, and she should probably get a shower to wash off the night and wake up more with a double dose of caffeine. Chris had kept her up until the wee hours of the morning.

"Same." Chris smiled, her cheeks flushing. It was adorable, and Ash couldn't resist as she leaned in for one last kiss. This time she lingered, dashing her tongue out as if doing that would keep the memory of last night alive for years to come. If this was the only time she was going to have that intimate touch, then she was going to take what was offered.

Jumping out of Chris' SUV, Ash nearly skipped up the front sidewalk to her house. When she got to her front door and had it unlocked, Ash glanced over her shoulder to find Chris still parked in front of the house, the window down as she watched. Ash waved before stepping inside. With the door shut, she leaned against it like she had the night before, her hand over her heart and a smile on her face.

That had been one of the riskiest things she had ever done. But it was absolutely worth it. She could still feel Chris' fingers inside her. And when Ash closed her eyes, Chris' tongue swiped at her again. Her cheeks reddened as her body was ready to go another round, but she'd known she had to get back to the real world. One night of happiness was all they had promised each other.

"Where the hell have you been?"

Ash jumped. Her heart was in her throat, the color and heat draining from her face. "Char!"

Char laughed, but she still looked a little gray at the gills. "Did you fuck her?"

"Damnit, Char!" Ash looked around the disaster of a house, making sure they were alone.

Char waved her hand. "I'm the only one here."

"I'm surprised you're even up this early."

"You know me and drinking. Late to bed and early up. Drove over here to get a start on finding your coffee." Char held out a mug. "Thought you might need it."

"I already regret giving you the spare key," Ash mumbled as she walked by her sister and toward the kitchen. Thankfully, Char had made enough coffee to last Ash half the morning. She was going to need more before lunch that was for sure.

"You'll love it, trust me."

"Sure I will." Rolling her eyes, Ash poured herself a mug.

"You're wearing the same clothes you were yesterday, your hair is a mess, you have that just-fucked look, and the car still isn't back. So...give me the deets."

Ash snorted. "Not happening."

"But your first time since Mari?"

That stopped Ash in her tracks. She had been doing so good that morning, well really since she'd stepped foot into Chris' place. But to have Char shove it in her face that she'd willingly had sex with a woman who wasn't her wife? Yeah, that stung a whole lot more than she expected. Ash closed in on herself, focusing on the coffee in her mug and the sinking feeling of regret and guilt that ate away the lining of her stomach.

"Oh Ash, I didn't mean it like that."

"It's nothing. Have you talked to Dad?"

"About what?"

"My car."

"Oh!" Char shook her head. "Nope. Mom texted and said they'd be around with breakfast at nine."

"Breakfast?" Ash got hopeful. She had no food in her kitchen yet. Her parents had taken the girls on a wild excursion yesterday to explore the town, leaving Char and Ash to do the dirty work, which they hadn't really accomplished without supervision, like usual.

"McDonalds, I think."

"Perfect." It wasn't exactly what Ash wanted. She was tired of fast food after driving a U-Haul across half the country, but since she wasn't buying and it was coming to her, she'd eat whatever they brought. "What are we working on today?"

"You're avoiding," Char teased.

"Damn straight I am." Ash walked away from her sister and into the bathroom. Shower first, and then she could get started on putting her house together.

She had just stepped out of the shower and wrapped the towel around her chest when she heard the front door slam shut. Well, her whole family was here now. At least she knew Char could keep a secret because her parents finding out she had a one-night stand wasn't something that she wanted to get out. She dried herself off and got dressed immediately.

The noise was unmistakable. Avonlee and Rhubie screamed bloody murder at each other as they came into the house, and Ash's spine was straight with tension in an instant. Avonlee had been antagonizing Rhubie every moment she had the opportunity to. Ash swung out of her bedroom and glared at Avonlee.

"What?" Avonlee snarked.

"Don't you *what* me!" Ash pointed at her. "I'm sick of the attitude. Enough."

Avonlee rolled her eyes, but she did stop. Begrudgingly. Ash straightened her back and put her hands on her hips, surveying her daughter. In two years, they had made very little progress in moving forward on what was coming between them. In fact, it was probably getting worse, and Ash was out of ideas on how to fix it or even work on it.

Therapy had failed. Patience had been a blunder. Ash was at a complete loss.

Rhubie ran up, wrapping her arms around Ash's waist and holding on tightly. Ash combed her fingers through her daughter's hair and bent down to give her a kiss on the head. "How was your sleepover at Pop and Gram's?"

Rhubie whined instead of answering. Ash had expected as much. She glanced up at her parents. "Do you want to help Avonlee set up her room?"

She hoped Avonlee would be nicer with them instead of her, since they always seemed to butt heads lately. In some ways they were way too much alike, and Ash missed seeing Mari in her oldest daughter as each passing month went by. Would they even remember her when they were grown up?

Sadness swelled in Ash's chest, choking her as she tried to focus on setting up Rhubie's room. If she let it settle in her for too long, she'd be a blubbering mess incapable of doing anything that day, and that was the last thing she needed. It had been two years already. She should be over this by now, shouldn't she? That was what her friends had told her, repeatedly. Or at least that it should be easier. It was easier. But it was also so vastly different that *easier* didn't quite encompass what she felt. Ash pulled out the frame for Rhubie's bed. That would be a good place to start.

They had the frame together and the mattress on top of it before Ash stretched her back and surveyed the room. This was going to take all day just to get the three bedrooms done, and she definitely needed more coffee. Stumbling her way back to the kitchen, she was pleased to see that Char was indeed being useful. Ash leaned against the counter, sipping her third cup for the morning.

"So...how was last night? You never really told me." Char kept her voice low, barely above a whisper.

Ash still wasn't comfortable talking about it with so many people around. Her cheeks were on fire when she answered. "Let's just say it was really good."

"Oh, me like-y. Are you going to see her again?"

"No." Ash shook her head. "One night of happiness. That's what we promised each other and that's what we got."

"Didn't you get her number?"

Ash frowned. She did have Chris' number. And now that Char brought it to her attention, Ash's phone burned a hole in her pocket. She wanted to snag her phone and see if it was still there, look at the numbers and memorize them. "I shouldn't have even allowed myself last night."

"Why not?"

"Because I'm not looking for a relationship," Ash hissed, her voice getting louder than she wanted. "I had the love of my life, Char. Mari was it. No one will ever compare to her."

"Ash." Char softened her tone. She feverishly looked around before stepping forward and touching Ash's shoulder. "Just because you loved Mari with everything you had, it doesn't mean you can't do that again."

Intuitively, Ash knew this was true. But she hated admitting it to anyone.

"It doesn't have to be with Chris. Just don't rule out the possibility, okay?"

"I love Mari." Ash rubbed her lips together.

"No one is asking you not to." Char went back to unpacking the kitchen.

Ash took the hint and went back to Rhubie's room. They would need to paint when they could, but she didn't have the time or the energy to figure that out now. She needed the girls to be sleeping so she could find the time for it between her new job —her first job back in an office in years—and being in a whole new place. She'd given up her career when she moved here, and that was going to be an adjustment for everyone.

Setting her coffee on the top of the dresser, Ash grabbed her phone and checked to find Chris' name and number right where it should be. She gnawed on her lip. She really shouldn't do it, but Chris had understood something so vital to who she was the night before that she couldn't let it go so quickly. Could she?

Rhubie glanced at her, her bright blue eyes and dirty blonde hair pulled back in a lopsided ponytail because Ash's mom still hadn't figured out how to do hair even after raising two daughters and having two granddaughters. Ash smiled and opened a new text message.

Ash 10:09 am - I know this is awkward, but I just wanted to say thank you again for last night. It was exactly what I needed.

Chris wouldn't answer. She would have to be stupid to text back. It wasn't like they had talked about what would happen next, but it was a general understanding of a one-night stand that they wouldn't talk again, right? Ash pulled over a box and started to unpack Rhubie's books.

She was halfway through the bookshelf when her phone buzzed twice in rapid succession.

Chris 11:39 am - You're welcome.

Chris 11:39 am - And I feel the same. I guess we both got what we needed.

That didn't leave a whole lot of room for more. Ash wrinkled her nose at the phone screen, her thumb hovering over the keyboard as she debated what to respond or if she even should respond. She'd broken the cardinal rule, and that left them both with the question of *now what?*

Ash was just about to put her phone away after staring at it for way too long, when another text came through.

Chris 11:41 am - Did you get your car started?

"Fuck!"

"Mommy, you said a bad word."

"I know." Ash pulled herself up with a groan. "Keep unpacking. I need to talk to Pop."

Ash stepped into Avonlee's room, the whine already so strong in there along with the tension that it was impossible to avoid. She stared around the room, finding it nowhere near ready. Seemed her parents were having just as much issue with Avonlee as Ash was.

"Daddy, I forgot to mention that my car died last night."

"What?" He immediately perked up, his bushy gray eyebrows raising. "What do you mean died?"

"Well, it won't start. I didn't look at it too much because it was late." And she had other things distracting her, but she definitely wasn't going to mention that. "Char and I left it at the restaurant until we could figure out what to do with it today."

Her dad sighed heavily. "Come on, let's go."

Ash hated putting him in this position. Not that he cared, but she hated having to ask for help with anything. Avonlee jumped into the back of her dad's truck, and they went to the restaurant. Ash nervously brushed her fingers along her thighs, wanting to be home to get her house ready, but realizing she really needed to be here, dealing with this, and removing Avonlee from the house would mean a lot more work would get done in the long run.

"There it is," Ash pointed.

Her dad pulled up alongside the car. "You're sure it's not the battery?"

"Not even a click."

He was under the hood in a minute flat. Avonlee stayed in the truck, glued to her tablet. Ash leaned against the side of her car, staring at the engine and pretending she knew what was going on underneath it. But she had no clue, and no one was fooled.

Ash 12:15 pm - We're just now taking a look at it, but short answer, no, it's not started.

Chris 12:16 pm - Bummer.

Bummer was right. Ash needed just one thing to go right in her life. Well, she supposed that could have been last night and Chris, and all that they had gotten up to. Her cheeks burned again, heat pooling between her legs at the mere thought of the memory. It didn't come as a surprise that she wanted to do it again. Chris was confident when it came to sex, though she seemed far less confident when it came to her own body. Ash could handle that. Mari had struggled with the same issues for years, and they had taken the time to work through most of that.

But in Ash's mind, Chris looked amazing. She wasn't a classic beauty, but everything about her was gorgeous, inside and out. From her confidence to her sex appeal, to her kindness and generosity. Chris was checking in on the car for Christ's sake. That absolutely said she cared to some extent.

"What put that smile on your face?"

"Uh...what?" Ash jerked her head up, making eye contact with her dad.

"I haven't seen you smile like that in years."

"Oh, it's nothing." Ash shoved her phone into her pocket. "So what's wrong with it?"

"Don't know. Why don't you get in and try to start the engine again?"

Ash did as she was told. Her dad shouted through the open

window at her from the front of the vehicle, "Give it a ton of gas!"

She did as she was told, and it took longer than it should have, but the car finally started. The engine roared to life. Ash was scared to death to turn it off again, worried that she wouldn't ever get it started. Her dad wiped his hands on his work pants and closed the hood on the car.

"I think it's something with the fuel injection system or the filter. We should get it to Alberto's and he can get it fixed up right."

"Okay." Ash breathed out. "How much is that going to cost?"

Her dad frowned. "It won't be cheap, but your mom and I can help if you need."

"I don't need help."

"You never do, but the offer is there when you decide to accept it." He patted the open window. "See you at the house?"

"Yeah."

"Want me to swing by somewhere and get lunch?"

"Sure." Ash watched as he pulled out of the parking lot. Deciding it would be rude to avoid Chris and not let her know the end to the car saga, she started another text.

Ash 12:29 pm - Got it started. Dad thinks it's something with the fuel something or another. Car lingo is not my lingo.

Chris 12:29 pm - Cute. Take it to Alberto's. He's cheap and does good work.

Ash stared at the text. Funny that Chris should suggest the same place her father had without prompting even. This Alberto must be good at what he does or something like that.

Ash 12:30 pm - Thanks. Going to eat lunch and unpack more. I don't think unpacking will ever end.

Chris 12:31 pm - I know how you feel. Good luck with it!

Satisfied the conversation had come to a happy conclusion, Ash put her car into drive and headed for home. She still had to get the girls' bedrooms ready before the end of the day. While Ash could sleep on the floor on her mattress—which reminded her thank god no one had asked where she'd slept the night before since the bed was still wrapped in plastic and vertical, leaning against the wall—she knew Avonlee and Rhubie would want their beds. She could do this. One day at a time. Isn't that what all the Al-Anon groups told her?

CHAPTER
Five

"WHAT DID you get up to this weekend?" Mel had her hands on her hips and a light in her gaze that Chris envied. But Mel could clearly sense something was different.

Chris had pep in her step when she walked into the school early Monday morning. It was the first time in years that she had felt so light, and she couldn't stop smiling. She didn't want to. She and Ash had texted on and off over the weekend. It had been hard at first to even contemplate continuing the conversation and relationship beyond Friday night, but she had wanted to check in and make sure that Ash had gotten her car working.

"I went out by myself."

"Did you go home by yourself?" Mel's voice rang through the hall.

Chris immediately put her hand out to quiet her down before grinning and shaking her head. "No, I didn't."

"Chris!"

"Classroom." She pointed toward Mel's kindergarten classroom, and they started walking toward it. She was stopped by tiny arms wrapped around her hips in a tight hug. Glancing down unexpectedly, Chris laughed and ruffled her hand through Anthony's hair before giving him a hug. "Hey, kid."

"Hi, Dr. Murphey!"

"You hanging out with your mom this morning?"

Anthony pouted. "Mom's got a meeting."

Chris cringed. She remembered that because Esther had requested the morning off while she dealt with some custody and harassment things with her ex. "Right. I forgot that. So are you hanging out with Mel?"

He nodded wildly. "I was until other kids showed up. Now I'm going outside. Bye!"

Anthony ran off—well walked with as much speed as he knew was allowable—toward the door that led to the playground. Chris laughed it off as she continued to walk with Mel toward the classroom. "He's so sweet."

"He's blossomed in the last year," Mel commented. "But tell me more about Friday. Sorry I had to bail on you, but Esther needed me to be home."

"I understand. Don't worry about it."

"And it clearly gave you time to meet someone." Mel stepped inside her classroom, shutting the door behind them so no one else could hear what was going on. "So who is she?"

"I don't know that much, honestly. It wasn't that kind of meet up." Chris crossed her arms, wanting to protect what little happiness she had found for even longer. It wasn't anything more than one night, at least that's what she kept telling herself. But it had spilled into Saturday and then into Sunday. Still, neither one of them had mentioned getting together again, and if it turned into a fun and beautiful friendship, Chris would take that too.

"You got together just for sex?" Mel's eyes went wide, and she fanned herself like she was suddenly hot.

Chuckling lightly, Chris shook her head. "No, it wasn't just for that. It wasn't even supposed to be that really. We were sharing a table at The Office, and one thing led to another, and we ended up back at my place. It was fun. That's what matters."

"Yeah, but do you want it to happen again?"

"I wouldn't say no if the opportunity arose, but I don't think that's going to happen."

"Why not?" Mel canted her head slightly to the side.

"Because it was one night. That's all it was ever meant to be, and unless we serendipitously end up in the same place again, which I doubt will happen, then there's no point in even contemplating it. Besides, she's younger than me, way hotter than me, and I'm pretty sure she wouldn't be interested in an old, divorced drunk who has seventy extra pounds on her and no future to think of."

"Chris." Mel's call of her name was sharp and biting.

Instantly, Chris cringed. She knew Mel hated when she talked about herself like that, but sometimes she just couldn't help it, especially when it came to relationships. "I know. I know."

"Good. Stop it before I have to slap that bad talk out of you."

"Like you would do that anyway." Chris' lips pulled upward. "It was a good night, one I'll remember for a long time."

"Good. You deserve to be happy."

"Andry said the same thing," Chris muttered, not sure why everyone kept telling her that lately. But for the few hours she'd spent with Ash, and the random texts they had sent throughout the next couple days, she had been happy. For the first time in a long time, and it had felt so good to be reminded of the fact that she wasn't as abhorrent as she thought. She was just dissatisfied with everything, especially herself, especially with who she'd become in the last ten years. Which was why she was working her butt off to change that.

"Andry was there?"

"Briefly." Chris waved it off. She really didn't want to talk about her ex-wife. "It was a fun night, that's what matters."

"It is." Mel agreed with a smile. "And I'm so glad that you had it."

"So fill me in on what's going on with Esther."

Mel groaned. "Well, Skip hasn't seen Anthony in six months,

and she took the first opportunity to file to change the custody arrangement. We set her up with a good lawyer this time to help, and with the harassment charges she filed along with the internal complaints at the district, she might stand a chance of getting it changed. At least Skip will have to meet her at a public place from now on to switch days."

"That's good." Chris had known about the internal harassment claim. She'd helped Esther file the paperwork at the end of the last school year and had willingly kicked Skip out of the school multiple times since then. But she hadn't seen him since the start of this year, or even heard from him. "I'm glad she's doing something about it. I can't imagine how hard it is."

"It is." Mel frowned. "But it's what's best for Anthony, and I think she sees that now."

Chris nodded, her mind already back on the million things she had to do that day. As much as she enjoyed catching up with her best friend and checking in on one of her other teachers, she had an entire school to run and mornings were always off with a bang when she least expected them to be.

"Think we can get together this weekend?"

Dragged back to the conversation, Chris looked at her long-time best friend. "Yeah, we can figure something out."

"You talk to Katie recently?"

Chris shook her head as the image of the last time she saw her daughter swam through her brain. It hadn't been a good conversation. Strained was the world she'd use. "She doesn't want much to do with me. I think Andry said something about her coming home for spring break."

"I'd love to see her if there's a chance. I miss her."

"Don't we all," Chris mumbled. She'd barely seen Katie over the Christmas break. She'd thought they were making progress on their relationship last year, but as soon as she'd gone to college, the little work they had been doing was snuffed out and hadn't restarted. "I need to make my rounds."

"Sure." Mel eyed her, as if not quite believing the change in topic.

Chris nodded and left. The halls were already filling up with students and staff. This was one of her favorite times of the day. This was when all her distractions were in place and she wasn't tempted to drink, she wasn't tempted to run away, and she knew she had eight hours of pure focus. Chris headed out front with her winter jacket on, gladly standing by and waiting for students to arrive with their parents and giving out more hugs and words of praise than she could count. This was where she felt most alive.

Her radio echoed next to her, calling her inside to the office to deal with something. She sadly and silently said goodbye to the kids arriving as she went to check in on what was going on. Ms. Linda sat at her desk in the main offices, a scowl on her face.

"We have a sub who's never been here before."

The woman had brown shoulder length hair, and when she turned around, Chris was somewhat surprised by how young she was. Raising her hand up, Chris held it out. "I'm Dr. Murphey. You can call me Chris."

"Heather Greene. I'm supposed to be subbing today, but no one told me where."

"Right." Chris glanced around the office. "That would be for Esther Dunja. I'll take you down to her class. She's hyper-organized, so I'm sure she left all of her plans on her desk." Chris pointed at Linda. "I'll be back."

"You got it, boss."

Chris walked Heather down to the classroom, calming the poor woman's nerves. It wasn't her first time substitute teaching, but it certainly was her first in that school, and she was still pretty new to the job. Once Chris had Heather settled, she went back to the office and stopped short in the doorway.

Ash.

Ash fucking stood in the school office.

Chris was an idiot.

She should have put this together so much faster than she had. Ash had kids. She'd said as much. But Chris had stupidly assumed that Ash's kids weren't elementary age, more middle school age. Not here. Not in *her* school. Chris clenched her jaw, not sure what the hell to do or say or even which direction to go. She wanted to turn on her toes and walk right out of there, hide in Mel's room until whatever Ash was doing there was finished and Chris could get ahold of herself.

Doing just that, Chris spun around and walked away from the office. Panic swelled in her chest. This wasn't good. No, this was worse than not good. This was a nightmare. And she had no one she could even call about it. The bell just rang, and her best friend was out on the playground getting her students, and everyone else she knew was in the same situation.

Except Andry.

Andry would have the same flexibility that Chris did, but could Chris really call her? Over something like this? Could she admit to her ex-wife that she'd slept with a woman on the first date that wasn't even really a date?

"Damnit," Chris muttered under her breath. She whipped out her phone and made the call, stepping out the back doors toward the staff parking lot to have what little privacy she could when not in her office. "Please answer."

"Hey, what's up?" Andry's sweet voice came through the phone.

Chris was nearly in tears. "I did something stupid."

"Well, that's not the first time." Andry laughed. "What is it this time?"

"That woman...the one from Friday..."

"Yeah, I remember her. Did you have fun?" Andry had no idea what she was asking, did she?

Chris whimpered. "Yesssss," she dragged out the word.

"And...?"

"And she's a parent at the school," Chris hissed. "What am I supposed to do?"

"You...wait...hold on. You don't just forget a face, Chris. You didn't knowingly *sleep* with a parent."

"No, I didn't." Chris clenched her jaw, crossing her arms and glancing around furiously. No one could hear this conversation. No one. "She's new to town. I didn't realize her kids were this young."

"How old did you think she was? Because she screams barely thirty."

Chris was still an idiot. "I don't know? I didn't do the math."

"How old is she?"

"I didn't ask!" Chris nearly screeched, but she bit her tongue to hold it in. "We didn't exactly look at each other's IDs to make sure we were legal."

"So you didn't know. Talk about it like adults, Chris. You're not an idiot."

How did Andry know she was thinking that? Chris shook her hand out and squared her shoulders. Andry was right. She didn't have any other choice but to walk back inside and deal with the problem in front of her. "What do I even say to her?"

"That you didn't know." Andry was probably rolling her eyes. Chris could see it now. She was leaning back in her chair in her office, rolling her eyes and thinking it was impossible that they were even having this conversation. "You need to be honest with her."

"I've never been anything but." Chris bit her tongue because that wasn't true, and she was covering up a lie with another lie. "No, that's not true. I know that, but it's not what I meant."

"I know what you meant." Andry's voice was drowned in pain and sadness. "You only ever lied about one thing."

"Right." Chris bit the inside of her cheek. "It was more than one night."

Silence permeated through the call, and Chris wasn't even sure Andry was still listening or if she was lost in her own chaos of hurt that Chris had caused in the past.

"Look, I'm sorry I'm an idiot. I lied to you for years when I shouldn't have. I lied to myself for longer. There's no excuse for it."

"I know." Andry sniffled. "At least you've come clean now."

The double meaning of Andry's *clean* didn't get past Chris. "I am, and I have come clean."

"How was it more than one night?" Andry seemed to snap back to attention.

"We've been texting, that's it."

"Then talk to her, Chris. You need to start on the right foot."

Chris knew Andry was right, even if she didn't want to admit it and she didn't want to do anything about it. "Thanks. I will."

"And Chris?"

"Yeah?"

"I still want you to be happy. Thank you for sharing with me."

"I panic-called you." Chris rubbed her temple.

Andry chuckled. "You did. Glad to know I still have some place in your life."

"You'll always have a place in my life, Andry. Please know that."

"I do." Andry sucked in a sharp breath. "I've got morning announcements."

"Crap. Me too. Talk to you later." Chris hung up without another warning.

Swiping her way back into the school, Chris started her long walk of shame. She had to get to the front office in one piece, because standing in front of Ash and having this conversation was going to take everything out of her. Did she want more? Yes. She was willing to admit that now that it wasn't even a possibility. Because she wouldn't date a parent. Not now. Not ever.

Not that she was worthy of dating to begin with. She was still an idiot. She was still a drunk. And as Andry had pointed out, she was still a liar. With her shoulders set, Chris trudged her way to the disaster waiting for her.

CHAPTER
Six

"I JUST NEEDED to bring in proof of residency and my kids' immunization records to finish registering them, right?" Ash's stomach was in knots. This was worse than the first day of school after Mari died.

The plump office admin sat behind her desk, staring at the papers Ash had handed over. She wasn't ready to move to Cheyenne. She wasn't fully ready to say that she was moving on, although that weekend had proved it, hadn't it? She'd had two full days to think about it, and that's all it had been. Ash moving on from the memory of her wife.

"That should be all we need, and a copy of their birth certificates."

"Right." Ash rummaged through her purse. She'd brought those with her, but she'd completely forgotten about them from the time it took her to get to the school and into the office. She handed the papers over.

"I'll just make a copy. Did you want to talk to Dr. Murphey? She should be back in the office soon."

"Oh, if she has time, I guess." It would be a prime time for Ash to fill the principal in on some of the issues Avonlee was having, maybe get a jump start on her individual education plan and a recommendation for a therapist since she was likely to need it at some point.

"I'm sure she'll have time." Linda smiled at her from the copy machine. "Maybe she'll even give you a tour and show you the girls' classrooms, meet their teachers before their first day."

"That'd be nice." Linda could probably put any nervous parent at ease. Ash was appreciating that ability right now. Her shoulders relaxed a bit, and she didn't feel like such an idiot standing there. Ash clasped onto the handle on her purse.

"Here's the paperwork back." Linda handed everything over.

Ash folded it up and shoved it into her purse. She really just wanted to get out of there and go home, so if the principal didn't show up in the next five seconds, she was gone. She was just about to ask if there was anything else when Linda jumped in first.

"Here's Dr. Murphey."

Ash turned around. Her stomach plummeted to the center of the earth. What kind of shit show was this? Her brain short-circuited as she tried to comprehend what was happening.

Chris.

Dr. Murphey.

Ms. Murphey.

Junior English.

Every fiber of her being told Ash to run. It told her to move back home to Seattle, get her kids back into a school with a principal who wouldn't hate them, someone who wasn't a bully, someone who was worth their salt and who would support her kids through everything. Chris wasn't that person. She couldn't be. She'd proven that to Ash decades ago.

"Want to talk in my office?" Chris asked. She at least had the audacity to look pale.

Though Ash couldn't be sure how true she was in that. Ash's voice wobbled, "Sure."

She wasn't sure why she did it, but she followed Chris into

her office. When the door shut, Ash's back was ramrod straight. What on earth could Chris have to say to her now?

"I should have figured out that your kids would be here," Chris started. "I made the assumption they were older...that you were older."

"Avonlee is ten, and Rhubie is seven."

Chris nodded, crossing her arms as she leaned against the table in the corner of her office. "And you're about five years younger than I thought. Add five to each of your kids' age, and you can see why I'd think they were older. I'm so sorry. If I had known you were going to be one of my parents, I wouldn't have..." Chris trailed off.

"Fucked me?" The curse burst from her.

Chris glanced around her toward the door. "This is my place of work, and it's the place your kids are going to be learning. I won't be their teacher, so there's that, but I would appreciate it if we can keep some kind of civility while we're here. And I know I shouldn't have to say this, but from the look on your face, you're probably in agreement that nothing can happen between us again."

Ash was very near tears. Her heart pumped hard, thudding up into her neck and clogging it with emotion. How was she even going to say this? "You don't remember me, do you?"

A deep line formed in the center of Chris' brow. "Remember you? From last weekend?"

Shaking her head, Ash tensed even more. Her chest was so tight that it was hard to breathe. She hadn't realized who Chris was, not until she'd seen her in this environment, seen her standing with the damn lanyard, the confidence in her shoulders, the power. "Regan High School. Junior English."

This was her worst nightmare coming true. Not only had Chris made her junior year of high school a living hell, but seventeen years later they'd fucked. And neither one of them had put it together. And now Chris—Dr. Murphey—was her girls' principal? She couldn't handle this.

"You were my junior English teacher. You *hated* me."

The light went off in Chris' eyes. She stilled, staring directly at Ash with a wide gaze and parted lips. "Ashton Garrison."

"Ashton Taylor now. My married name."

"Oh my god." Chris covered her mouth with her hand, still staring, still in total shock.

To be fair, Ash was too. She had never thought that she'd see this woman again. She'd always thought she'd recognize her in an instant, but seventeen years, different states, what was the likelihood that they would run into each other? It had to be completely improbable.

"Oh my god!" Chris said louder. "Holy..." she trailed off, not finishing out the curse that Ash knew was on her tongue. "And I didn't hate you." Chris stood up, straightening her back but still keeping her distance.

Ash was so grateful for that, because she couldn't be sure what she'd do if Chris came any closer. Run. She'd definitely do that, but to bring her girls back? That wasn't ever going to happen.

"I really didn't hate you," Chris said softer, her hand out in front of her as if she was going to touch Ash, but at the last minute, she pulled back. "You were my favorite student."

"Favorite?" Ash screeched.

Chris once again furtively glanced toward the door. "Yes, my favorite. I was working on my master's, Ash. I didn't know a lot of what I was doing, but you were so brilliant with words. You were amazingly creative in your assignments."

"You constantly told me that my stuff was shit."

"No." Chris shook her head. "I told you that you could do better, because you could."

"You're such a *liar!*" Ash stepped forward, suddenly finding that grit she'd needed earlier. "You made my life a living hell. There was nothing I could do that could please you. You were always telling me that I could do better, that I wasn't good enough. You're the worst teacher I ever had."

Chris' lower lip quivered. "I'm so sorry. I...I didn't know."

"No, how could you? You didn't care about us. All you cared about was you." Ash was on a roll now, and she wasn't sure she wanted to stop. "My friends used to call you a bitch behind your back, and they were right. God, I can't believe I had sex with you." Reaching up, Ash grabbed her hair and pulled at it hard. "How stupid could I be?"

"You're not stupid," Chris murmured, her voice raw. "You're not. You're brilliant. I wanted to challenge you back then. I'm not lying when I say that you were one of the best students I had, Ashton. Your writing is brilliant."

"Was," Ash spat.

Chris shook her head in confusion.

"You know what? It doesn't matter. I gave up writing, and I'm not going back to it." Her career was dust, and she was back to working in the real world.

"Going back? Ashton, you're going to have to fill me in on what you're talking about. It's been seventeen years—"

"Like I said, it doesn't matter. Let's just forget last weekend ever happened, because it *won't* happen again. And not because you're my daughters' principal, but because you're a bully. If I could move my kids to another school, I would."

"I'll sign the waiver if that's what you want. If that's what's best for them." Chris seemed to shrink before Ash's eyes, her entire body becoming even smaller if that was at all possible. She looked meek almost.

Ash hadn't even considered a waiver. But she'd worked her kids up to going to school here, and to change the plan again would only devastate them both and probably push Avonlee further behind than she already was. That and it was an argument she absolutely didn't want to have with Avonlee.

"Ashton, I promise you I didn't remember who you were. If I had, then Friday night never would have happened."

"Of course it wouldn't. I wouldn't have allowed it." Ash

clenched her jaw hard, glaring with everything she had. "I can't believe they let you continue to be a teacher."

"I know I'm not perfect," Chris stated, her voice soft as if she was placating Ash into something she didn't want. "No one is perfect."

"What are you saying?" Every word was still an accusation. Ash wasn't going to let this go. Chris had been awful to her.

"I'm saying that I mess up, and I will continue to mess up." Chris collapsed into the chair at the table, her hand covering her eyes. "This is a perfect example of that. But I promise you that I was a good teacher, and that I am a good principal. It's the one thing I manage to do right in my life."

Empathy tickled the back of Ash's heart, despite the fact that she didn't want to feel it. Was this just another trick? Chris had been particularly hard on her when she was a kid, always giving her a grade just below what Ash thought she deserved, talking only to her about the problems in her assignment. Chris never did that with anyone else.

"Yeah, well, we're all screw ups in one way or another." Ash slid into the seat next to Chris, not sure why. She'd much rather leave and never come back, but if her girls were going to school there, they'd have to figure out how to see each other. "Friday shouldn't have happened, for so many reasons."

Chris frowned, looking over her head. "Well, if there was one way you pleased me, it was that, but it certainly hasn't been the only way."

Ash chuckled, a smile tugging at her lips that she worked hard to contain. This wasn't a funny conversation. This wasn't any type of talk that was amusing. Except Ash wanted to laugh. She brought her hand up to her lips to try and stifle the snort. She shook her head, unable as the laugh bubbled up from her chest. "What?"

"I don't know." Chris laid her hands flat on the table and leaned back in the chair. "I don't know anything anymore."

Chris looked devastated. The lines in her face were deeper,

her gaze was glued to some spot on the other side of the table, and her entire energy was deflated. Ash hadn't done that, had she? No, she couldn't feel bad for her bully. Ash pulled herself back together and ran her finger in a circle on the tabletop.

"I expect my girls to be treated in a way I wasn't."

"They're with two of my best teachers." Chris still didn't look at her. "Ms. Walsh is an amazing teacher, she's been teaching almost ten years now—she'll be Rhubie's teacher. And Ms. Dunja will be Avonlee's."

"I'm sure you say that about all your teachers."

Chris cut Ash a look. "I don't play you for a fool, so don't act it."

The wind rushed out of Ash's lungs. She sat there stunned. *That* was the Ms. Murphey that she remembered. The one who didn't hold back when she had something to say or a point to make. Ash pursed her lips.

"You're still as cruel as you were back then, aren't you?" Ash scoffed. "Great. Just where my girls needed to end up." Ash stood up, not willing to put up with any more of Chris' bullshit. She'd been here before, and she wouldn't stand for it again. "If you pull any of the crap on my kids like you did on me, you can bet your ass I'll be filing a report on you."

"I would expect nothing less." Her tone was so flat. Chris knocked her chin up, her jaw clenched tightly.

Ash scoffed again. "You haven't changed at all. Were you sleeping with students back then, too?"

Chris slapped her hand on the table before fisting it, as if catching herself. "I've never slept with a student."

"What would you call me?" Ash's heart was in her throat, her entire reaction riding on Chris' next answer.

"An unfortunate mistake."

"Unfortunate?" Ash was worked up again, ready to defend herself no matter what Chris threw at her.

Chris stood slowly, staking her ground in her office. Ash was suddenly reminded that this was Chris' world that she stood in, not hers. She saw the cameras in the corners of the office and tightened again. What was going on? What mistake was Chris talking about?

"I wanted so much to like you," Chris whispered.

"I thought I was your favorite student," Ash fired back.

"You were." Chris softened instantly. "You were. And for Friday?" Chris paused, her gaze dropping from Ash's eyes to her mouth and back up again. Chris shrugged slightly. "I wanted to like you for that, too."

"Wanted to?"

"Did," Chris corrected. "But I can see how it was a mistake now, and I apologize for the harm I've caused."

What the hell was Ash supposed to do with that? It wasn't like Chris had forced Ash to sleep with her. She'd willingly gone with Chris. They'd screwed each other's brains out for hours. So many orgasms that Ash had lost count. And then they'd texted. God, they had texted all weekend, slowly getting to know each other when they'd already known each other. It was a betrayal, but clearly not one that either of them had intended. This was just going to take some time to get used to. That was all it was.

"Don't mess with my kids."

"I would never dream of it," Chris responded, her voice monotone.

There was no emotion coming from her, and Ash craved it. Any kind of response was better than this one. Ash almost stepped in closer, almost touched Chris' shoulder, her arm, her face. Biting the inside of her cheek to stop herself from doing something stupid, Ash froze in place.

"I'll see you tomorrow, Dr. Murphey."

Chris whimpered.

Ash's mind went right back to Friday night, to a different kind of whimper, to Chris' fingers sliding in and out of her. She shuddered, her nipples hard, and that pull to touch Chris again was so strong and next to impossible to resist. But she did resist. Because this was Ms. Murphey, the teacher she hated and the teacher who hated her. This was her girls' principal. And they'd already decided Friday would never happen again.

Sex was sex, no matter how good it was. And no bully like Chris could replace what Ash had with Mari. No one in the world could replace that. Pulling her lip into her mouth, Ash steadied herself. She found her resolve. She stared down her nose at Chris and said nothing as she walked out of the principal's office and straight out of the school.

CHAPTER
Seven

"DO YOU THINK I'M A BULLY?" Chris sat across from Mel at the table in the lounge. Mel had her lunch in front of her, and Chris had her fifth coffee of the day.

"I'm sorry, what?" Mel's face pinched.

"Just something someone said," Chris mumbled into her mug before taking a long sip. She hated that it was still bugging her, but for two whole weeks she hadn't been able to think of anything but. No one had ever called her a bully before. She wasn't one, was she? "No, answer that. Do you think I'm a bully?"

"I'm pretty sure every teacher here would attest to the opposite. You can be demanding, but I don't think I'd call you a bully. What's going on?" Mel took a bite of her sandwich.

"Nothing."

"This isn't nothing." Mel pointed her sandwich toward Chris. "You don't mope for nothing."

"Sure I do." Now what was she trying to pull? She did mope, frequently, she just didn't let other people see it—ever.

"Nope. You don't, not like this anyway."

Chris frowned. "This isn't something I can directly talk about in this building."

Mel frowned at that, setting her sandwich down. "Did one of the teachers call you a bully? Did someone file a complaint? Linda?" With each question, Mel's voice rose higher.

Chris shushed her, moving her hands in a downward motion. "No, no one filed a complaint."

"Then who called you a bully."

"A parent," Chris mumbled, trying to keep her voice low. The last thing she needed was to accidentally start rumors about herself. "And it wasn't in any specific conversation."

"I'm confused."

"Like I said, not here. But she called me a bully, and I've been trying to think back to everything I did, and I honestly can't come up with anything. I mean I was firm, I pushed her to do better, I made sure she had the tools she needed."

Mel tsked. "You're not making any sense."

Chris wrinkled her nose. She hadn't told anyone about the conversation in her office with Ash, not even Andry—though Andry had called to check in about how that had all gone. If they'd been together in person, there was no way Chris would have been able to hold back on that. Chris scratched her scalp and winced. "What's it like to have kids in your classroom when you also taught their parents?"

"Oh, well, that's been rare so far. It's only happened once or twice."

Chris remained riveted to Mel. She'd been teaching in this district for over twenty years, and she knew everything. Well, Chris liked to think she did on days like this. She needed to confidently believe that Mel would and could catch her when she fell. And if she were to sink deep into what was going through her mind right then, she was falling hard.

"What makes you ask that?"

"We have two new students, and I taught their mom in high school." Chris' cheeks heated. She definitely wasn't going to add in exactly who Ash was and what they had done a few weeks ago. Mel knew about that, but she didn't know everything.

"High school? You haven't taught that since..."

"Since I was working on my doctorate." Chris grimaced. "Seventeen years ago, when I was working on my master's, however, is when I taught this parent. She was in one of my junior English classes."

"Oh, well this gets more interesting by the minute. And she called you a bully for what you've done to her kids or what you did to her?" Mel ripped off the wrapper on her pudding cup.

Chris was sure her look said it all. She couldn't even make herself look Mel in the eye because she would see everything. Like she'd told Ash, she wasn't perfect, no one was. So had she made mistakes that year? Absolutely. She just hadn't thought that Ash was one of them. In fact, she'd thought that Ash Garrison— no, Ashton Taylor—was one of the few good things she had managed to accomplish that year.

Ash had wanted to be a writer, and Chris had given her as much encouragement and mentoring as she possibly could. Maybe she'd just been too intense. She had at least been accused of that before. Chris still wasn't sure where to go with this, but her radio echoed with her name. She snagged it.

"Dr. Murphey, you're needed in the office."

Perfect. Chris saluted Mel with her mug of coffee and started toward the office, which was directly across the hall. Linda knew where she was at, but it was easier to just use the radio where everyone could hear that she wasn't in the office rather than simply get up and walk the twenty steps to her. It was an annoyance of Chris' but also not something she wanted to deal with —ever.

As soon as Chris stepped into her office, she found Avonlee sitting with a pout and a glare at the corner table. Managing both those looks at once was quite the feat. Chris glanced at her and then looked to Linda to figure out what happened.

"Ms. Dunja needs to speak with you, immediately."

Well, this is going to be good. Chris said nothing as she left the office and marched down to Esther's classroom. She was waiting.

She stepped out into the hallway and lowered her voice to just above a whisper, her hair pulled back in a slick pony that day. Esther crossed her arms.

"I didn't know what to do other than to send her down to the office."

"Start with what happened." Chris crossed her arms as she leaned more on one leg than the other.

Esther drew in a sharp breath and held out her hand with a chain and ring on it. "This fell out of Avonlee's pocket, best as I can tell."

Chris reached forward, plucking it from Esther's palm. It was a pearl ring, three small pearls situated at an angle with a string of diamonds glittering across it on either side. The ring was clearly big enough for an adult, not a child, and Chris wasn't sure she'd ever seen a child with such an expensive piece of jewelry—certainly not one that would be worn to school.

"So what's the drama with it?"

"When Avonlee realized she'd lost it, she panicked. She's been searching frantically for it for the last part of the day today, unable to contemplate focusing on anything else. That's not the real issue though, despite her being disruptive to the rest of the class. Kelli found it."

"And refused to give it back?" Chris turned the ring in her fingers again. It was a beautifully delicate ring. She'd never thought of pearls quite that way before.

"Yes, and teased Avonlee about how attached she was to it."

"You didn't send her to my office for that?"

"No." Esther heaved a sigh. "Avonlee attacked Kelli, trying to rip it from her fingers."

"Attacked?" Chris' back went up.

Esther waved her fingers. "No damage was done, but there was yelling, screeching—which was barbaric—and I was able to put a stop to it before anyone was injured."

"By sending her to me?"

Esther nodded. "She wouldn't give it up. With the expense of that, I decided it'd be better for me to keep it for the rest of the day, but Avonlee was still disruptive because she didn't have it with her."

"All right, I'll deal with it." Chris started to walk away, but Esther stopped her with a hand on her arm.

"It's her mother's." The weight of Esther's words weren't lost on Chris, but the meaning was.

She was missing something. She nodded sharply, as if she understood, and started back toward her office with the necklace laced between her fingers. It was a gorgeous ring, but her mind was spinning with just exactly what had set Avonlee off to that point. She'd only been at the school a few weeks, and while Esther had remarked that she was a difficult student, nothing like this had happened yet.

Chris walked back into her office and crooked her finger at Avonlee, beckoning her into the office with her. They sat at the table in the corner in Chris' office with the door cracked open still so anyone could see what was happening inside.

"Want to tell me your version of what happened?" Chris set the necklace and ring on the table in between them.

She was surprised when Avonlee didn't immediately reach out for it. Instead, she crossed her arms tightly and stared at it, her gaze unwavering.

"I can't help you if you don't tell me what happened."

"Nothing happened." Avonlee's words had a sharp bite to them.

Chris leaned back slightly. "You can have the necklace back. I'm not sure you should bring it to school because we don't want it to get lost again—"

"I didn't lose it! Kelli stole it!"

"Ah." Chris relaxed. That had been the way to get her to open up. Though it was a bit more explosive than Chris had hoped for. "And if she didn't?"

"She did!"

"But if she didn't, if she just found it, are you more upset that she had it or that you didn't know where it was?"

Avonlee pouted after letting out a snort. Chris had figured that one out in a second. This child was hurting. Something deep inside her was broken, but Chris had no idea what it was or what the cause was.

"Ms. Dunja said it's your mother's. It's beautiful. Is there a representation for the three pearls?"

Avonlee flicked her gaze up to Chris, a tense pause before she finally broke the silence. "For me, for Rhubie, and for the baby Mom lost."

Chris' heart shattered in front of her.

Avonlee leaned forward and pointed to the string of small diamonds that bridged over the pearls. "These are to show what ties us all together."

"Love?" Chris asked, trying to hold back her own tears.

Avonlee nodded slightly. When she locked her gaze on Chris, those bright blue eyes reflected back at her weren't Avonlee's but were Ash's, except the shade was different, the innocence and experience in them was different.

"Avonlee, I can't have you disrupting the class when everyone is trying to learn."

"I know," Avonlee mumbled.

"I know this ring is important to you, but you might not want to bring it to school with you. It's too important to accidentally lose. Or maybe wear it?" Chris was out of suggestions. It was as if she'd lost all words to comfort and console, as if she wasn't sure what she was supposed to do as a principal with a child in front of her was achingly sad about something. "Do you want to stay here for a little bit before you go back to class?"

"Are you going to call my mom?" She seemed almost scared but far more remorseful.

"Probably. Don't you think she should know what happened?"

Avonlee pursed her lips, staring down at the ring again. "She'll be mad."

"Are you supposed to leave the ring at home?"

The nod confirmed everything.

"Do you think you'll get in trouble for bringing it?"

"I know I will." Distressed, Avonlee fidgeted her fingers in her lap.

"All right, well, I'll see what I can do about that. For now, do you want to leave this with me until school is out so you don't lose it?" Chris normally wouldn't give a student an option, but this ring and necklace had way more meaning than Avonlee was letting on.

"No."

"Then I suggest wearing it instead of keeping it in your pocket. Would you like some help with that?"

Chris snagged the necklace up and clasped it around Avonlee's neck. The girl's entire mood changed as soon as the necklace was back in her possession. Chris would have to figure out what that was all about later.

"Why don't you go back to class, and maybe, you can focus on learning for the rest of the day."

Avonlee nodded sheepishly and headed out of Chris' office. Chris stayed at the table for another minute before finally standing and walking to her desk. Calling Ash wasn't something she wanted to do, but this was also a conversation they probably needed to have. She could brush it off on Esther if she really wanted to, but she didn't. She wanted to hear Ash's voice again. She wanted to prove to Ash that she wasn't a bully.

"Hello?" Ash sounded worried. She probably would be since it was a call coming directly from the school.

"Ms. Taylor, this is Dr. Murphey." Why was she being so formal? She'd literally had her fingers inside Ash so many times she'd lost count and now suddenly her brain decided to be professional? Who was the idiot now?

"Oh."

"I'm calling about Avonlee."

"Is she sick?"

"No." Chris tapped her fingers against her standing desk. She needed something to do with her hands, anything to make this conversation more comfortable. "There was an incident in the classroom I wanted to talk to you about."

"Her teacher couldn't talk to me?" Ash's retort was sharp.

"She could have, but I wanted to be the one to make the call."

"Why?"

Chris sighed. "Because I'm concerned about Avonlee, Ash, nothing else. She brought a necklace to school today, one with a ring on it."

"She shouldn't have done that." Ash's voice softened, disappointment in each word.

"Right, she told me she wasn't supposed to bring it, but what's the significance behind it? She was very upset by not having it, and while I'd rather her leave something so expensive at home, I'm not going to deny her bringing it either."

"I'll talk to her about it." Ash's answers were back to short and clipped.

Chris clenched her jaw tightly, staring out the small window to her office. She should have just let Esther make this call. "I'm concerned about her, Ashton. That's what I'm trying to get across to you. She's struggling."

"I know." Ash sobered instantly. "I know she is."

"I wasn't insinuating you didn't, but I'd love to work on a plan so that she can start to enjoy life again. She looks so upset half the time, and the other half she's angry." Chris waited for any kind of response, but she was only greeted with silence.

Ash finally broke it. "Do I need to come get her?"

"No. I'll talk to Ms. Dunja about scheduling a meeting with you to work on some of the issues we've noticed so far. Is Rhubie struggling? I haven't noticed anything, but I haven't had a chance to speak with Ms. Walsh yet either."

"No." Ash sounded choked up.

Chris wished she could see Ash's face, know what she wasn't saying, find a way to pry it out of her. She'd broken the trust between them though, somehow seventeen years ago, Chris had broken the delicate trust between teacher and student. She might never be able to make amends for that.

"I'll continue to watch out for them and make sure they have everything they need. I promise."

"Forgive me for not believing you."

A male voice could be heard through the phone. Chris didn't strain to hear it, but when Ash came back, she said she had to go and hung up quickly. Chris frowned as she stood at her desk. What had she done that was so bad? She just wished she knew. Not because she thought she could change Ash's mind, but at least she could apologize.

CHAPTER
Eight

ASH WAS ready to pull her hair out. First the phone call from the school and now this? She stared at her office that she hadn't even had time to settle into and wondered not for the first time why she had decided to take this job. Working at a nonprofit that helps homeless families get back on their feet had always been a dream of hers, but she had been thrown into the fires of a brand new job when she'd spent the last seven years working from home on her true passion, and she was regretting her choices.

The flu.

That was her current problem. The flu was going around the house, and multiple people had it, which meant that she was struggling to find coverage for overnight staffing, and it wasn't like she could just step in. Not like she would have done when Mari was around or even before that when she'd been single. No, now she had two kids, and it was obvious they needed her attention. Today was proof of that.

"Ash." The knock on the door startled her. Jack stepped in just a little bit, but he had a smile on his face. Her program director was proving to be worth everything in the last few weeks as she'd tried to get her feet wet in the nonprofit sector again. "I found someone."

"Who?"

"She's a volunteer, but she's done overnights for us in emergencies before, and has all the requirements. She'll be here at seven but is in meetings until then. Can you cover the break in between? I can't miss this appointment."

"Yeah, I can stay until seven." She would owe Char a bottle of wine for taking the girls until she got home, but she could afford that.

"Good. I've got to run!" He was already walking out the door before she could catch him to figure out exactly who was coming and how to get ahold of her if she didn't show up on time. Trusting wasn't in Ash's nature in general, but especially when it came to volunteers.

The house was still quiet, with most everyone gone for work and the kids out for childcare. Ash blew out a breath and rubbed her temple. She was overwhelmed. The weight of the world was on her shoulders, and she had no chance to share the load anymore.

What on earth had she been thinking? Moving her kids across the country and going back into the workforce—this was a disaster in the making. She'd willingly walked into it too. But she needed a job, so that one wasn't really an option any longer, and she needed the support of her family. She wished her parents had agreed to move out to Seattle. Her mom had been there for most of the first six months after Mari had died. Ash wasn't sure how she would have survived without that.

But it had been two years, and while she was back on her feet, there were things that still weren't quite right. She just wished it was easier to fix the problems in her life. Then again, nothing could fix the devastation they had been through. This was their new reality.

Time sped by, but Ash managed to drag herself out of her office long enough to help the families with making their dinner.

She kept glancing at the clock, waiting for this mysterious volunteer to show up. It was five minutes to seven when there was a knock on the front door.

"Finally," Ash murmured. She needed to get home. She needed to find her quiet space again and unwind from the day.

She swung the front door open, ready to meet the volunteer, get her set up, and go home. Except she was frozen to her spot. Speechless.

"Chris."

Chris' lips slowly curled upward, but it didn't reach her eyes. Her hair was around her shoulders like it normally was. Ash wanted to reach out and touch it. She wanted to wrap her arms around Chris and let Chris hold her and take away the stress of the long day. But she still couldn't move. Her chest was so tight, cold washing through her until her toes were frozen.

"What are you doing here?" The accusation was stark, but Ash had no idea what else to say.

"Jack called me. You needed someone to stay the night."

"You're my overnight..." Ash trailed off. She stepped out onto the front step and shut the door behind her with a loud snick. "You volunteer here."

"Yes." Chris canted her head to the side. "I have for the last three years."

Ash rubbed her hands over her face roughly. "Do you just follow me everywhere?"

"No, I don't." Chris sighed heavily. She put her hands on her hips, parting the sides of her down jacket to reveal her blazer and T-shirt she'd worn to school that day. The bag at her feet must have her overnight stuff in it. "I guess we just keep running into each other."

"You're the last person I wanted to see."

"I'm sorry that I am." Chris frowned.

Guilt punched Ash in the gut. That had been cruel to say, but she was still so shaken by everything that had happened in the last few weeks. She clenched her jaw and looked Chris directly in the eye. "I'm sorry. That was mean."

"Not anything you don't feel, and you're entitled to feel whatever you want." Chris shrugged. "Am I allowed in?"

"Is this really why you're here?" Ash didn't want to believe that Chris could be this kind, not with how she'd been when she was growing up. "You didn't decide to follow up on the phone call from earlier?"

"Ashton, how would I have even known you were here?"

Why was Ash being so unreasonable? She fisted her hand and then stretched out her fingers. She had to get a hold of herself. "Fine."

"Thank you."

Chris still didn't move, and neither did Ash. They stood in the doorway, staring each other down, like they were going to battle each other to the death.

"And stop calling me Ashton. I hate that name."

"In high school, you told me to call you that. You said if your parents had wanted to name you Ash, they would have."

Ash's jaw dropped. "How do you remember that?"

"Like I told you before, you were one of my favorite students. I tend to remember my favorites." Chris' eyes are dark in the lack of light, but the intensity of her gaze was clear.

There was no escaping her. Chris had haunted her dreams for years after that class. Ash had almost given up writing because of her, but then in college, Chris' voice had been in her head every time she'd started a new story.

Make sure it's a strong start.

Finish every scene with a hook.

Use a variety of words.

Follow the arcs of the plot, of the characters.

Make your reader feel something profound.

It was all simple instructions, but repetition had forced them into Ash's brain throughout the years. Even when she'd been writing her books and publishing them, Chris' voice was still in her head. She'd been with her every time Ash had sat down at a computer to type.

So why did Ash want to lean in and kiss her? Why did she want to curl up in Chris' arms and be held? Everything in her body pulled her closer to Chris. Ash stepped off the porch onto the sidewalk so she wasn't towering over Chris anymore.

"How many times have you stayed the night here?"

"At least a dozen last year alone." Chris remained steady.

"And why do you volunteer here?"

Chris stayed put, but Ash took another step closer, unable to resist being as near as possible. Her breathing came in shallow gasps, and her head spun from something she wasn't quite ready to name yet.

"I like to give back to my community, but it started with tutoring. I needed to keep myself busy, and tutoring was a natural place for me to do that."

Ash bit her lip. "Tutoring?"

"For GEDs for the adults and anything else they might need, and for the kids, whatever subjects they needed help with. You'd be amazed what you can learn with three degrees in education."

She had no doubt of that, and the reminder of Chris' education, of her tenacity for studies, of her willingness to put in the hard work wasn't what she needed right now. "We have four families in the house right now."

"Busy busy."

"Seven adults and twelve kids total."

"I'm sure they're all well versed in the program."

Ash shook her head. There was one family that was continuously having issues following the program, and she was probably going to have to make the hard choice to kick them out within the next week.

"Some of the kids are unruly."

"You would be too if you didn't have any structure or place of security."

Ash's lips parted, instantly thinking of Avonlee. That had

been swiped from them all in one fell swoop, but Avonlee had dealt with the biggest blow from it. At least for now.

"What?" Chris touched Ash's arm. "What are you thinking about right now?"

Tensing, Ash stared down at Chris' fingers, warm, comforting. "Avonlee."

"She's hurting, Ashton."

"I know." Ash looked up, meeting that unwavering gaze. How was Chris so much the same and so different at the same time? "You haunted me."

"Haunted?" Chris withdrew her hand.

Ash missed the touch. "You still do."

"How do I haunt you?" Chris whispered the words, as if they were a caress against Ash's skin.

Oh, what would it take to lean in a little more? To have Chris' hands on her? To shut up that voice, that lecturing voice, that Ash had memorized? "Why didn't you ever leave me alone?"

"I don't know what you're talking about. I wish I did." Chris shuddered in the freezing air. "But you don't have to tell me if you don't want to. You feel I was awful to you, and that's your right."

"Of course it is," Ash murmured, her gaze drawing down over Chris' body again. She wanted to talk. She wanted to tell Chris everything, but the words got stuck in the top of her throat, and she couldn't force them out.

"Look, I know that this is hard." Chris' voice was raw, emotion clasping onto every syllable. "I don't want to put the onus on you to help me right my wrongs, but I will listen if you ever want to tell me."

"Chris." Her name cracked at the end. Ash closed her eyes, sucking in a deep breath of the freezing air and using it to center herself. "I have to go home and talk to Avonlee."

"Don't be too hard on her about today. It was an honest mistake."

Ash found herself nodding, but she wasn't sure why. "Um, I guess I should take you in."

"It'd be preferable to standing out in the cold."

The air finally broke through Ash's clouded mind, and she realized just how cold it was. She laughed lightly before keying in the code to the door and letting them inside. "Even if you can only stay one night, it'll be helpful. But I'll warn you, the flu is going around."

"Ashton, I'm a school teacher. I don't get sick."

"I wish I had your stamina." Ash's cheeks were instantly on fire, remembering their one night of happiness. Despite everything that had happened in between then and now, Ash was amazed that it hadn't turned into a nightmare yet.

Chris stopped in the doorway, snagging Ash's hand briefly before letting go. "Can we talk? Truly talk, outside of here and school?"

Ash paused, not sure how to answer. She wasn't sure she wanted to. Well, she did, but that would open a world she hadn't dared enter in years. "Do you know where the room is?"

"Ashton," Chris pleaded.

"I'll show you." Ash led the way into the basement, away from where the families stayed and toward the offices. She would introduce Chris to everyone next, make sure everyone was settled, and then she'd leave for the weekend.

Chris followed her dutifully down the stairs. They dropped her bag off, and Ash introduced her to everyone. She stayed another twenty minutes before grabbing her stuff and heading for the front door. She had to escape. Because Chris was going to talk to her, she knew it. There was no escaping Chris Murphey.

Sure enough, Ash was at the front door when Chris caught her by the elbow. "Give me another minute."

"I'm tired, Chris."

"Glad to hear you use my first name again." Chris kept her voice quiet, as if anyone could overhear them at any moment, which was probably true. "Please talk to me in the morning. We've been avoiding this far too long."

Ash's voice caught in her throat again. Her mouth was open like she was going to speak, but she couldn't form the words. Why couldn't she just find the words? Not here, not in her writing. It was as if they had vanished from her in the loud crack of a vehicle against cement. Her eyes watered, her nose stinging as her cheeks heated. She shook her head slowly.

"Ashton," Chris whispered, empathy filling her gaze.

Doing the only thing she could think of, Ash wrapped her arms around Chris' shoulders and held on. She buried her face in Chris' neck, the scent from her shampoo filling her, the warmth of her body surrounding her. Ash clung tightly.

"Oh, Ashton," Chris murmured in comfort along with a caress. Her hands pressed against Ash's back, pulling her in even closer.

This was perfect. If Ash could live here, right in the circle of Chris' arms, she knew she could find her words again. She knew without a doubt that she would be safe again. "Don't let me go."

"I won't." Chris tightened her grip. "Just tell me what you need."

Ash shook her head, the tears flowing freely down her cheeks and disappearing into Chris' hair. "I can't."

"Okay." Chris rubbed circles into Ash's shoulders. "Okay."

"I'm sorry." Ash pulled away suddenly, wiping her fingers against her cheeks. "Tomorrow. I'll text you."

She ran out the front door of the house before she had a chance to regret her decision. Ash gathered herself throughout her drive home, and when she pulled up into her driveway, she was happy to see the warm house in front of her. She didn't hesitate walking inside, or feel weighed down by the responsibilities on her shoulders. Rhubie ran up and wrapped arms around her in a hug. Ash looked over Avonlee, sitting curled up on the couch with her *Nintendo Switch* and a blanket.

Char looked confused, but Ash smiled at her before walking

to the couch and pulling Avonlee into her arms. She dropped a kiss onto Avonlee's head, nuzzled her nose into her hair, and hugged her tight. "I heard you had a rough day, baby."

Avonlee said nothing, but the sniffle was loud enough for the entire house to hear it.

"Want to have a calm relaxing night?"

"You're not mad?" Avonlee squeaked out.

"No, baby. No, I'm not mad."

This was what Ash had needed more than anything. Rhubie slid against Ash's other side, cuddling into the crook of her arm. This was Ash's happiness, and she never should have thought otherwise.

CHAPTER
Nine

WERE THEY MEETING?

Or were they not meeting?

Chris hadn't really gotten that question answered. Ash had said something about tomorrow. Well, it was tomorrow. And she still didn't know if they were meeting or not or when or where. She sighed, tossing her hand over her eyes as she laid in the uncomfortable bed in the basement of the transitional housing building. Jack had asked her to be there all weekend, but Chris suspected that Ash was unaware of that, especially based on their conversation the night before.

Taking a risk, Chris grabbed her phone and sent the text she had been avoiding all night.

Chris 6:59 am - Just to clarify, are we meeting today?

She held her breath as she waited for a response, but she also didn't expect one. Without Ash right in front of her, it would be easier for Ash to avoid. Which she seemed rather good at doing. Something they had in common, actually. But Chris didn't want to avoid this any longer. Two weeks of it was enough, and if she could help resolve some of that conflict, it would probably go a long way for both of them.

Ash 7:03 am - Yes.

Chris nearly jumped out of bed with excitement. She hadn't honestly thought it would happen. She'd been convinced Ash would back out by now, but she wasn't. With the house slowly waking up, Chris got dressed and ready to leave. Overnights at the house were the easiest, and she only had to wait until nine for her replacement to show up and then she could meet Ash somewhere. Neutral ground might be the best option for this conversation, but Chris would take it wherever she could have it.

By nine she was out the door with her bag in hand and sitting in her freezing cold car. She always forgot to warm it up on days like this. Rubbing her fingers together as she sat outside the transitional house, Chris snagged her phone and sent another text.

Chris 9:07 am - When and where?

She wanted the conversation to happen immediately, but she also knew that Ash had to be the one to direct everything. Chris drove back to her place, starting up coffee because she needed more in order to make it through the day before going back to the transitional home. She had two more nights there before Jack said they'd evaluate who was going to replace her. She didn't look forward to starting a week of school with a lack of sleep, but it was for a good cause.

Chris had just plopped down on her couch with her coffee when there was a knock at her door. Frowning, she stood up to answer it, sloshing a bit of her coffee over the rim of her mug and onto her thigh. Cursing under her breath, Chris moved to the door and opened it.

"Ash." She breathed out Ash's name, surprise echoing. "Did you remember where I lived?"

"I sent a pin to my sister with where I was that night. Just in case anything went bad." Ash shoved her hands into her pockets and pushed up on her toes. "Got time to talk?"

"Yeah." Chris' stomach twisted with nerves. She hadn't expected this, and she wasn't sure what was going to happen next. Fear ramped right back up into her chest, and she'd thought she'd gotten rid of it. Everything about their conversation the night before had been on edge, and she hoped they'd be able to dig a little deeper this morning with clearer heads and sleep—though the amount of sleep Chris had got couldn't be considered much.

"Got any coffee?" Ash pointed at Chris' mug still in her hand.

"Sure. How do you like it?"

"Black is good."

Chris still wasn't sure what to do. She needed to focus on the conversation, but her mind was in overdrive as she thought about the possibilities of what could happen, about the fact that Ash was back in her space, what they had already done here. Chris bit the inside of her cheek to keep herself in check. She couldn't be thinking like that. Ash had made no inclinations that she wanted that to happen, and it had just been one night. Those boundaries were set from the start, but with all the recent discoveries, everything was a disaster.

With Ash's coffee poured, Chris led the way back to the couch. Then she regretted it. This had been where they'd first fucked, and the scratchy fabric of the couch against Chris' skin was most memorable. Ash seemed to hesitate briefly before sitting down.

"You wanted to talk," Ash whispered, not looking at Chris. Her eyes were glued to the coffee.

She was uncomfortable. But Chris couldn't tell if it was because of the topic of conversation or the fact they were in the room together. Chris pressed her lips together hard, choosing her words carefully. "I wanted to listen."

Ash raised her gaze then, meeting Chris'. "Listen?"

"Yeah." Chris sipped her coffee. "Listen."

Blowing out a breath, Ash set her coffee on the table and relaxed back into the couch. But her entire body was still tense. If Chris didn't know better, she'd say she was anxious. "You made junior year a living hell."

"How?" Chris genuinely wanted to know. She wanted to see if there was anything she needed to change for the future, something that she could be doing better than she had in the past.

"Do you remember when you told us we could write anything? Just some fictional story, any genre, our choice?"

Chris nodded, though she didn't remember what Ash had written. It wasn't that unusual for her to give that assignment, and she had done it for years before switching into an administrative role.

"You hated my piece."

"Hated it?" Surely Chris would remember that. She tried to think back, tried to pull the pages from the back of her mind, but she couldn't for the life of her remember it. "I doubt I hated it. I never hated anything you wrote."

Ash snorted loudly. "You put red marks over everything."

"That's my job as a teacher."

"No one else had red marks like that!"

"Did I say anything mean?" Chris held her mug tightly. "Did I say anything that was out of line?"

Ash sat still for a few moments, thinking before she slowly shook her head. "You weren't unnecessarily cruel."

"So how did I bully you?"

"I didn't want your extra attention." Ash clenched her jaw tightly. "I wanted you to leave me alone."

Chris nodded slowly, trying to take that in. What was she supposed to say to that? She ran her finger around the rim of her mug as she thought. "I'm sorry I didn't see how you were interpreting my actions."

Ash sighed. "But you did help me."

"Help?" Chris raised her eyebrow.

"I was a full-time author until a few years ago when I stopped writing. That's why I'm back to working in the nonprofit sector." Ash wrung her hands together tightly.

"You're a published author?" Chris couldn't stop the grin from reaching her lips. "So you actually did what you said you would do. You did it, Ash!"

When Ash turned and looked at her, there were tears in her eyes. Again, Chris couldn't place the cause. She wished she knew, but those weren't tears of joy. Reaching out, Chris settled her hand on Ash's to calm her. "Look, I know you don't trust me, but if you ever want to talk about what *that* is, please, talk to me."

Ash's lips parted in surprise, but she shook her head. "It's nothing."

"You said you stopped writing. Why?"

"Life." Ash shrugged. "Life got hard with two kids and drama, and I stopped to focus on my family."

"That's understandable. Will you go back to it?"

"No," Ash whispered. "No, I don't think I will."

"Pity. You were my best student, and few have come close to your abilities since. You have an innate sense for the written word and for storytelling. That's all I was trying to encourage you toward." Chris squeezed Ash's fingers and let go, not wanting to linger too long and make her uncomfortable.

"Avonlee likes you," Ash croaked out.

Chris jerked her head back in surprise. "I barely know her. That's the downside to being principal. I don't get to know the kids as well as I used to when I was teaching."

"Well, she likes you. It's one of the few things she confessed to me last night." Ash rubbed her palms together before grabbing her mug. "Should be some consolation."

"She's struggling. All I wanted to do was to help her."

"Well, it worked, for now at least. She was calmer last night."

"You didn't yell at her for bringing the necklace, did you?"

"Hmm, no. I figured she felt guilty enough about it." Ash ran her fingers through her hair, the strands loose around her shoulders today, still damp from a shower.

Chris readily resisted the urge to touch them and held onto her mug. "I'm glad. Is the ring yours?"

Ash nodded slowly, her gaze flicking to meet Chris' eyes before dropping back down. "I suppose she told you what it was for."

Chris shrugged, a noncommittal response. "After our first kid, Katie, Andry and I struggled to have another. Nothing worked."

"How old is your daughter?"

"She just turned nineteen. First year in college." Chris finished her coffee and was reluctant to set the mug down. It was a good distraction for her hands and to keep her body to herself. She and Ash weren't the same people who had met all those weeks ago or all those years ago, and she had to tread lightly if she didn't want to mess this up any more than she already had. "Both Andry and I struggled, so Katie is our pride and joy."

Ash reached out and gripped Chris' hand tightly, squeezing once before letting go. The touch of her fingers lingered on Chris' skin, a ghost that was already gone and cold. But that meant Chris was moving in the right direction, wasn't it? Chris rubbed her hands along her thighs. Why were they here again?

"Ms. Dunja loves having Avonlee in her class, and after the incident Friday, I checked with Ms. Walsh about Rhubie, and she said she's doing really well in class."

"Rhubie is my rockstar, always able to hold her shit together until the weight becomes too much and she cracks. But then she's right back to her normal self the next day."

Chris raised an eyebrow in curiosity. Just what had this family gone through? She was tempted to research it, see if she could figure it out, but she also wanted to honor Ash's privacy and the fact that this was her story to tell. Chris couldn't force her into it if she didn't want to share.

"Avonlee is too much like me. React first, ask for forgiveness later." Ash's cheeks tinged red. "Is Katie more like you or Andry?"

"God, I hope she's more like Andry, but I fear she's way too much like me."

"Is she enjoying college?"

Chris paused. She wanted to be as honest as she could be, but she also didn't want to drop too many bombs into this relationship that already seemed to be littered with landmines. "Katie and I don't talk a lot, not since Andry and I separated. I think she's enjoying school."

"Oh." Ash turned her chin up. "I'm so sorry."

"Don't be. It's my own fault. I wasn't a great parent for a number of years, and Katie is still suffering from that." Chris hated admitting that, but it was true. She had done irreparable damage to their relationship, and as much as she hoped for some sort of reconciliation, she wasn't sure it was even possible. They'd tried a number of times but had always failed after a few months.

Ash looked shocked.

Chris' lips parted as she looked directly at her. "What?"

"Most people can't admit that, or anything close to that."

"I've done a lot of work on myself in the last few years. Sometimes it pays off to be self-aware."

"And other times it's devastating with how shitty a person you've been?"

"Most days." Chris gave Ash a wry smile. "Like bullying my student."

"I guess you weren't really a bully. But you were a jerk."

"Fair." Chris didn't want to stop smiling. The lightness that had entered the conversation was something she appreciated, and she wanted to keep it. "So where are the girls today?"

"Char took them to Denver to the zoo. I'm supposed to be

finishing more unpacking." Ash shrugged slightly. "I'm so tired of boxes."

Laughing again, Chris relaxed back into the couch and stretched her arm out along the top edge of it. "I swore after I moved out of the house when we separated that I'd never move again."

"And did you?"

"Three times already, and moving Katie into her dorm." Chris rolled her eyes. "Never say never. Isn't that what they always say?"

"Yeah." Ash's tone turned breathy, a look of longing crossing her features before she masked it.

Good, so they were both on the same page there. Sex between them wouldn't ever happen again. This was simply putting water under the bridge, which was something they both needed to do.

"Why do you volunteer at Hope in Action?"

Chris hummed, debating once again on how honest to be. It wasn't that she didn't want to share everything with Ash, but Ash was still a parent at her school. She had to keep some sort of boundaries between them, and it was her job to do it. "It keeps me out of trouble, and I like giving back to my community. Truly. Some of the kids who have been through the house have been my students, and they need as much support as they can possibly get."

"That's admirable."

The compliment was unexpected. Chris wasn't sure what to do with it, so she remained silent. What were they supposed to do now? They'd talked, though Chris wasn't entirely sure they had gotten everything out of the way yet, but one conversation wouldn't accomplish that.

"Are we...okay?" Chris finally asked, stumbling over her words.

Ash jerked around to face her. "Okay?"

"With each other. With everything that's happened..." she

trailed off, not quite sure how to even begin to put all of that into words. "I just want to make sure that we're okay."

With a slow shake of her head, Ash stared, dumbfounded. "Why wouldn't we be okay?"

"Ash, you called me your high school bully."

"But...but I was wrong, okay? I was wrong." Ash leaned in closer, her eyes so sincere. "You weren't my bully."

Relief washed through Chris. "So are we okay, then? I don't want to make this any more difficult than it already is."

Ash's lips parted like she was going to object again, but Chris stopped her with a quick shake of her head.

"You can't deny that this is a complicated situation."

"It is." Ash sighed. "My life is complicated."

"Whose isn't?"

CHAPTER

Ten

ASH WASN'T SUPPOSED to be here. But with the girl's at her parents' house for the day and night, she had nothing else to do. As soon as she opened the door to Hope in Action, she was surprised to see Chris sitting at the kitchen table. Chris had spent the entire last weekend at the house, but since then, Ash hadn't seen her. Not at school during the week, and certainly not any time after school hours. Not since the conversation in Chris' living room. Not since she'd asked the question, *Are we okay?*

A question that still haunted Ash every day. Chris' voice echoed in her mind as she heard her ask it, over and over again.

Because no, they weren't okay. Every time Ash was in the room with her, she wanted to know more, she wanted to touch and feel and go back to that night of bliss when she'd been able to forget those pesky complications for a few hours. The complications of pain and hurt and grief and devastation.

"What are you doing here?" Chris asked from the kitchen table, pulling Ash right back to the present moment.

Cold rushed over her. "I thought I'd get some work done."

"Boundaries are a thing for a reason, Ashton."

That firm voice, the commanding tone, sent a shiver through Ash, straight between her legs and settled into the pit of her stomach. God, what Ash would give to hear that tone again in an entirely different way.

Stop.

She had to stop thinking that. One night of happiness was all it could ever be, and she knew that. Why was she thinking otherwise?

"Ash?"

"What?" Ash jerked her head up, her cheeks red as she'd been caught with those thoughts in her mind.

Chris pushed out from the table and came over, concern lighting her gaze. "Everything okay?"

"Uh...yeah. Just wanted to get some work done."

"Where are the girls?"

"Grandparents. I honestly didn't think they'd be gone this much with family." In all honesty, it made Ash uncomfortable. She hated being alone, and the last two years, she had been with the girls almost every waking second she had with them.

"The novelty will wear off, I promise you." Chris skimmed her hand down Ash's arm and then dropped her hand to her side.

Ash shivered. She could blame it on the cold from outside if she needed to, but she knew the real reason. They both probably did if they thought about it. Ash hummed to herself. "I'm going to get some work done."

"Your choice, but there is such a thing as overworking."

"Speaking from experience?" Ash stared directly into Chris' dark brown eyes.

"Always." Chris ducked her chin before backing away. She went to the table and slid into the chair, pulling over a notebook that a current resident had been writing in.

Just what was Chris doing? Ash wanted desperately to go see, but she restrained herself, barely. It was a bit of her business, but she also had that new pesky word in the forefront of her mind. Boundaries. Why did Chris have to put it like that?

Ash stood at the door to her office, watching Chris as she tutored. She was kind and gentle in her approach. Was this

Chris' true passion? She'd said something about missing connections with the kids. Did she find that here? Sliding into her office for safety and comfort, Ash collapsed into her desk chair.

Ash had been on the receiving end of that attention from Chris so many times in her life. It surprised her to realize that she wanted it again. She wanted to feel Chris over her shoulder, reading whatever she had written, and commenting on it—good or bad. Ash bit her lip and closed her eyes. She hadn't felt that pull to write something since Mari had died.

She'd assumed it was gone. Vanished. Never to return. Maybe the move hadn't been in vain for everything. Then again, she wasn't sitting at a computer typing. Nope. She was daydreaming. About Chris' breasts against her shoulder, the scent of her hair, the scent of her arousal, the taste of her pussy. Ash's breathing increased. Closing her eyes, she felt Chris against her. Those soft caresses. The feel of her fingers curled around her neck, just enough pressure to make Ash wonder what she would do next and know that Chris was in complete control.

"Ash?"

Startled, Ash jerked upright with a start. Chris stood in her doorway, a curious look on her features, as if she knew what Ash had been thinking about. But she couldn't have known, right? "Uh...yeah...what's up?"

Chris crossed her arms and leaned against the doorframe. "Donald has his GED test in a couple weeks. I was wondering if I could come in and tutor him until he takes it."

"Sure." Ash choked on the word. That meant they would see even more of each other, and while Ash was fine with that on one hand, on the other, she wasn't. She needed to keep her distance, because Chris was pulling things out of her that had long remained buried.

"Thanks." Chris nodded and turned back around to leave.

"Chris?" Ash called, not sure where she was even going with the conversation, but she knew she didn't want Chris to leave yet.

"Yeah?" Chris once again leaned against the doorframe, looking like she owned the building. She belonged there more than Ash did.

Ash panicked. She had to come up with something to say now because just staring at each other wasn't an option. But Ash couldn't drag her gaze away. Chris looked so sexy standing there, her semi-professional workwear, her hair haloed around her, and her eyes bright with brilliance.

"Um...never mind. You're welcome to tutor here whenever you want."

"Great." Chris flashed her a beautiful smile. "You should call me if anyone needs something that I can help with."

Ash nodded, choking on more words. She was completely lost. When she didn't say anything else, Chris stepped into the room and shut the door behind her. She moved around the desk and sat on the edge of it, her knees parted. Ash swiveled her chair slightly so she was very nearly planted between Chris' legs. There was so much she could do in this position if she wanted to, but they were in her office in a house with a dozen other people in it. And Ash didn't want that, did she?

"Is everything okay?"

"Yeah. Why?" Cold washed through Ash. How could Chris tell so easily when she was off-kilter?

Chris quieted, holding the tension between them. Finally she placed her hands on either side of her and leaned down slightly. Her voice was quiet, as if anyone could hear them. "I don't want to overstep."

"Overstep what?"

"This line we've formed."

Ash wanted to tell her that she should overstep. That the thing she wanted the most was for Chris to lean down and kiss her again and take away all the worries and fears she had rampaging through her brain. Ash wished Chris understood that the line had already been washed away.

"I get the sense that not everything is quite right in your

world, more than the average person. You always seem like you're on the brink of shattering."

It was difficult to pull air into her lungs, her breath raggedly filling her chest. What magic was this? Ash stared directly into Chris' kind eyes. Where was the woman who had been so firm with her in high school? Where was the teacher she had hated for all those years? Because this wasn't the same person as then. Swallowing hard and clenching her jaw, Ash remained completely still.

"It's okay to break, you know." Chris leaned in even more. "Because unless we break, then we don't know what we can withstand."

"I'll keep that in mind," Ash whispered, her gaze immediately drawn to Chris' lips. What she was really thinking about was what it would feel like to taste her mouth again, the warmth and pressure of another body firmly against hers.

"Don't think you have to go it alone."

"Now you sound like my family."

Chris hummed. "Family is worth its salt most days."

"Char thinks she's the center of the world."

"Really? I didn't get that sense from her." Chris' wink belied her actual thoughts. "Still, they're not wrong. You don't have to go through whatever it is alone. Take it from someone who believed that for far too long."

Ash cocked her head. "Are you ever going to tell me about whatever you're avoiding telling me?"

"If you'll share yours, I'll share mine."

"Maybe someday." Ash's lips curled upward, happiness bubbling in her chest again. It was as though they weren't talking about the darkest hours of her life in such a casual way. Ash leaned back in her chair, crossing her legs and shaking her head. "How do you always get me like this?"

"Like what?" Chris rocked back, amusement flashing in her eyes.

"Vulnerable." The word escaped her lips quickly, but there

was no denying the truth of it. Even in the vulnerability that Chris compelled her to feel, Ash was safe. For some reason, she knew that. Whether it was because they had known each other all those years ago in a different context or if it was because Chris was such a damn good listener, she wasn't sure, but Chris made her feel perfect in her brokenness.

Chris stilled. "Vulnerability isn't a weakness, Ashton."

"No, it's not." Ash stood up, stepping right between Chris' legs so she had the upper ground. "It's a point of strength and control."

With her chin tilted upward, Chris raised an eyebrow. "So why are you saying it like it's something bad?"

"Because it's you, and I'm not supposed to like you." That was about as close as Ash could come to saying it. She wasn't ready to dare herself to breathe more life into what was impossible. Because the hope shouldn't be there. But that was the odd thing about hope, it often bloomed when least expected and when most unwanted.

Chris reached forward and snagged Ash's hand. She rubbed the pad of her thumb across Ash's skin in a slow, tender motion. Ripples of that hope she'd been avoiding rolled through her, cascading down her spine and settling into the depths of her body. Was this something she should even dare to dream of happening? Or was it only night two in their one night of happiness?

"Come to dinner with me," Chris said, her voice firm but still quiet.

"Dinner?"

"Yeah." Chris smiled, finally roving her gaze from Ash's hand, up her body, over her breasts, her lips, to her eyes. "Dinner."

"Like a date?" Ash swallowed down the sudden rise of fear. She didn't need a date or another love. She'd already had that once, and no one was going to replace Mari.

"If you want it to be. If not, then it's two *friends* having dinner after a long, stressful week." Chris hadn't dropped her hand yet, and that rhythm of Chris' thumb across Ash's skin hadn't stopped.

"Where will we go?"

"The Met? It's a fancier place in town, but still low key."

"Okay," Ash answered before she could even think about the potential consequences. But she was alone that night, and the last thing she wanted was to be stuck by herself in her house. She wasn't used to it, and it wasn't something she wanted to get used to either.

"Let's go then." Chris squeezed Ash's hand. "That is if you're done with whatever you came here to do tonight."

I came to escape. The words were on the tip of her tongue, but Ash wouldn't let them out. Not yet. Not without more trust built between them. Instead, she said, "Let's go."

CHAPTER
Eleven

WHAT ON EARTH had she been thinking?

Chris cringed. She was supposed to be putting up boundaries and keeping them, not tearing them down every second she got. She needed a meeting to get her head on straight. She needed to talk to her sponsor and her therapist, and figure out exactly what she was supposed to be doing, because it surely wasn't this.

It didn't take her long to pull up outside the restaurant and park. She had no idea how far behind her Ash was. But the question asked lingered in her mind like a siren shouting out a warning.

Is this a date?

Perhaps the more important question for Chris to answer was, did she want it to be a date? She was so used to helping bleeding souls and not taking care of herself, that she had a tenuous line to walk. Ash was hurting over something, but Chris had to remind herself that she didn't have to be the person to fix it.

That wasn't her job.

Chris stepped out of her car and pulled her down jacket tighter around her shoulders. The cold air was coming in right at the beginning of February like it always did, and she knew the next two weeks were going to be some of the coldest in the year. Ash probably wasn't prepared for it. When Chris got to the front of the restaurant, she was surprised to find Ash already there.

"Hey," Chris said, awkwardly. Where was this person coming from? She was never accused of being timid.

"Hey there. Long time no see." Ash's cheeks had a beautiful red to them. She'd pulled her hair back in a messy bun on the way there. Her nose and ears were red from the cold, and Chris wanted to kiss away the chill.

Those thoughts had to stop immediately. They'd made it very clear from the start that it was a one-night stand and nothing more. Chris didn't want anything more than that. Or did she? Because she'd certainly thought about it more than just the one night. Despite her many attempts, getting Ash off her mind wasn't easy.

They moved to the dining portion of the restaurant, sitting across from each other. Chris ordered a soda and waited with interest to see what Ash would order. Once again, she ordered a non-alcoholic drink. There was definitely more to that than being responsible. Chris wanted to find out what it was.

"Too quiet at home?" Chris asked.

She could tell by Ash's response that it was unexpected, but she wasn't going to hold back, at least not on this. Chris leaned back in her chair and waited for Ash to start to open up a little more. It seemed both of them were too used to having the reins on their life tight, but each time they had these quiet moments, that grip loosened.

"I suppose you would understand that."

"That was the hardest part about separating from Andry. Well, aside from the ending of the relationship. Learning to sleep in a place on my own again was devastating."

"I never thought I'd have to do it. In Seattle, we didn't have any family around, so it was always me and the girls."

"Never sent them to the grandparents for a week?" Chris

played with the napkin on the table, needing something to do with her hands otherwise she might be too tempted to touch Ash's fingers again. While that had been nice, the word *boundaries* echoed back into her brain again. That was her one and only job in this, and she was already on the wrong side of that line.

"No." Ash thanked the waiter when their drinks arrived.

They ordered their food and settled in to wait for it. Chris couldn't keep her eyes away from her. Ash was beautiful. She'd grown up since high school, because Chris had never looked at her like this then. Ash was a woman now, and honestly, had that one night of happiness not happened, Chris wasn't sure that she would have ever looked at Ash like this. But mistakes were mistakes, and she probably shouldn't repeat them.

"I always enjoyed when Katie would go to my mom's for a night here or there. Gave me time to spend with Andry doing something fun."

Ash's cheeks paled. Chris had no doubts that she was a single parent, but despite what the kids had told her, and Ash, no one had explained what had happened to their other mother. And Chris wasn't about to ask either.

"Do you want to take kid-talk off the table for the night? Sometimes it's nice to have a break from all that." Chris watched Ash carefully, trying to detect any signs that Ash was distressed or uncomfortable. While she did look tense, Chris couldn't quite tell if it was because they were out at dinner or if there was something else going on that she didn't know about.

"That'd be nice," Ash answered. "I do miss adult conversation."

Chris chuckled. "So...what brought you into the nonprofit sector?"

"I've always volunteered for something. It's how Mari and I met, years ago."

Mari. The name rang a bell in Chris' mind, but she struggled to place it.

"We volunteered together to build houses, and when I started working there after high school, I couldn't avoid what I'd been feeling for her much longer." Ash's face lit up, her eyes gleeful with the memory.

Chris ran her thumb along the pads of her other fingers, focusing on the gentle touch as a way to center herself. "And you just continued to work in it?"

"I did. Mari left and got a job as a bank manager. It was the only way we could afford to live in Seattle." Ash chuckled lightly. "But I've always loved it, so when I gave up writing, it seemed like the perfect place to step back into the world."

Chris wanted to talk about that. She wanted Ash to go back to her passion and thrive in it, though she couldn't be sure that still was Ash's passion. Chris smiled as their food was put in front of them. "So what have you written?"

"Uh uh uh, teach. That is the whole point of a pen name."

Chuckling, Chris shook her head. "There are many reasons for a pen name, Ashton." If Ash was going to play the teacher card, then Chris was going to push right back on it. At the very least, they seemed to have moved beyond that barrier.

"Oh, I know." Ash winked. "Marketing is among the top reasons for one. I'm honestly surprised you haven't read any of my books."

"Books?" Chris settled her fork on the edge of her plate. "So you have multiple books out?"

"And I write young adult."

Chris sucked in a breath. She was usually quite up-to-date on what new books were out there, but she hadn't seen any that she would suspect were Ash's in the last few years. Then again, she had pretty much stopped reading in the last five. Giving up, Chris went back to eating. "You'll have to tell me some day if you want. That way I can read them. Maybe I'll make the entire school read them for a contest."

Ash laughed, but the nervous energy flowed through it.

With the fork poised for another bite, Chris froze on the

spot. Andry and Isla walked into the dining room, hand in hand. She never could escape, could she? She cringed, knowing exactly what Andry was going to think, catching her out twice with the same woman. Chris settled her fork back down and sent Ash an apologetic look. "I'm so sorry."

"For what?"

"Chris." Andry's warm tones rushed over her.

Drawing in a steadying breath, Chris folded her hands together and looked up at her ex-wife. The woman she had called in a panic when she'd found out she'd had sex with a parent, with the very woman sitting across the table from her now. And she'd never called her back to tell her exactly who Ash was. "How's it going, Andry?"

"Good. I didn't expect to see you here." Andry's smile was sweet and honest. She always was. Chris missed that some days, and still found comfort in the fact they could maybe be friends again.

Of course Andry didn't expect to find her there. Chris clearly had to get some new dinner spots if she was going to keep dating. Nope...that's not what they were doing. It wasn't that she minded seeing Andry, but being out on what could have been called a date, twice now, and running into the ex-wife really wasn't what Chris wanted to keep everything flowing in the right direction. Again, not the direction she really wanted it to go.

"Just thought we'd grab a late dinner." Chris' shoulders were rock hard from the tension.

"That's what we thought too." Andry pointed toward Isla who was already sitting down.

Of all people, Chris had expected Isla to come over and talk to them. She was the chattier of the two, but then again, maybe she wasn't as comfortable with the dynamic as Chris had originally thought. Or maybe Andry was pushing buttons that Isla didn't agree to. Either way, Chris wasn't going to step into that argument. It wasn't her battle to fight. What she wanted was for

Andry to vanish so she could finish her meal with Ash and run out of there.

Ash's knee bumped hers under the table. Chris flicked her gaze to Ash curiously, and once again, Ash pressed her knee up against Chris'. Was this a show of comfort? Solidarity? Or was it a damn coincidence that Chris was reading way too much into? Either way, Chris was going to take it for what she needed in that moment, which was knowing that she wasn't alone.

"I guess it shouldn't come as a surprise that when you're with someone for seventeen years you learn to like the same places."

"Probably not." Chris sounded light-hearted, yet she was anything but. The tension in her shoulders and neck tightened.

"It was good seeing you again, Chris."

"Always a pleasure, Andry." She didn't mean it as a dig, but she was pretty sure it came out that way. Chris was always the one fucking things up in their relationship, not Andry, so if her sarcastic comment pertained to anyone, it wasn't Andry.

Andry faltered in a step before waving her hand and looking directly at Ash. "Good seeing you again. I hope you're keeping her in line."

"It's not my job to keep anyone in line," Ash countered.

"Ah, well, then, my mistake." Andry blushed before nodding her head and finally walking away.

"Well, that was weird." Ash picked up her fork, but her leg didn't move. In fact, now half her leg was against Chris'.

"It can be." Chris blew out a breath and tried to focus on her dinner, but the appetite she'd had minutes ago was completely gone. What was the tension in her belly? Whatever it was, she wanted it gone.

"Do you think it'll ever get easier?"

Was Ash a mind reader? Chris looked her directly in the eye, wondering how someone so young was so wise. Then she realized how, and all those strained emotions and control in holding them back came to mind. Ash had experienced a wealth of terror and trauma—there was no other explanation for it.

"This is easier, believe it or not. Last year? It was way worse than this. We barely functioned to talk about financial aid stuff or buying a car for Katie."

Ash knocked her knee into Chris' a little hard, proving that the touch wasn't just accidental. "Hey, I thought you said no kid talk."

"What I should have said was no ex-talk."

"Fair, fair." Ash was smiling again, and Chris already felt lighter. The conversation slowed, and when Chris looked back up, Ash was staring directly at her. "Do you want to go?"

"We're not even done with eating," Chris protested.

"I don't get the sense you're very hungry anymore."

Oh, Chris was hungry all right, just not for the food in front of her. She raked her gaze all over Ash's face, to her lips, and down to her chest before slowly moving back up to meet her eyes.

Ash giggled. "Never mind!"

"I never can keep a blank face."

"No, no, you can't." Ash grinned broadly and grabbed the bill that had been brought over to pay for their meal. "But that's what I like about you so much. You never hold anything back."

"Ash, you don't have to pay for my meal." Chris reached for the bill, but Ash jerked it away.

"It's only fair since you paid the other night."

Chris sighed but let Ash pay. They didn't even ask for boxes as they got up and left. The cold air outside was a welcome reminder of what was inside, and a nice jar back to reality. Chris couldn't be doing this. Ash was her former student, a current parent, and quite frankly, Chris was so messed up that no one deserved to walk into that disaster-in-wait.

"Take a walk with me." Ash wrapped her arm in Chris'.

"I don't think that's a good idea," Chris finally said what she'd been avoiding. Chris turned and faced Ash, looking up into her eyes. Ash had to understand what dire circumstances they were under, right? What a bad decision this was?

"Why not?" Ash was smiling again, but it didn't fully reach her eyes.

"Ashton," Chris murmuring her name disappeared into the wind. "I'm their principal."

"I know. But this isn't anything we haven't done before."

"What is *this*?" Chris wanted to plant her hands on her hips, give Ash the patented principal look, but Ash still had her hands curled around Chris' bicep as she hung on.

"I don't know." Ash canted her head to the side, something running through her mind because her features went from contemplating to devious. "I guess we should find out, huh?"

"What's that me—" Chris was cut off when Ash pressed her lips against Chris'.

Humming, Chris' eyes fluttered shut. She was surrounded by a mix of sensations, the warmth of Ash's body with the cold air and biting wind. Her heart fluttered rapidly but her mind moved like molasses. Chris stepped in closer, letting instinct take over.

She had to stop thinking. She had to stop coming up with excuses and reasons they shouldn't be doing this because the more she did that the more she wanted it. Chris parted her lips and tilted her head up, capturing more of Ash's mouth with her own. She wrapped her fingers in the back of Ash's hair, pulling her in closer and melding their fronts together.

This was everything.

Whatever *this* was, Ash had been right. They just needed to test the waters and find out. Chris pulled away enough to nip at Ash's lower lip and dive back in. Everything was like that second kiss they had had only better. This time it wasn't two strangers fucking in the middle of the night. This was actual happiness, with barriers down, with vulnerabilities out in the open. This was joy.

Chris' eyes teared up, watering in the corners as she snaked her free hand around Ash's back. Heaven had to be this. Everything was so different even though they had already done this. Honesty and truth were the words that came to mind, dragging

Chris deeper into the embrace. Their tongues touched, tangling together and heating up even more.

She didn't want to let go. The idea struck her harder than she expected, and Chris doubled down on her efforts to keep Ash against her. She moved a hand around to Ash's front, against her hip bone, sliding her fingers upward and under Ash's shirt. If they didn't stop now, Chris wasn't sure she was going to be able to.

The clearing throat froze her.

Chris broke away, her heart racing and her breathing shallow. She looked into Ash's eyes and feared who she would see next.

"Sorry for interrupting."

No she isn't. Chris stopped that line of thought. She had to give Andry the benefit of the doubt. Chris straightened her shoulders and faced her ex-wife down.

"What's up?"

"Katie just texted that she's coming home for spring break. She asked me to tell you."

"Sounds good. I'll see if we can get together when she's here."

Andry nodded, her lips curling up in the corners in a beautiful, true smile. "Enjoy your night, you two. You deserve it."

Andry walked away without another word. Chris' cheeks were on fire. Nope, that was a lie. Her entire body was on fire. How much more embarrassed could she possibly be?

Leaning in, Ash kissed Chris' cheek tenderly and squeezed her hand. "It's probably a good thing she stopped us, because I was just about to fuck you against the wall."

Chris groaned, her eyes closing as heat licked its way through her again. "Do you ever stop?"

"You know, this is the first time I've been interested in sex in a long time. You should be proud it's all because of you."

Chris faced Ash, the sincerity in her gaze sure. "You have to stop keeping so many secrets."

"That goes both ways, Chris." Ash kissed her on the lips,

lingering but not deepening. "I'll see you at drop off on Monday."

With that, Ash was gone, and all Chris could think about was being fucked against a wall by her former student and one hot MILF.

CHAPTER
Twelve

ASH HAD MASTURBATED. Not only was that an amazing step in and of itself, but she'd thought about Chris while she'd done it, the way Chris' body moved against hers, the heat, the passion, the pleasure. And on Monday morning at drop off, Chris was waiting outside with her coffee cup and a sexy smirk on her lips that Ash definitely wanted to test out.

She shuddered out a breath when she dropped the girls off for the day, waved to Chris who gave her a small wave back, and then left for work. Was she ready for more than one night with Chris? Ash wasn't sure, but that kiss had been enjoyable, probably one of the best she'd had in a very long time. Their relationship was something new and exciting, which meant that she couldn't stop thinking about it.

The entire morning she was in a good mood. Jack even commented on it a couple times, but Ash wouldn't tell him why. She hid in her office for the first few hours, trying to power through a lot of the work that had been missed because of so many people being out sick.

It was just before lunch when her phone rang again.

The school.

Her stomach sank.

One call last week was enough, wasn't it? Ash snagged the phone, and her hands shook when she answered it. "Hello?"

Maybe it was as simple as they ran out of lunch money or something. Or maybe one of the girls was sick. Except somewhere deep inside her, she knew that wasn't possible. This wasn't going to be one of those conversations, as much as she wanted it to be.

"Ash, it's Chris."

She wanted to cry. Tears prickled her eyes, and she dropped her head into her free hand. "What happened?"

"I think you better come down here."

Ash groaned. Her mind spun with all the possibilities. Avonlee was forever getting herself into trouble. The number of times she'd been called down to the school in the last couple years were too many to count. Ash had been foolish to think that moving there would change that. "What happened?"

"She's not being suspended, but I'm not sure she's going to want to be here the rest of the day."

"Not suspended?" Her heart thudded loudly. "Chris, quit being vague."

"There was an incident in the classroom, nothing major. But if it continues to happen it'll lead to suspension."

Ash bit her lip hard, pain searing its way through her skin and reminding herself that she had to be the parent. There wasn't another option. The old bitterness she had managed to push to the side in the last few months came rushing over her. She hadn't missed it.

"Is this something I can deal with at the end of the day when I pick her up?" Ash was trying to find any excuse to avoid going down there, avoid the role she knew she had to play but didn't want to. Her support was gone, and she hated having to be the only one everyone relied on.

"No, it's really not. I'm so sorry to call you in on this. If it could wait, I would say it could."

Ash knew that. But she still didn't want to have to drive all the way back to the school in the middle of the day if it wasn't something that could be dealt with over the phone. "I can be there within the hour."

"Okay. I'll see you soon."

Racing to finish up everything as quickly as possible, Ash then made her way back to the school after taking a half day at work. Her stomach was in a bundle of knots as she parked in front of the school and got out of the car. She wanted to break down and cry, but she couldn't. This was the time she had to be strong for Avonlee because she had a feeling she knew exactly what was setting her off. And Chris wouldn't have a clue.

Ash pressed the button to be buzzed into the school. As soon as she stepped around the corner in the hall toward the office, she was met by Chris, who had a pained expression on her face. Ash melted, however. Chris might not be Mari, but if there was anything about the last few days and observing Chris at Hope in Action, Ash had a sense that Chris was on Avonlee's side, which was exactly what her daughter needed right then. Ash needed it too, for that matter.

"She's not in trouble, mostly," Chris started.

Resisting the urge to wrap her arms around Chris in a hug that would set her right was harder than she anticipated. Ash clenched her fists against her sides and schooled her features. Everything in this moment was about her daughter, not about what Ash wanted.

"What happened?" Ash felt like she was on repeat. No one had told her anything yet, and she desperately wanted to know what was going on with her baby.

"Let's talk in my office."

The last thing Ash wanted right now was to be in a confined space with Chris. Her veins were still alive with electricity from the weekend and *that* kiss. Ash said nothing as she walked alongside Chris to the offices. Avonlee sat at a small table in the corner of the office, Ms. Linda watching her. Avonlee didn't get up. She looked at Ash and shook her head slowly before dropping her gaze back to the floor.

Ash's heart broke for her.

"Your mom and I are going to talk for a few minutes, and then you can come in and talk with us, okay?" Chris explained.

Avonlee didn't even move to recognize that she'd been spoken to. Ash frowned deeply. Was she despondent because she was guilty or was there something else going on? Ash was going to have to figure that out. Bending down next to Avonlee, Ash put a hand on her daughter's arm and squeezed.

"You okay, baby?"

"Yeah, Mama."

"Okay. You going to be good to sit out here for a few more minutes?" Ash kept her voice as calm and comforting as humanly possible. She didn't want Avonlee to be in any more dire straits than she already was.

Avonlee nodded her response but stayed silent.

Ash squeezed her arm lightly and stood back up, indicating to Chris that they could go to her office now. Stepping inside this time was vastly different than the last. Ash was far more comfortable, even though this brought back the memory of what it was like to be in Chris' gaze as a teenager. It was tolerable now when it wasn't before.

"You need to tell me what happened."

Chris sighed and sat at the small table in the corner of her office, clearly a place where she met with many people since her desk was a standing one. Ash hesitated only for a moment before sitting down and crossing her legs. Tension strained through her shoulders and up into her neck and head. She'd be lucky if she didn't get a migraine from this.

"With the incident the other week and this, Ms. Dunja is concerned about Avonlee's mental wellness."

Who isn't? Ash certainly was, and she'd meant to find a therapist in town, but they were hard to come by and those who were accepting new patients? Impossible to find. Not to mention the last one didn't exactly help any.

"The class had a project about family lineage. They're studying some genetic traits and genealogy."

Ash hadn't known about that. Then again, Avonlee rarely talked to her about anything. If she asked how school was, then she was given a standard *fine*, in response. Getting answers to actual studies was impossible. But she could already see where this problem was going.

"The assignment was to draw out a family tree, starting with immediate family and moving beyond that, then list some basic traits and characteristics and trace those back."

"So what happened?" Ash was getting tired of asking that question.

"There were some girls who made fun of Avonlee for her family tree."

Ash jerked her head back. "Made fun of?"

Chris rubbed her lips together, looking very uncomfortable. "Cheyenne isn't as progressive as Seattle."

"They made fun of her because she has two moms?" Ash's eyebrows rose to her hairline. "You've got to be kidding me."

"I'm not, unfortunately."

"And what are you doing about them?"

Chris canted her head to the side. "I can't tell you that, or who they were, though I'm sure Avonlee will tell you who they are. I can tell you that the situation is being handled on all sides."

"What do you mean *all sides*?" Ash hissed the last part of her question, anger simmering to a boil. "My daughter is the victim."

"Well, she would have been."

"Would have? Chris stop talking in riddles."

Chris touched Ash's hands gently, and as much Ash didn't want to admit it, the caress calmed her. "Avonlee retaliated very quickly. She hit one of the girls and shoved another one. She didn't talk to Ms. Dunja about it, so the initial report that came in was that Avonlee had started a fight."

"In response to being bullied."

Chris shook her head slowly. "I'm not convinced this is a case of bullying, not yet. But yes, they were trying to get her in trouble."

"And where are they?" Ash looked around the office, as if trying to make her point.

"In the classroom, and yes, I already talked to their parents." Chris retreated.

Ash knew it was because she was essentially attacking Chris —again—for her ability to do her job, and the bully word had already come between them before. "And why isn't my daughter there?"

"She's upset, Ash, and she asked not to go back today. I was respecting what she wanted, and I'd hoped you would have some compassion for her."

"You're the principal here." Ash's voice lowered. "How can you stand for hatred like that?"

Chris jerked her head back, her eyes wide. "I don't."

"They're still here. In school."

"Yes, because everyone has a right to an education. If it continues, more drastic measures will be taken, but as it stands, this is the first incident—"

"First hate crime of many." Those words would sting, she knew it. But she said them anyway, not caring how much harm she caused Chris if it meant protecting her daughter.

"Ash." Chris' voice was full of power and command. "I don't allow any kind of hatred, against sex, sexual orientation, gender identity, race or anything else in my school."

"Clearly, you do." Ash grasped at straws. She needed to be angry. It was the easiest emotion to feel right now, and she clung onto it with everything she had.

"No, I don't." Chris glared. "And don't you of all people accuse me of that."

Ash dragged in a deep breath, trying to calm her racing heart. She wasn't mad at Chris. She really wasn't. She was ticked because she'd brought her kids to a place where they wouldn't be fully accepted, and she was really ticked at Mari. Because Ash was left cleaning up all the messes that were left behind because of Mari's stupid, stupid decisions.

"What kind of project is that even? Is there just the assumption that everyone has a traditional nuclear family in this school?"

"Quite the opposite, actually." Chris leaned back in the chair. "Ms. Dunja is very adept at navigating non-traditional families, and that's part of the point of the project. She adds in a concept on nature and nurture, what we learn and pick up from others."

Ash pursed her lips at being proven wrong. "I'd like to take Avonlee home."

"She's all yours, and she's not in trouble just to make that abundantly clear. But if she continues to react rashly and violently, there will be consequences next time." Chris stood up and called Avonlee into her office, shutting the door as soon as she was inside.

"Avonlee, I was talking to your mom about what happened today." Chris sat back down and pulled out a chair for Avonlee to sit in.

Avonlee looked so tense and scared. Ash wanted to gather her up in her arms and hold her tight.

"What the other girls did wasn't right, and we all know that in this room." Chris eyed Avonlee carefully. "I want you to know that you can always come talk to me if you need to, okay? If the girls start up that kind of talk again, you go to Ms. Dunja and you tell her you need to talk to me."

Ash stared directly at Chris, confused with how soft she was being with Avonlee, yet how harsh she had been with Ash just moments before. Still, knowing that Avonlee would have a safe space with Chris was exactly what Avonlee needed. Ash faced her daughter and did the unthinkable. "Baby, if anyone starts to give you a hard time about mom or me or how our family is built, you come talk to Dr. Murphey, okay? She's..." Ash paused, trying to figure out how to say this so everyone in the room would understand. "...Dr. Murphey is part of the family, okay?"

Avonlee's face pinched in confusion.

Chris immediately jumped in. "I'm like your moms, Avonlee. Do you understand?"

"Yeah. I think so." Avonlee nodded, and suddenly she looked so much more at ease. "So, are you married to a girl?"

Chris shook her head. "No, but I was."

"Mama was too." Avonlee sniffled, her entire face going red. "But Mom died."

Ash's world rocked hard. The issue with the family project hadn't been the fact that Avonlee had two moms. It might have been that for the other girls, but every moment of that project was a stark reminder that Mari was dead. Ash crashed, cold washing over her instantly. She should have figured that out as soon as the project was laid out in front of her.

When she finally gathered the courage to look up, Chris was staring directly at her. Shock. Disgrace. Secrets laid out flat in front of everyone. Chris barely moved her gaze over to Avonlee. "I'm so sorry, Avonlee. No one should ever have to go through that."

Avonlee swallowed hard and wrinkled her nose, but that was it. "Can I go home now?"

"I want to talk to your mom alone again for a quick second, is that okay?"

"Yeah." Avonlee stepped outside of the office.

As soon as the door clicked shut, Ash's discomfort snapped. "Don't say anything. Please."

Chris sighed heavily, reaching for Ash's hand. As much as Ash didn't want the touch, she welcomed it. She flipped her hand and curled their fingers together. Chris slid forward on the chair and wrapped her arms around Ash's shoulders and pulled her into a tight hug. Ash buried herself into Chris' strength. She held on tightly, not wanting to move away. Ash couldn't let go.

Running hands up and down Ash's back, Chris held on. She stayed silent as Ash craved the touch and familiarity. She stayed there, breathing in Chris' scent and using it to comfort herself, using the gentle touch, the rhythmic motion to center herself. Ash took her time pulling away.

Chris brushed her fingers across Ash's cheeks, wiping away her silent tears. "I'm sorry your secret came out this way."

Ash gave a hint of a smile. "I have to remember that it's not only my secret to share. I just don't want to always be seen as the grieving widow. And to be fair, Mari isn't a secret. She is the love of my life, always and forever."

"I understand." And Chris looked like she did too.

Gathering herself, Ash stood. How could Chris possibly begin to understand? "Thank you for all you've done today. Hopefully tomorrow will be a better day."

"It will be."

"I'll see you around, Chris." Ash walked out of the office, put back more right than she'd been when she entered it. She snagged Avonlee and walked out of the school with a lightness in her step that she hadn't felt in years.

WITH HER DOWN JACKET ON, Chris stepped out onto the playground during the end of the day rush. It had been a bit since she'd managed to get out there and see the parents picking up the kids. The energy and excitement that filled the playground this time of day was exactly what Chris needed to keep her mind focused.

Chris couldn't get Ash and her family out of her thoughts. She'd even stopped by Isla's classroom, despite the awkwardness, twice to check on Rhubie, but she seemed to not have as many issues as Avonlee. Still, Chris watched the girls for any sign that they were struggling more than typical. But since she'd come out to Avonlee, Chris hadn't noticed any struggles. As much as she would love to tell her that Esther was also a part of that community, she wasn't willing to out anyone else. Her job was to protect her teachers as much as possible, and Esther had enough going on at the minute that she didn't need any more drama in her life.

Avonlee raced by her toward the second-grade door and snagged her sister in a big hug. Chris' lips quirked up as she watched the reunion. It was probably the first time she'd seen Avonlee be cheerful. They moved rapidly to the playground set and started running around on it together, ignoring all the other kids around them.

Chris talked with a parent here or there and hugged kids as they trickled home. It didn't take long for Ash to show up, but the playground was half empty. Chris smiled to herself as she walked over to where Ash was looking for the girls.

"They're playing," Chris answered, shoving her hands into her jean pockets and rocking up on her toes. "Avonlee ran to snag Rhubie from her teacher, and they're on the play equipment."

"Oh, well, that's good I guess." Ash sent Chris a shy smile, her cheeks red, but Chris couldn't tell if it was from the chilly air or something else.

It was finally a decent day outside, so Chris didn't mind staying out there longer than she normally would. They stood shoulder to shoulder, watching the girls play and other kids started to disappear. Chris realized belatedly that they were the only ones on the playground.

Ash caught her attention, another slow smile lighting her lips. "I wanted to thank you for the other day."

Which day? The impromptu but interrupted make out session? The dinner? The fill in at Hope in Action? Or the awkward reveal about Mari in her office?

"Avonlee has been a lot more relaxed since talking with you about your sexuality. I think she felt a bit slighted and on her own out here, honestly."

"Ah." Chris smiled, warmth filling her chest. "I'm glad she's coming into her own."

"She's more comfortable now. I think Kelli has still been giving her issues, though."

So Avonlee had told Ash who it was that was primarily bugging her. Chris hadn't heard of any other incidents involving the girls that week, but that didn't mean it wasn't happening. It just meant that it wasn't as bad or that it hadn't been reported. Chris rolled up on her toes again. "I'll keep an eye on it."

Ash drew in a sharp breath. "And thanks for giving me a few days to recover."

Chris turned sharply then. Confusion swam through her, and she eyed Ash down. "Recover?"

"I sometimes forget how much it hurts that Mari isn't here anymore. Being the only parent isn't only traumatic but exhausting." Ash frowned. "I hate sometimes that there's no backup."

"Oh, Ash." Chris reached out and touched her arm lightly, squeezing through the thick down jacket. Once again, her heart was breaking for this family. "I'll back you up as much as I can."

"I know that now."

"Forgive me for the cruel question, but how did Mari die?"

Ash sighed heavily and nodded toward the small bench on the side of the playground. Chris followed her to it, realizing belatedly that this was going to be a much longer conversation than she'd originally anticipated. It was a good thing it was a rare warm day that February.

They settled onto the bench. Ash's gaze never left the girls playing. Chris could understand that. They were an easy and good distraction, but Ash probably also wanted to protect them from the conversation that was about to happen.

Ash's face didn't change. She folded her hands together and leaned over her knees, her head downcast. The anticipation of what she was about to say built up in Chris' chest. She desperately wanted to know, but she didn't want to force Ash to share either.

"Mari was in a car accident."

The words jarred her.

Chris blinked sudden tears away. Reaching out, she covered Ash's clasped hands and rubbed her thumb along the smooth skin. "I'm so sorry."

Ash shrugged slightly, but Chris couldn't tell why. Either it was because she didn't see it as a big deal or she was trying to make it seem like she didn't. Chris suspected the latter, because no sudden death of a spouse wasn't a big deal.

"It was a single car accident." Ash's jaw tightened. "She survived the accident, initially. What killed her was what happened afterward. She was in ICU for weeks before she finally succumbed to the injuries and everything else going on."

Chris wanted to know what everything else was, but she hesitated to ask. She wanted Ash to guide the story, share what she felt comfortable disclosing.

"It was a long winter break."

"I can't imagine." Chris squeezed Ash's hands before breaking the contact and leaning back into the bench. The girls played together as if nothing had happened, giggling and laughing. They were completely untouched by the conversation happening at the moment, though both obviously deeply wounded by the death of their parent.

"No one can. I can barely believe it myself half the time. But it's been two years, Chris. Sometimes it feels like yesterday, other times it feels like ten years ago, and some days—the worst days —it feels like it hasn't happened yet." Ash wiped away the tears falling down her cheeks.

"You've been through so much." And everything Chris had thought about the past few weeks was proven true again. "You can't expect to have dealt with it completely."

"Do you ever?" Ash let out a wry laugh.

"Probably not." Chris licked her lips and watched the girls go down the slide one after the other. They were so joyful. It was hard to imagine the devastation they had survived. "You're stronger than your trauma. You know that, right?"

"Doesn't feel that way."

"No, no, it doesn't." Chris stretched her arm across the back of the bench.

They fell into a comfortable silence. Avonlee ran up to them, asking to show off some trick she mastered on the monkey bars. Chris clapped her hands and cheered as Avonlee landed. Rhubie climbed up to try her hand, but she slipped off almost immediately. She'd get there, eventually. She needed to grow another six inches to really be able to grasp on better.

"Do you have time today?" Ash asked suddenly.

"Time for what?" Chris was confused by the turn of the conversation. She furrowed her brow and looked into Ash's bright blue eyes. Waves of emotion swept through them, but it was too quick for Chris to completely decipher.

"For this. I know you usually have meetings after regular school hours."

"Oh." Chris looked at the building, then back to Ash. She shook her head slowly. "Actually, today I don't have any meetings."

"Is that rare?"

"Yeah." Chris smiled. "Seems like a good day to be without, though."

"I'm keen to agree with that." Ash looked lighter than she had moments before, the weight of the conversation easing as it naturally should. "Do you remember what I turned in for that paper?"

"Seventeen years is a long time." What she didn't add was the drinking had made it longer and killed a lot of her brain cells in the process. "I barely remember any specific papers. I wish I did, though."

"I wrote a story about a nymph who was lost in the woods and ran into another nymph, also lost."

"Delfina." The character's name came back to Chris suddenly.

"Yeah." Ash's lips curled upward. "That's the first book I ended up publishing."

"Is it?" Chris' brow creased.

"It's completely different now than it was then. I promise you."

"Didn't want to publish your first draft?" Chris knocked her shoulder into Ash's. "I really am proud of you for doing that, you know. It's the one thing you always said you wanted."

"It was." Ash's voice became sad again. "It's not now."

"I can respect that. But don't give up on dreams just because trauma gets in the way. Promise me that." Chris was touching Ash's hand again, this time, letting her fingers linger in a way that was wholly inappropriate for a principal and a parent. But Chris didn't want to let go. She threaded their fingers together, clamping down and waffling their hands. This felt perfect. She hoped Ash thought the same, but then again, how could she? She'd just revealed one of her deepest secrets, which meant that Ash wasn't in the right state of mind for this.

Rhubie ran up, and Chris instantly dropped Ash's hand. The girls couldn't see this. No one could see what she was doing. They were sitting in the playground at the school for fuck's sake. Chris had to stop taking so many risks. That was what had sent her down the rabbit hole of drinking to begin with.

"Mama! I'm so cold."

"Let's get going." Ash sent Chris a look of disappointment. "Dr. Murphey and I are done talking anyway."

Ash gathered the girls up along with their backpacks. Chris walked them to the corner of the school property closest to where Ash had parked before she dipped back into the building. She was just about to head to her office when she stopped in her tracks, Mel staring at her with a stern look on her face.

"You have some 'splainin' to do, Lucy."

Chris' stomach dropped. She shook her head and pressed a finger to her lips. "Not here."

Mel snagged Chris' wrist to stop her from sneaking by. "My house. You have one hour to get your butt there before I chase you down."

Chris knew better than to argue with her best friend, so when her hour was up, she found herself at Mel's house and sitting on the couch with Esther in a chair and Mel next to her. She had no idea where to start but she was pretty sure Mel had already figured it out.

"Please tell me you didn't know she was a parent when you took her home."

"I didn't," Chris squeaked out, taking a large sip of cold water.

Esther rubbed her temple. "So you're in a relationship with Avonlee's mom?"

Chris shook her head rapidly. "No. No, I'm not. I'm not doing that at all. We had sex, once, and that was it." Except it was way more than that, and Chris hadn't even scratched the surface. "And then we kissed once, about a week ago. And she's my former student."

"What?" Esther and Mel said at the same time.

Chris went through the whole story from start to finish, her cheeks heating at the parts she really didn't want to share. She was crossing so many lines with them, but she and Mel had always managed to walk the line of boss and employee while maintaining their friendship. She had to believe they could continue that.

"Are you drinking again?"

"No." Chris sneered. "I swear I'm not."

"Okay, just checking, because this is a wild story."

"I know." Chris closed her eyes and rested her head on the back cushion on the couch. "What am I supposed to do now?"

"Nothing. You're not supposed to date a parent."

"Says you." Chris shot Mel a dirty look.

"Hey, Esther is a teacher, too."

Rolling her eyes in an exaggerated motion, Chris stayed still. Mel did have a point. But she already knew the decision was made. As much as she might want Ash, they couldn't have a relationship. Not now, and probably not ever for that matter. Still, it didn't mean that she didn't want to try at some point. Ash made her feel like she mattered, as though she wasn't as screwed up on the inside as she'd originally thought.

"Just be careful, Chris. I don't want you to do anything stupid."

"Stupid and me? Ha!" Chris gave an odd grin, halfway between a grimace and a laugh because she knew without a doubt, Mel was right.

Stupid was her middle name.

CHAPTER
Fourteen

Ash 8:53 pm - Thank you for today.

ASH STARED AT HER PHONE, wondering exactly what she was doing. They had been so careful to put up boundary lines between them, but at every turn, Ash barreled right over them. From the conversation in her office at Hope in Action, to the dinner that was definitely a date, to the kiss afterward.

Pausing on that last thought, Ash closed her eyes as she sat on her couch. The house was quiet. The kids were in bed and should be falling asleep shortly if they weren't there already. It had been a good day, one of the rare ones she had with Avonlee lately, and she wanted to revel in it.

Chris 8:56 pm - Anytime.

Disappointment surged through Ash. She wanted more than a simple conversation with Chris. She wanted to dig deeper now that the intimate bond between them had increased. Snuggling down into the couch with the television playing quietly in the background, she knew she had to be clear in what she wanted.

Going through part of Mari's story earlier that day had been tough, but it had also been freeing. It wasn't the first time, but it was still rare for Ash to talk about Mari without crying. Chris had made it so easy for her.

Ash 8:57 pm - What are you doing tonight?

She wasn't going to give up, that was for damn sure. With her warm tea in hand, Ash pulled her legs under her body and flicked her gaze up to the screen in front of her. She'd completely lost track of what was on it and realized belatedly that it was still the kids show she had yet to turn off. Reaching for the remote, she changed it to something else.

Chris 8:58 pm - Was just settling in after finishing up work.

Ash 8:58 pm - Me too. Girls are asleep, hopefully. But I'm watching TV. Can't remember the last time I did that.

Chris 8:59 pm - Raising kids is hard work.

Ash's lips curled upward. The conversation between them deepened right as she anticipated and in the way she wanted it. It was Ash's turn to take this another step further, in the direction she wanted. Her thumb hovered over her phone. Was this really what she wanted? To step into another relationship? Even if it was only potential, was she ready for it? Were her girls?

Ash 9:03 pm - I can't stop thinking about the other night.

Chris 9:03 pm - Which night?

That was an apt question. Ash pulled her lip between her teeth, staring at the screen even more. There was no doubt in

her mind. She wanted this. To know that Chris was just as interested in her, to know that she had support outside of her family,
that her girls were looked after—it was exactly what she wanted.

Ash 9:05 pm - Snagging on the sidewalk.

She could almost see Chris' laugh and smile in reaction to her
chosen words. She'd specifically picked them, hoping to get that
rise. She just wished she could actually see Chris now, touch her,
be snuggled against her. But with her girls sleeping mere feet
away, that wasn't going to happen. Ash bit her nail, waiting for
any kind of response to know if Chris was thinking about it or if
they were not on the same page.

Chris 9:06 pm - That was an unexpected but pleasant surprise.

Giddiness coursed through Ash's chest. Was this actually
happening? With full awareness of who they were to each other,
were they actually going to go beyond this mere friendship they
seemed to have struck up?

Ash 9:06 pm - I would love to kiss you again.

Chris 9:06 pm - If only.

Ash paused. Was she pushing too much? Her nerves kicked
into high gear, and she wasn't sure which way Chris wanted to go
with the conversation. Or if she was being obvious enough with
what she wanted. Ash hovered her thumb over the phone and
decided to just come out with it.

Ash 9:08 pm - I can't stop thinking about fucking you.

Chris 9:08 pm - Fuck.

She wasn't getting what she needed to know where to go with this. Ash was just about to write something else back when the three little dots appeared, indicating that Chris was typing something. She held her breath as she waited for the response.

Chris 9:09 pm - What are you doing, exactly, right now?

Was this the invitation Ash had been waiting for? She looked around her house, the door locked, the bedrooms quiet. She did what she'd wanted to do for hours now and stretched out her legs on the couch, pointing her toes before picking up her phone again.

Ash 9:09 pm - Touching myself.

Chris 9:09 pm - Are you thinking about me?

Ash 9:09 pm - Your mouth against mine, fingers inside me. Can you make me come?

Since Ash had told her as much, she slipped her hand under her loose pajama bottoms and pressed three fingers against her. Her skin was hot, burning and ready, her outer lips already swollen. When had she gotten so aroused? She dipped two fingers farther down and gathered some of her juices, moving the pads of her fingers back to her clit and starting slow circles.

She couldn't believe they were doing this. Nothing had indicated that they were going to move beyond what they'd already found, but Ash still knew without a doubt that she wanted more. She kept the pattern between her legs steady and calm, waiting to see what Chris would say and do next. She would love if Chris would direct this, anything that would put the image of Chris being in control back in her mind.

Chris 9:11 pm - Do you have any idea what you're doing to me?

Ash 9:11 pm - No.

Was Chris as turned on as she was? Fuck, Ash wished they were in the same room, or that she could hear Chris' voice. But she didn't quite have the guts to call her, not yet, not without knowing more. Ash let out a grunt, hitting her swollen clit just right. Her body begged her to give more, but she was still hesitant.

Chris 9:13 pm - Are you touching yourself?

Why was she asking again? Ash closed her eyes, her mind racing while her fingers kept up the gentle rhythm.

Ash 9:14 pm - Do you want me to? Do you want me to think of you while I do it?

Chris 9:14 pm - Yes.

Relief flooded through Ash, taking over her entire being. She hadn't realized just how much she was holding back because she didn't have permission, not yet. Spreading her legs and scooting down farther onto the couch, Ash relaxed into the gentle play of her fingers between her legs. She kept her right hand free so she could freely text, needing to know what Chris wanted her to do.

Ash 9:16 pm - Tell me what to do.

Ash loved a demanding partner. Chris had proven herself to be that when they'd been together the last time. Maybe it wouldn't be their only time. But for now texting and Ash's own hand were going to have to do. What was taking Chris so long to answer? Ash just needed to know what to do next.

Chris 9:21 pm - What toys do you have?

Ash 9:21 pm - None.

Chris 9:21 pm - Really?

Ash 9:22 pm - I have small kids, and we moved. I wasn't using them so figured why keep them.

Chris 9:22 pm - Because you're not a nun.

Ash smiled at that. She had been pretty much sexless until the day she'd moved here. It had been a good start to living here. A small downhill afterward, but nothing major that they hadn't handled well. Ash gripped her phone tightly.

Ash 9:23 pm - Tell me what to do.

She knew she was pushing Chris. This didn't seem to be anything within her comfort zone from what Ash had seen, but she could always be surprised. She and Mari had sexted a few times throughout their relationship, but Ash always preferred to have a warm body against her instead.

Ash 9:25 pm - Chris. Tell me what to do.

Those three dots shown on the screen. Then disappeared. Then started again. The anticipation was almost worse than whatever Chris was going to tell her to do. Ash gathered more moisture, needing the lube on her clit to make the stimulation feel better. She didn't even have lube for this. She cringed. She shouldn't have gotten rid of everything when she moved. That had been a stupid idea.

Chris 9:27 pm - Two fingers. Pound yourself. Pretend it's me.

"Yessss," Ash hissed, sliding two fingers inside her. Heat and wet surrounded her hand, spilling into her palm. This had been exactly what she needed. Ash curled her fingers up and did exactly as she was told.

Ash 9:28 pm - This feels so good. You would feel better.

Chris 9:28 pm - Maybe someday.

Ash 9:29 pm - I wish I had your mouth on me.

Ash was being so vulnerable, willing and able to put everything into this conversation to get what she needed out of it. She bit her lip, her eyes fluttering shut as she focused on what her body was telling her. She rocked her hips into her hand, imagining Chris' fingers were her fingers, that Chris' mouth pressed kisses to her bare thighs. Damn it, she should have taken her clothes off before doing this. She should be in her bedroom doing this, where she could be louder and less constrained.

Chris 9:30 pm - Are you close?

Wanting to be and being there were two different things. Ash wasn't going to lie to Chris. Was she closer than she had been five minutes ago? Yes. Was it going to take probably another five to ten minutes? Also yes. Pursing her lips, Ash took deep breaths to steady herself as she debated on what to say because she for damn sure wasn't going to lie.

Ash 9:31 pm - Getting there.

Chris 9:32 pm - Next time we do this, do you want me to come packing?

Ash groaned out loud. That image put everything into the right place in her mind. The feel of Chris sliding between her legs, not just her fingers inside her but a thicker and fuller toy. Ash fluttered her eyes shut, a wave of wetness pooling between her legs at the images that text created.

Ash 9:32 pm - Fuck yes.

Chris 9:33 pm - Can't wait. Move harder and faster.

Following directions, Ash did as she was told. The angle started to make her wrist ache, but she kept going because Chris had told her to do it. She tried to shift her pants around to loosen them up and give her more room, and when she lifted her hips to help, she let out a vivacious moan. When had she become a loud lover? Especially when no one else was there with her.

This was better than the last time she'd touched herself. Even just having Chris' voice in her head through the texts, taking the decision-making away from her sent an added thrill through her. Pressure built up between her legs, the sweet telltale signs that she was getting closer and closer to her orgasm. It was exactly what she needed.

Chris 9:37 pm - Rub your clit with your thumb. Think about it as my tongue, teasing you. Tasting you.

Ash pulled her lower lip between her teeth and bit down to try and contain herself. If Chris was there, she wasn't sure she'd be able to hold back. She would want to let everything go, all those tenuous lines of control that she held so firmly. And she could trust herself to do that with Chris. The conversation after school proved that, didn't it?

Ash 9:43 pm - I'm close.

Chris 9:44 pm - Perfect. Don't stop. Don't change anything. I know how amazing you taste.

Grunting, Ash clenched her eyes and focused on her body. Goosebumps rippled up her arms, her stomach tensed, her thighs tightened. She brought her knees up slightly as she lost some of that control she had. Ash turned her face into the back of the couch and ground her teeth down to keep her noises to a minimum.

She wanted to tell Chris exactly what it felt like, what coursed through her, the pleasure that overtook her. Ash gasped. Her entire body jerked tightly as she creamed her fingers, her pussy clenching hard and deep, pulling her fingers farther inside. It took her longer than she anticipated to catch her breath, but when she turned onto her back again, Ash removed her hand and wiped her fingers against the fabric of her pajamas.

Ash 9:51 pm - That was amazing. I'm not sure I can stand yet.

Chris 9:52 pm - Well you're going to have to.

"What?" Ash stared at her phone. Chris wasn't typing another response. She could mean anything, really. She could mean Ash had to get up and clean up, could mean that she assumed Ash wasn't in her bed. They hadn't really talked about any details. Texting back and asking for clarification was exactly what she did.

The rapid succession of four knocks on the front door, soft but loud enough for Ash to hear from the couch startled her. Ash glanced at her phone and then the front door. Her heart was in her throat as she forced herself to stand.

Flicking on the porch light, Ash prepared for whatever might be on the other side of the door. Unlocking it, she twisted the knob and pulled it open. Chris stood, haloed by the porch light, her hair around her shoulders, and a small bag in her right hand.

"Chris," Ash breathed out her name like an answer to a prayer she'd never said.

Staying put, Chris looked Ash directly in the eye. "I know I shouldn't be here."

CHAPTER
Fifteen

CHRIS PANICKED. Ash said nothing as she stood on the other side of the door, staring at her dumbfounded. She had overstepped. This was a bad idea. She should just go back to her car and go back home and forget this happened. She tensed and was just about to turn around when Ash stumbled a step forward and opened the screen door.

"What *are* you doing here?"

"You really can't be asking that after those texts." Chris' heart was in her throat. Should she go inside or not? The warmth from the house rushed against her cheeks, but that didn't mean she would be welcome in.

"No, of course not." Ash pushed open the door wider. "Are you coming?"

Chris nearly groaned at Ash's choice of words. While Ash had gotten off, assuming she hadn't lied about it in the text, Chris hadn't. She was worked up beyond anything she could recently remember, and she'd just wanted to find some relief. Stepping into the house, Chris was overcome with nerves.

She really shouldn't have just assumed that she'd be welcome here. "I'm sorry if I'm interrupting."

"Chris." Ash smiled, shutting and locking the door. That

sealed it. "If you're here to make good on those texts, I'm glad you showed up."

Breathing a sigh of relief, Chris awkwardly stood in the front entryway. "I didn't want to assume."

"Safe to assume on this one." Ash took her by the hand and led the way barefoot through the house. Chris followed her through the kitchen and down the stairs into the basement. "The girls' sleep upstairs. This way we can make a bit more noise."

As soon as they stepped into the playroom down there, Chris was jarred back to reality. The girls were here. Of course they were, and of course Ash was leading her someplace where they didn't have to worry about being interrupted. There was a bed in a white room, with nothing but sheets on it and nothing else in the room. Not even a dresser. It was obviously a guest room still in the progress of being furnished.

"This isn't because I don't want you in my bed." Ash shut the door and flicked the lock.

Chris stood in front of her, awkwardly. All the smoothness of her flirtations and seductions were gone in an instant. Ash gripped the lapels of her jacket and dragged her. Chris stumbled and nearly fell into Ash's body, smooshing her between the door and her body.

"But I do want you in a bed with me." Ash crushed their mouths together in a brutal kiss.

Chris dropped the bag she'd brought, moving her hands up to Ash's body. She skimmed fingers over Ash's breasts, her nipples hardening on contact. Palming Ash's left breast, Chris squeezed it lightly, diving deeper into the embrace and tangling their tongues. This was so much better than the brief but intense kiss they'd shared after dinner.

Confidently, Ash snagged Chris' chilled fingers and shoved them down her pajamas and underwear, right against her crotch. Chris chuckled and pulled back from the kiss. She canted her head to the side and stared directly into Ash's eyes. "You're demanding."

"Sometimes. But your fingers are so much better than mine."

"My hand is half frozen."

"Perfect," Ash purred. "Take me already."

Chris put their mouths together, nipping at Ash's lips and then her neck. She sucked hard, hoping to leave a mark for the morning when Ash would remember everything they had done together. But Chris didn't move her hand, despite Ash wiggling against her to try and get more contact.

"I can't wait to taste you," Ash whispered, dropping her hips down as if that would get her what she wanted from Chris. "I can't wait to be between your legs."

Shivers ran through Chris' body. She couldn't believe that Ash wanted her so much. Despite what she was saying, that niggling voice in her head still whispered quietly that she was too screwed up for this. But Ash's voice was louder. Ash pushed at Chris' jacket, trying to tug it off. Chris was going to have to move her hand for that, and she wasn't sure Ash would want that.

But at Ash's insistence, Chris moved away and tugged off her jacket. As soon as her hand was free, Ash clung to it desperately and put it right back between her legs. Chris chuckled loudly, slowing down her kisses as she pressed them against Ash's neck and to the top of her cotton T-shirt.

"Chris," Ash whined. "Fuck me already."

Laughing again, Chris shook her head. "Patience is a virtue for a reason, and you've already gotten off once, which means we can drag this one out."

"The first one doesn't count." Ash pouted. "You weren't here."

Chris moved her free hand up and wrapped it around the side of Ash's neck. She slid her thumb across Ash's throat, feeling her pulse quicken. Ash stilled, but the desire in her gaze deepened, and Chris' fingers became wetter. "Do you like this?"

"Your hand around my neck?" Ash breathed the words. "Yes."

"What else do you like?"

"Hard. Fast. Repeatedly."

Chris' lips curled upward. "We really should have stopped to talk more that first night."

"It was worth it. The orgasms were good."

"These will be better."

"Yes," Ash moaned out the word as she undulated her hips against Chris' unmoving fingers.

Cocking her head again, Chris eyed Ash carefully. Just what was she going to do with this one? She pressed in a little harder against Ash's neck, tightening her grasp but not enough that Ash would struggle to breathe. Just the threat of it being there was likely enough.

"Chris." Ash strained. "I've been thinking about this for weeks."

"Me too." Chris stepped in closer, using the weight of her body to add pressure to Ash's. "But I didn't think you'd want to."

"I didn't for a while." Ash's breathing became labored. "But I just can't stop thinking about you."

Chris drove two fingers into Ash, pushing into the wet heat. She sighed, more connected than she ever had been before. Starting at a slow pace, Chris pumped her fingers in and out while Ash writhed on top of her. Little noises emitted from Ash's throat, spurring Chris to maintain every ounce of control she had left in the situation.

"Yes," Ash whispered, throwing her head backward into the door. She raised her leg up, resting it on Chris' hip, deepening the angle and thrust. "Yes."

"I love how you love this." Chris nibbled on Ash's neck, licking the bare skin that she could find and swirling her tongue in tight circles. She wanted Ash to think of her mouth elsewhere, exactly like she'd told her before. Bending her head, she captured one of Ash's hard nipples through the fabric of her shirt and sucked it between her lips.

The wet fabric against Chris' tongue was rough and a stark contrast to what she knew Ash's skin would be like underneath. She desperately wanted to feel the press of their bodies against each other, smooth flesh to hot skin. But that wasn't in the cards for right now.

Ash groaned, her voice reverberating around the room and wrapping around Chris. Moving to Ash's other nipple, Chris started the same process. Licking. Sucking. Enticing. She wanted Ash as worked up as she could be.

"That feels so good," Ash's voice was barely above a whisper.

Reaching out, Ash clung to Chris, digging her fingers into the sensitive flesh at the backs of her arms. She lifted up on her toes. Chris kept her pace the same. It would be slow, torture by pleasure, which was exactly what she wanted for Ash. This was everything she'd wanted to tell Ash via text, but she didn't have the courage to put it into writing. This was so much better.

"Tell me when you're getting close."

"So you can stop?" Ash let out a breathy laugh. "Not a chance."

"Do you like edging, Ash?"

"Sometimes. Not tonight." Ash tightened her grip and tugged Chris closer. She pressed their mouths together in a heated kiss. "Don't make me wait."

Chris increased the pressure and speed of her fingers. She was going to give and give and give. Ash deserved everything. The door echoed as Ash's body moved into it with each thrust of Chris' fingers.

"You're next," Ash murmured through grunts. "I want you to come apart."

Chris eyed Ash thoughtfully and shook her head slowly. "I think you're going to want to wait before you decide that."

"Wait?" Ash's nose wrinkled, and she let out a wild groan. "I'm not waiting."

"You might for this." Chris circled her thumb around Ash's clit, pressing in to increase the pressure. "Close enough yet?"

The small tells were already there. Ash's body was moving outside of her control, her cheeks were red with arousal, and her lips were parted but filled with a smile. Chris loved seeing her like this, drenched in pleasure.

"Don't be so cocky."

Chris' chuckle was slow and sure. "Don't be too sure about that."

Ash gasped, holding onto Chris tightly as her face screwed up in pleasure. She pulsed as Chris continued to drive her fingers in that steady rhythm. Finally, Ash clasped both her hands against Chris' cheeks and dragged her in for a sloppy kiss.

When they broke apart, Ash rested her forehead on Chris' shoulder to catch her breath. They stood against the door, breathing heavily, Chris' fingers still between Ash's legs, the scent of Ash's arousal reaching their nostrils. It was heaven. Chris didn't want it any other way.

"What were you going on about?" Ash asked, breathy.

"You asked me to come packing the next time."

Ash's eyes widened with surprise before her lips settled into an excited grin. "Did you really?"

"Yes. If you'd like—"

"Hell yes!" Ash pushed Chris away and immediately stripped out of her clothes.

Chris was slower to move. She also had a lot more clothes to dispense of. By the time she was naked with the strap in place, Ash was already on the bed, stretched out with her arms above her head and her legs spread wide.

"How are we doing this?" Ash giggled. "It's been so long since anyone has taken me like this."

"Flip over." Chris climbed onto the bed, her clit already tingling from the press of the base of the toy against it. "Put a pillow under your hips."

"One of my favorite positions." Ash raised her eyebrows twice in succession before moving.

Chris had lubed up the strap even though she wasn't sure

they'd need it. She didn't want Ash to be sore tomorrow when she had to deal with the kids and work. Straddling Ash's legs between hers, Chris leaned over her and positioned the toy just at her entrance.

"Are you ready?" Chris breathed, not sure if she was asking Ash or herself.

"More than ever," Ash answered, lifting her butt up and tightening her legs.

She had definitely done this before. Chris pressed in slowly, the consistent pressure against her clit adding relief but also building her up even more. She was going to love this. As soon as she was all the way inside, she leaned forward and gripped Ash's wrists tightly. Ash had shown every sign of loving being restrained, and Chris wasn't going to give up the golden opportunity while she had it.

The first thrust was slow. Ash hissed, her eyes closed.

"Feel okay?" Chris double-checked.

Ash nodded. "Yes. So much fuller than fingers can get."

Understanding the sentiment, Chris pulled out and thrust back in. Their bodies rocked together, the movements becoming smoother and more practiced as they continued. Ash grunted a steady stream with each thrust. Chris couldn't believe it, but she was so very near to coming herself. She tried to hold back, really wanting Ash to be against her and in her.

Reaching down, she wiggled her fingers between the bed and Ash's body, finding Ash's clit and teasing her again. Chris fumbled so many times, but Ash seemed alive with the pleasure she received. Chris was just about to come when Ash cried out. Stopping sharply, and breathing deeply, Chris managed to stave off her own orgasm. She closed her eyes, every nerve alive and waiting for touch, craving it.

She could so easily get addicted to this. She already had an addictive personality, so it wouldn't be out of bounds for her. But the way Ash made her feel alive was more than Chris had ever hoped for. She was wanted. She was *desired*.

In a sudden twist, Ash turned and flipped them over, Chris landing on her back with a thud. The wind rushed from her lungs. Before she knew what was happening, Ash had two fingers inside her and her lips surrounding the cock still strapped to Chris' hips. This was sexy as hell. Reaching down, Chris brushed Ash's hair to the side so she could see her face, her eyes.

"How do you taste?" Chris asked, because she had yet to get her own taste that night.

"Like you know what you're doing." Ash thrust back in, curling her fingers up and right into Chris' g-spot.

Groaning, Chris bucked her hips up into the touch. Ash pulled aside the dildo as much as she could and dove right in. She covered Chris' clit with her mouth, sucking desperately. Chris groaned loudly as ringing took over her ears. She clenched her eyes tight. She was already on the edge. Her heart raced, and it didn't take long for pleasure to overtake every sense she had.

She collapsed onto the bed, and Ash put the dildo right back where it was. Ash straddled her, kissing Chris senseless again. Chris' heart raced as she ran her hands up and down Ash's back and settled into this perfect feeling. But it scared her. She wasn't ready for it. And that niggling voice in the back of her mind got just a little bit louder.

"I'm going to ride you next," Ash whispered, giving love nips all down Chris' chest. "If I'd known you had this the last time, I would have made you use it."

Chris laughed, still out of breath. "Last time we were just getting to know each other."

"True that." Ash chuckled as she raised her hips up and slid down. "Are you ready?"

"I don't think I'm ever going to be ready for you."

"Same here." Ash kissed her desperately.

It started out fast, as if Ash was clawing at some semblance of reality, but it slowed and eased. They became comfortable with each other again. Ash rocked her hips, then moved them in a deliberate circle. Chris' clit was already on fire, not having calmed from Ash's first onslaught of touches.

"Feel good?" Ash had a satisfied smirk on her lips. "Or do I need to do it harder and faster?" As soon as she said the words, Ash mimicked them with her movements.

Chris hissed. "You're going to keep me up all night."

"No doubt about it." Ash bent down and kissed her again with a tease, but she sobered quickly. "But the girls—"

"Don't worry," Chris interrupted. "I understand completely. I'll be gone before they wake up."

"But not yet." A tinge of worry filled Ash's voice.

"No, not yet. I still need to catch up with you."

"Now that we can manage, I think." Ash rotated her hips again, and at Chris' surprised groan, she didn't stop.

CHAPTER
Sixteen

"COME ON! Come on! Let's get going!"

Ash couldn't wait for morning drop off. It was only a few hours since Chris had snuck out of the house after they'd caught a quick nap together, and Ash wanted to see her again already.

Who am I?

This wasn't like her at all, but the secrecy, the sneaking around, the newness to everything was a thrill she was loving. Ash didn't want to give it up. The girls were moving extra slow that morning, still half asleep as if they'd been the ones up all night instead of Ash. But she was excited. She had a plan in place, and she wanted to make sure that it happened.

As much as Ash knew this was what she wanted, that didn't stop the nerves from battling away in her belly. She snagged her coffee mug and slid into the driver's seat of her car while the girls climbed in the back and buckled up. It was so cold outside, and she knew the girls would be inside in their classrooms that day because of it instead of on the playground, which afforded her the perfect opportunity, didn't it?

Instead of pulling up the drop off lane, Ash turned the corner and parked on the street. Avonlee and Rhubie looked very confused, but Ash said nothing to them as she took a long sip from her coffee to continue to wake up her brain. But her body was absolutely alive. Chris had made sure of that last night.

"What are you doing?" Avonlee asked.

"I need to talk to Dr. Murphey for a minute." Ash glanced over her shoulder. "Nothing bad and nothing about you two, I promise."

Rhubie took that answer easily, but Avonlee didn't. She stared at Ash suspiciously.

"I promise it's nothing about you." But that did bring into question just when they would tell the girls, assuming the conversation went according to Ash's plan. She didn't want to talk to them about that for a while, not until she knew what direction the relationship was for sure going. But Chris was a mom, surely she'd understand that, right?

Ash tugged her jacket a little tighter around her chest as she got out of the vehicle. She forgot just how damn cold it got here. Char had warned her, and she'd been out to visit several times in the last few years since they'd moved there, but she hadn't spent much time in Cheyenne in the dead of winter. Shuddering as the warmth from her car left her, Ash got the girls out of the car and made her way to the front doors of the school as quickly as possible.

One of the teachers was there to open the door as soon as they stepped in, not letting the kids linger outside very long. The hallways were alive with children and people. Ash wasn't sure she'd ever seen the school this busy before. But it really shouldn't surprise her. Everyone was inside. She took the girls to their classrooms and hugged them goodbye.

Her next mission was to find Chris.

Heading to the office while wading through small children, Ash's hands became clammy. Sweat pooled at the small of her back and in her pits. Was it just nerves or was it because it felt like six million degrees in here? Her heart raced. Was she really doing this?

Yes. Because it was exactly what she wanted.

Ash stepped into the front office, and it was so much calmer in here than anywhere else in the school. Ms. Linda smiled at her and looked up expectantly. Ash started, "Hi."

Her nerves were so bad.

"I need to talk to Dr. Murphey."

"She's somewhere. Hold on a minute." Ms. Linda rustled around on her desk for a walkie-talkie. Ash had seen most teachers who were on playground duty with one and Chris carried one. "Dr. Murphey, there's a parent here who needs to speak with you."

"On my way." Chris' voice was firm and confident as she spoke back.

Ms. Linda pointed to a small chair in the corner of the room. "If you want to just sit and wait, it might be a few minutes."

"Right." Ash nodded and moved awkwardly to sit down. She was crazy for doing this, right?

Every second that passed, Ash's nerves got worse. She shouldn't be doing this here. It was a mistake. She was bringing the personal into the professional, and Chris had been so careful to keep those boundaries in place. Ash was breaking all the rules they had. She had been from the start.

"Ashton." Chris' tone was firm, edging on scolding.

Ash jerked her chin up, making eye contact with Chris' dark brown eyes. She looked amazing this morning. That fresh-fucked glow did her wonders. Ash swallowed the fear in her throat, but it made its way back up.

"Are you okay? I said your name three times."

Shaking her head in surprise, Ash licked her lips. "Uh...yeah. I can talk to you another time, if you're busy."

"No, now is fine." Chris held her hand out toward her office, indicating Ash should make her way there.

Ash hesitated. Her feet rooted to the spot and her butt glued to the chair. Chris took a step back in her direction, her head tilted down as they locked eyes. What was Ash supposed to do now? She needed to back out of this conversation yesterday. This was such a bad decision to have the talk here.

"Ash," Chris said calmly. "Let's talk in my office. Come on."

"Right." Ash finally pushed herself to stand.

Chris had locked her hands in her pockets, and Ash was pretty sure it was so she wouldn't be tempted to touch. Ash should have done that, because all she wanted to do was reach out and run her fingers over Chris in some way. Remind herself that whatever was between them was real. Because it had felt so real the night before.

The door clicked shut loudly. Ash jumped. Chris furrowed her brow and crossed her arms, leaning against her standing desk. "What's going on? Is everything okay?"

Ash pulled her lip between her teeth and shuddered. "Yeah, everything's fine."

"So what are you doing here? I thought we left last night pretty clear." Chris wasn't speaking at full volume, and Ash leaned in to hear her better.

"We did. You're right." Ash gnawed on her lip. This was such a stupid idea. "I was just dropping the girls off."

Chris nodded, as if she understood what Ash was going on about, but she didn't. She really didn't. Ash wasn't even sure what was holding her back from this conversation other than the fact that they were standing in the middle of the principal's office at her daughters' school. She should have talked to Chris off property. But when?

They rarely managed to see each other outside of these walls.

Ash fisted her hands and glanced out the large windows alongside one wall. Kids ran inside from the playground, huddled down because of the weather. If teachers looked out their windows and into Chris' they could potentially see them. Ash couldn't touch Chris. That would break the rest of the rules they had.

Dragging air into her lungs, Ash stepped backward and toward the door. She had to get out of there. This was a mistake.

"Ash," Chris crooned so gently. "What's going on?"

Shaking her head, Ash froze again. She'd ridden the high of sex, that was it. She'd expected that high to last, but being thrown back into reality was what crashed everything down around them. Chris immediately walked forward and grabbed Ash by the shoulders.

"Look at me."

Ash struggled. Raising her gaze to meet Chris' was incredibly difficult. She didn't want to look and see pity. She'd seen that enough over the last few years, and for Chris to look at her like that would be the end of what was just starting.

"Ash," Chris whispered. "Don't be scared."

Chris used the side of her finger and raised Ash's chin up. Ash closed her eyes, fighting back the tears that threatened to slide down her cheeks. She wouldn't cry. She'd come in today to follow her heart and now her heart was stuck back in that damn grieving well she never managed to get out of.

"Talk to me."

"I've never done this before, not really." The words rushed from Ash. "With Mari we just kind of fell together."

Chris' eyes crinkled as she smiled, and when Ash expected her to move away, she stepped in closer. "I'd say we kind of fell together, wouldn't you?"

"Many times." Ash's cheeks were kissed with heat. "After last night...I want to change the rules."

"What rules?" Chris' brow furrowed, confusion flashing in her eyes.

"One night of happiness?" Ash's lips pulled up to the side. "We said this was only going to be one night."

"But then there was last night." Chris's pink tongue dashed across her lips, wetting them.

Ash desperately wanted to lean in and kiss her. Her heart raced at the mere thought of it. "Yeah, last night. It was amazing."

Chuckling, Chris nodded. "I can agree with you on that."

"But I want more than last night." Ash held her breath, wondering just what Chris' reaction was going to be. They hadn't discussed anything more than this, and Ash hadn't asked someone out in more than a decade.

Chris slid her hands down Ash's shoulders, to her elbows, tugging her in even more. They stood a breath away from each other, the tension between them rippling in an instant. Ash was choked from the emotion welling up. She wanted this connection with another human being, and Chris couldn't be a better person for it to happen with.

"I want to go out with you."

"Like a date?" Chris asked, sliding one hand down to Ash's and clasping their fingers together.

Ash nodded, her lips pressed together as she stared down into Chris' eyes. She was at a loss for words. What if Chris didn't want that? She'd never even thought about that possibility, but they'd agreed to one night and Chris might just want to keep it sex between them. But Ash couldn't do that. She craved a deeper intimate connection.

"Where will we go?" Chris asked, whispering. "Because we've gone to my few favorite date spots already."

"I don't know. I haven't lived here very long."

Chris hummed. She moved her left hand to Ash's side, then slid it around to the small of Ash's back, tugging her in even closer. "Then I guess I better step up my dating game."

Relief rushed through Ash, the anxiety that had bubbled up completely dissipated. "Does that mean a yes?"

"You haven't actually asked me on a date, so let me unburden you from that." Chris pressed her fingertips in, a gentle pressure that pulled Ash toward her. "Will you go out with me, Ashton?"

"Yes." Ash giggled, the weight completely off her shoulders. "When?"

"Whenever you want." Chris moved up on her toes and pressed their lips together.

This was what Ash had needed before. She moaned lightly,

this kiss freer than the ones last night. They kept the embrace light, but Ash smiled as she pulled away. Complete joy filled her, and she couldn't stop smiling. "I'll text you."

"Please do." Chris winked. "But unless you want a repeat of last night, let's keep the texts PG."

Laughing, Ash kissed Chris again. "Will do. Promises. Mostly."

Chris stepped away, putting space between them. Ash took that as her sign to leave. She was close to being late to work that day anyway. Rolling her shoulders, she glanced at the door and then back at Chris. "I'll see you around."

"See you, Ash."

Her step was so much lighter as she walked out. She waved at Ms. Linda as she left and bundled up as she raced with her head down toward her car. It was freezing outside, but she was so happy and warm inside that she wasn't going to let the cold bother her.

As soon as she was in her car with the engine running, Ash called her sister and put it through the car speakers. She had to share with someone, and since Mari wasn't there—not that *that* wouldn't be an awkward conversation, but she was still so used to sharing everything with her late wife—her sister got the honor.

"Char," Ash breathed heavily, the same excitement as before rushing through her.

"What? It's early."

"Shut up. You're going to want to hear this." Ash pulled away from the curb.

Silence reverberated through the line. Ash had to look and make sure the call hadn't disconnected somehow.

"I asked her out."

"Asked who out?"

"Chris!" Ash couldn't stop the smile.

"The teacher you hated?" Char sounded either disappointed or confused. Ash couldn't quite put her finger on what.

"Uh...yeah, that one."

"You asked out your bully?"

Well, when her sister put it like that, it didn't sound good at all. Her defenses went up in an instant, her shoulders tensed, and the joy that she'd just found was quickly pulled out from under her. "She's not a bully."

"Ash." Char grumbled, "You ranted about her your entire junior year of high school. You hate her."

I love her! But the words wouldn't leave her chest. Ash clenched her jaw tightly as she pulled out onto the main road. How was she supposed to defend against this? Char hadn't seen them together. All she'd known was they'd had a one-night stand and Ash had been devastated to find out that Chris was the principal at the school. She'd done a poor job of keeping her sister up to date on her life. Her stomach twisted hard because she didn't want to lose the happiness that she'd found.

"I didn't like her then," Ash finally said. "Now it's a completely different story."

"Stories." Char sighed heavily. "She's not bullying you into this, is she?"

"No." Ash gnawed on her lip again. "No, she's not. I asked her out." It was mostly the truth. Char didn't need the details until she was ready to hear them. "I want this, Char. You've been telling me for months now that it's time to get my feet wet. I thought you'd be happy for me."

"I am happy." Char paused. "I just want to protect you. You're my baby sister, and I know what you went through after Mari died."

"Yeah. It sucked. And it still sucks. But I can't live in the past anymore. Maybe someday I'll be able to think about Mari without wanting to cry, but I'm not going to give up on happiness until that happens."

"Good for you, sis." Char sighed. "I am happy for you. I promise."

"Thanks." It wasn't quite the reaction that Ash had wanted

to get, but she would take it. And she would focus on Chris and just how much joy she got from their relationship. And maybe she would find hope in love again.

CHAPTER

Seventeen

THEIR SCHEDULES WERE A MESS. It took an entire week to find a time when they could get together, and Chris had to skip her regular AA meeting for it. She hesitated as she drove through the snowy streets toward the steakhouse. She should have planned the date at her place, made it more intimate, but Chris wasn't sure they were ready for that.

A date.

She almost couldn't believe that she was going on one. It had been so long since she'd truly thought about this being a possibility, about the fact that it might be worth it again. But Ash was shockingly insistent, and quite honestly, it just felt good to be around her.

Chris wished the kiss in her office the week before had been better—longer, smoother, more intense—but she was hyperaware of anyone who could walk in on them at any minute, and the fact that the school had cameras everywhere. When she'd been with Andry, they'd never minded about those things, but they'd moved to the district already married. This was dating, which was different, and Ash was still a parent at her school.

Pursing her lips, Chris turned into the parking lot and tried to find a spot near to the door, but it was packed. She was glad she'd put her name on the waitlist. Then they wouldn't have to wait for so long, hopefully. Maybe Ash was already inside.

She was so nervous.

Ripples floated through her, daring her to stop what she was doing and run back to her AA meeting where she knew she was going to be safe. This was a risk, and even though she was sober for nearly two years now—that anniversary was coming up quickly—Chris wasn't sure she could handle this. Going back to her life of AA meetings and work seemed like a much better option.

Then she saw Ash, bundled, head down, as she raced through the parking lot toward the front door. All that tension inside her chest eased instantly, and Chris wanted to be inside with her already. Parking, Chris pocketed her keys and raced toward the front doors of the restaurant. They could do this. She could do this. It would just take some strategy to make sure she didn't get off track.

When Chris stepped inside, the blast of heat and warmth filled her. She brushed off her jacket and her hair from the snowflakes that still clung to her and immediately unzipped her jacket. She looked around the waiting area until her eyes landed on Ash. She was stunning. Her brown hair was loose around her shoulders, soft and big waves of hair. She'd done up her makeup a little more than usual, especially with eyeliner and lipstick.

Warmth spread through Chris' entire body, and she wanted nothing more than to take Ash home right then and there and forget they'd even agreed to dinner. She found herself smiling as she rubbed her palms together to warm them up.

"Hey," Ash said, coming to stand close to Chris and grabbing her fingers. "You're so cold."

"Yeah. It's freezing outside if you didn't notice."

Ash bent forward and kissed Chris' fingertips. "Guess I'll just have to warm you up."

"We're in a steakhouse, Ash." Chris laughed. "I'd agree to that if we were at home."

Ash's cheeks went pink. Chris leaned in and kissed one before turning around to find the hostess. She wanted to get seated as soon as possible. Luckily, their wait wasn't long. Chris followed the hostess to their table with Ash's fingers curled in hers. She was going to touch Ash as much as she possibly could that night. It was one of the few things that centered her lately.

They sat across from each other in the booth, even though Chris would have much preferred to sit side by side. They ordered drinks and then food, and within what seemed like minutes, Chris' entire focus was on Ash. This was exactly how it should be.

"I can't believe we're doing this," Ash whispered, as if them being out was some big secret.

That ate away at Chris. She didn't want to keep secrets. She'd kept enough of those throughout the years, and this one would just eat away at her too, but then again, she didn't want to share it with anyone just yet, either. Maybe Andry, since she'd been such a good listener so far, and Mel. Chris wrinkled her nose at that thought. What was she even doing? She was a principal to Ash's girls. She shouldn't be here at all.

"Chris," Ash said sternly. "I lost you there a minute. What happened?"

"Nothing." Chris grabbed her drink and took a sip of cold water.

"Talk to me."

"I can't stop thinking about the girls." Chris winced. "This is complicated."

"It is." Ash frowned slightly. "But I've never been in a relationship that hasn't been complicated."

"I guess." That did make Chris feel slightly better. If she thought about her relationship with Andry, it was the same. Everything came with its own complications. "But I'm their principal."

"And my former teacher." Ash gave her a brilliant grin. "I

think if we can get over the student-teacher thing, then the principal thing isn't so different."

Chris wasn't so sure about that. And she also wasn't sure she wanted to be bringing up such a serious conversation during their first date. Chris really had to bring up the fact that she was a drunk, well, in recovery as her sponsor would say. She still felt like a drunk most days. But she had no idea how to actually bring that up in conversation in a way that wouldn't completely put them on the outs.

Chris wasn't the teacher she used to be.

And she wasn't the principal she used to be either.

Which meant she was left in recovery, not even two full years yet, and still struggling with her addiction every day.

"Are you regretting this?" Ash asked after the waitstaff placed their food in front of them.

Chris really had to think about that because initially her answer was no. She didn't regret going out with Ash. But she still had a whole lot of hesitations about it, and she did need to work on resolving those one way or another.

"I'm not regretting being with you," Chris answered honestly, glad that she'd taken the time to figure it out for herself. "But I am concerned about how some of this is going to work."

"It's our first date, Chris. Can't it just be that?"

She wanted to say yes. She wanted to calm down her anxieties and let this just be, but that wasn't who she was. Protector at heart. Chris always looked for ways she could protect those around her, including herself, and that meant she was hyperaware of how every possible thing could go wrong. Except she failed at that too sometimes. Like with her drinking. And Chris found herself back in the vicious cycle she always struggled to get out of.

"Chris?" Ash set her fork down. Her bright blue eyes dampened with concern, and Chris hated seeing that. "Talk to me."

"I'm just a worrywart." Why did she always brush these

things off like that? She should be better at this by now, shouldn't she?

"It's more than that." Ash softened her tone.

"It is, but I'm not sure we're ready for that yet."

Ash chuckled. "When are we going to be ready for it?"

Chris wanted it to be hopefully never, but she knew that couldn't make this relationship work. But she really didn't want to talk about it today. Cutting into her steak, Chris took her first bite, chewing but not tasting. When she swallowed, she looked Ash directly in the eye. "Maybe someday."

"Seems to be our standard answer, doesn't it?"

Chris couldn't agree more. "How will we navigate the principal part?"

"Well..." Ash trailed off as she took another bite. "I don't exactly want to tell the girls right away that we're dating. I think we need to be together for a while first."

"Good idea." Chris had thought similarly, so she was glad Ash was on the same page with that. "Are they ready for you to be dating?"

Ash blew out a breath. "Rhubie will probably be fine with it. Avonlee is a different story."

"She seems to be on the struggle bus."

"Well, she does take after me in a lot of ways."

"How is that?" Chris studied Ash carefully. Was this okay conversation? It seemed odd to be talking about kids on a date, but kids were also so much a part of their lives that she couldn't imagine a conversation without them. Which led her right to Katie. Her own daughter. And someone she had largely avoided since becoming sober because again she just didn't know how to start those hard conversations.

"She doesn't have a lot of filters, but mostly just tries to suppress her feelings if they're not good. Then they explode in unhealthy ways."

"Sounds like what's happening at school."

"Yeah," Ash agreed.

Chris would have to do better at observing Avonlee to make sure she was on track with everything and that she wasn't going to have any outbursts. She'd talk with Esther about it. Then again, should she be doing that? Was that a conflict of interest? But she couldn't *not* help Avonlee if she saw issues, right? That would also be an ethical issue. The complications from this made her brain hurt, and while Chris would love to ignore it, she wasn't sure she could.

Maybe Mel could help with that particular issue.

It was so much easier to think about these things when she wasn't in the center of them. For now, she just wanted to enjoy the first proper date she had been on in years, and maybe just maybe she could go home having enjoyed tonight instead of finding it stressful.

Chris was just about to ask Ash a question when her phone buzzed in her pocket. She frowned but reached for it. Katie's name appeared across the screen—a text message. Chris flicked her gaze to Ash, issuing an apology before she opened her phone and read the message.

Katie 6:56 pm - Mom, I need to talk to you.

Chris 6:56 pm - Anytime. When?

Looking up at Ash, Chris shook her head. If she hadn't been in such a vulnerable state before, she definitely was now. "My daughter texted."

"You look like you've seen a ghost."

"Yeah, well, we don't talk much. This is the first time she's texted me something other than a meme in a month." Chris stared down at her phone, waiting for Katie's answer. "We've had some issues in the last few years. It's hard to work through those."

"It is," Ash commented. "But it sounds like you're open to working on it."

"Always. She's my baby." Chris smiled, remembering the last time she called Katie her baby and the smart retort Katie gave her. But it never would matter. Katie was her baby no matter what.

"Yeah, I get that." Ash smiled fondly. "Avonlee gets so mad when I call her that."

"Katie too." Chris was enjoying the small talk, but also the tender conversation they were having together, a connection point that she'd been missing minutes before.

Katie 6:58 pm - I'll meet you at your place.

Chris stared at her phone dumbfounded. She had said anytime. She just hadn't meant now, had she? Her heart was in her fingers as she typed back a quick response and then stared at Ash.

"I'm so sorry to have to do this."

"Do what?" Ash put her fork down.

"Katie wants to talk. Now."

Ash frowned, flicking her gaze from Chris to her phone. "Now?"

"Yeah. I'm so sorry." Chris couldn't move. She wanted to stay there and finish their date, but the call to parenting and maybe beginning the hard work on her relationship with Katie was so strong. "I have to go."

Ash blew out a breath. "I understand. I'm disappointed, but I understand."

"Me too." Chris swallowed the fear in her throat, hoping that it would vanish, but it didn't. Maybe she wasn't as scared about her date as she thought, or maybe her fear now was all about Katie and just what this conversation that couldn't wait was about. "We need to reschedule."

"I'm not sure when we'll get a chance. My parents are going out of town for a couple weeks. And Char is only helpful to an extent." Ash fingered her napkin that she'd set on the table.

"We'll find a time. I promise." Chris reached across the table and covered Ash's hand with her own. "I don't want to give up the possibility of us, not yet."

"Me either." Ash softened. "I guess just text me, then."

"Yeah, I will." Chris was about to stand up, but she stopped. "Fun texts, sexy texts, all texts are welcome, just to be clear."

Ash's cheeks turned a bright red. "Duly noted."

"See you around, Ash." Chris bent down and pressed her lips to Ash's cheek. Then Ash turned and their mouths connected in a brief but intimate kiss. When she pulled away, Chris found herself smiling. "See you."

"Yup. See you."

Chris walked toward the front of the restaurant, paid for the meal on her way out, and then climbed in her car. Immediately, she called Andry. She needed to know what this was about before she stepped full force into a potential ambush she didn't know was coming. And Andry would help her. She always did.

CHAPTER
Eighteen

"THAT WAS SHORT," Char commented as soon as Ash walked into the house.

"Yeah." Ash blew out a breath and smiled at her girls. "Want to stay a bit while I get them to bed?"

"Is it a good story?"

Ash shrugged. "Not sure on that one yet."

"Oh, that sounds juicy." Char rubbed her hands together. "Get those kiddos to bed."

Rhubie clung to Ash's leg, and she didn't even feel bad about it. She needed the physical affection and reminder that Chris hadn't left the date because of her. She deeply understood the need to take care of family first, but Katie was an adult, which was so different than Rhubie or Avonlee who were still very much kids.

Bending down, Ash wrapped her arms around Rhubie's shoulders and gave her a kiss on her cheek. "Why don't you go get in your jammies, and we can snuggle."

Rhubie squealed as she raced toward her bedroom. Avonlee stayed staunchly on the couch. Ash flopped next to her and let out a sigh. She wrapped her arm over Avonlee's shoulders and tugged her into her side, kissing the top of her head.

"How about you? Do you want snuggles tonight?" Ash wished Avonlee would say yes, but she was pretty sure it'd be a no.

With a shake of Avonlee's head, Ash had her answer. She patted Avonlee's knee and relaxed into her couch while she waited on Rhubie. It didn't take her long to get her daughter to bed, and the twenty minutes of snuggles that she got was exactly what she needed. Ash clung onto moments like those, ones where she knew she'd remember them for the rest of her life. The ones where she missed Mari being there with her.

Sneaking out of Rhubie's bedroom, Ash wandered into the living room. Avonlee was still on the couch, staring at the television screen. Ash sent Avonlee off to bed, and Char raised an eyebrow and nodded toward the kitchen. Ash followed her.

"So what happened?"

"Her daughter texted and needed to meet with her."

"And it couldn't wait?" Char asked, grabbing the juice from Ash's fridge.

Ash shook her head. "Apparently not."

She frowned as Char poured each of them a drink. They moved to the small table Ash had shoved against the far wall and sat down. She wasn't sure where to start, because the date had started off well, but then they'd taken a deep dive into life drama and struggles. Not exactly first date material. She hated that she couldn't separate her trauma from her life.

"What really happened?"

"That is what happened." Ash looked at Char over her glass. Though she knew what Char meant. Something else was going on with Chris, those deep secrets coming up again, and they hadn't shared them. "I promise you. She even paid for the meal."

"She ditched you, Ash."

"I don't think she did." Ash spun the glass on the table. "But it didn't go as smoothly as it could have."

"Why's that?" Char finished her juice and stared at it. "I wish you had something harder to drink."

Ash shrugged. She hadn't had a drop of alcohol in her house

since Mari had died, and she would likely keep it that way for a long time. "I miss Mari."

"Marigold Taylor." Char laughed lightly, but her eyes misted over. "I miss her too. Fuck, I miss her."

Ash grimaced. She nearly forgot sometimes just how much the rest of her family went through those steps of grief as well. She hadn't really been able to focus on them because she was so worried about her daughters and making sure they weren't going to go down the well of despair she'd found herself in.

"Being with Chris has brought up so much of that. I'm just not sure this is the right time."

"It'll never be the right time, Ash." Char reached over and touched Ash's hand lightly before pulling back. "And Mari was an amazing woman. It's impossible to replace her."

"I don't want to replace her. She's the love of my life. I can't just go on and pretend like she never existed." Ash's heart raced. How could Char even think about something like that? She wanted nothing more than to be at ease with this pain, but it came back to bite her in the ass when she least expected and least wanted it. On tonight of all nights? It was more unwelcome than Katie's interruption.

"No one can do that. Poor choice of words on my part." Char blew out a breath. "I'm sorry."

"I just don't know what to do."

"Take it one step at a time."

Ash finished her drink, and they went into the living room. Lounging with her big sister was exactly what Ash needed that night. She had to sort through these emotions that kept running face first into her, the despair but also the hope. She needed to figure out what she wanted in order to move forward. They may have only had one date, but it broke the rose-colored glasses that Ash had put on before. She wasn't sure she could do this because she didn't want to fall in love.

They were through the second episode of the true crime show they were watching when a piercing scream resounded from Avonlee's room. Ash and Char were on their feet in an instant, racing down the hall to Avonlee's bedroom. She screamed again.

Ash's heart was in her throat as she flung open the door to find Avonlee thrashing around on her bed, the covers twisted around her ankles and wrapped around her hips.

"Wake up!" Ash nearly shouted, failing to control the adrenaline rushing through her. "Avonlee, wake up."

Ash shook Avonlee's shoulder while Char tried to grab her hands and hold her still. Another scream tore through the room just before Avonlee jerked with a start, her chest rising and falling rapidly as she looked around the room wildly.

"Baby, it's okay. I'm right here."

Avonlee shook her head sharply. "I don't want you."

"I know, kiddo. I know." Ash reached forward and held her daughter tightly in her arms. She tugged Avonlee into her chest and rubbed her hands up and down Avonlee's back in a soothing motion. She would sing like she had when Avonlee was little, but the last few times she'd offered that, she'd been told to stop.

"Stop it." Avonlee pushed at Ash's arms. "I don't want you!"

"Avonlee," Char said, sitting on the edge of the mattress. "You had a nightmare. We're just trying to help."

Avonlee shook her head forcefully from side to side and backed into the corner of her bed. She held her knees to her chest, her entire body shaking. Ash's heart broke. It seemed she wasn't the only one wanting Mari back, not that she was surprised by that. Avonlee had missed her mother since before Mari had died. She just likely wasn't to remember that.

"I don't want you." Avonlee glared.

Ash bit her tongue and held herself still. She didn't want to lash out in anger, but what she really didn't want was for Avonlee to see just how hurt she was. It was good to an extent, she knew, to let her daughter in on her own feelings, but right now it wouldn't do either of them any good for it to happen.

"Get out!" Avonlee screeched, her cheeks red and tears streaming down her face. "Get out! Get out! Get out!"

"I'm just trying to make sure you're okay," Ash started, regretting her words in an instant.

Avonlee's face morphed from anger to utter anguish. "Okay? I'm not okay, Mom. I'll never be okay. You killed her. You should have been the one in the car that night! She should be here. Not you!"

Ash's heart ripped in two. Char reached out and put a hand on her shoulder, her lips parted in surprise. Hatred was the only word that came to mind when Ash looked at her daughter. Avonlee hated her. Ash's heart thundered, catching in her throat.

"I didn't kill her."

"You should have been the one driving! Not her. If you'd been driving, then she wouldn't be dead!"

"Enough!" Ash's raised voice cut through the tense air in the room. "Enough already. She was drunk, Avonlee. I didn't know she was drunk, and she shouldn't have been driving that night, but she was. I can't go back and change that."

Avonlee's jaw dropped. She paled. She clasped her knees tighter, as she stared wide-eyed at her mother. "She was drunk?"

"Mom had a drinking problem, and I tried to protect you from it, but I can't anymore. Mom was an alcoholic, and the night that she died, we went out, and I thought she wasn't drinking all night so I let her drive home, but she had been sneaking drinks. I didn't know." Ash's heart caught in her throat. Tears flooded her eyes, flowing down her cheeks and matching Avonlee's. "I didn't know."

The silence in the room was palpable. Char sat on the edge of the mattress completely still, her gaze focused on Avonlee. They'd all done such an amazing job at keeping this secret, but Avonlee deserved to know the truth. Ash couldn't hide it any longer.

"Mom had a drinking problem for years. I didn't find out how bad it was until she was in the hospital. She didn't die from the car accident. She died withdrawing from the alcohol in the hospital after."

"You're lying," Avonlee threw the accusation.

Char held her hand up. "She's not, Avonlee. I promise you, she's not."

Betrayal flashed through Avonlee's eyes. Ash understood that. She'd felt the same way when she'd woken up in the hospital after the accident, when she'd learned just how drunk Mari had been. She sucked in a shuddering breath and tried to keep herself together. She didn't want to fall apart in front of Avonlee. She didn't want to shatter.

"I put Mom on a pedestal, baby, and you do, too. It's normal to do that." Ash's voice was raw. "But we have to stop doing that, because it's not right. Mom wasn't perfect. She loved every fiber of your being and every fiber of Rhubie's, but Mom wasn't perfect."

Avonlee released her knees and wiped the tears on her face. "I don't want to believe it."

"Me either, baby. I don't want to think about Mom like that, but sometimes we have to." Ash stayed planted on the mattress, hoping that Avonlee was finally reaching her breaking point. She would give anything to have Avonlee in her arms, just so Ash could hold and cradle her.

"So what actually happened?"

That question broke Ash's heart into a million little pieces. She'd always told herself that someday she would have to share the whole story, but she never wanted that day to actually happen. Sighing, Ash rubbed her temple and tried to pull herself together for the sake of her daughter. "We were driving home after going out on a date, and I don't really remember much after that. It was rainy, and the highway was wet. The police officers said we hydroplaned. That's when the car kind of floats on top of the water instead of sinking to drive on the pavement. It means Mom was going too fast."

"She always liked to drive fast," Avonlee mumbled.

Char smiled at her fondly, and Ash understood it. Remember the good so long as she could. That was what she had to do. "Yeah, she did, didn't she? But that night she was going too fast, and she crashed the car. I woke up in the hospital, but Mom didn't. They tried to save her for weeks, remember? But they couldn't."

Avonlee looked so innocent, staring at Ash with hope that the story would change, that something would be different this time. As much as Ash wanted to give that to her daughter, she couldn't. The story wouldn't change. Mari was still dead. Ash was still left alone to parent their daughters. She was still alone.

"I'm so sorry, baby." Ash opened her arms, and Avonlee crawled into the circle of safety that Ash offered.

Finally, she cradled her baby, hugging her, squishing her, kissing her. She wasn't going to let go a second sooner than she had to. They needed each other through this.

"Does Rhubie know?"

"No, she's too little to understand." Ash dropped another kiss into Avonlee's hair. "I don't want you to forget her, ever."

"I won't. I promise."

"Good." Another kiss, and Ash closed her eyes, relaxing finally.

It was the first time in years that she felt completely connected to Avonlee. They had struggled so much, especially these past few weeks since moving there, but this was the breakdown of those walls. Ash couldn't give that up. And she also couldn't deny the fact that tonight was so similar to the night Mari died. She'd been out, on a date, and her kids had needed her. She wasn't there for them when they needed her the most.

"I love you, Avonlee."

"Love you, too," Avonlee mumbled into Ash's shoulder.

Ash stayed with Avonlee until she fell back asleep. Exhausted, she walked into the living room to find Char still waiting for her with the television on. As soon as she saw her,

Char stood up and wrapped Ash in a hug. "You're so fucking strong."

Ash whimpered.

"I really should get going."

"Yeah." Ash dragged her fingers through her hair.

Char grabbed her jacket and her purse but not before sending Ash a concerned look, a line forming in the center of her forehead. "Don't tell me you're going to back off now."

"I don't know," Ash whispered. "But I do know that I need to get my priorities right, and this is where they're at."

"But Ash—"

"Drop it, Char. I love Mari, and I'm never going to stop loving her."

CHAPTER
Nineteen

THE BASEMENT of the church was oppressively warm. Chris had been there so many times throughout the last two years that she knew the way down the hall like the back of her hand. But leading the way for Katie wasn't something she ever thought she'd be doing.

Three days ago, Katie had begged her to go to a meeting. Chris had only hesitated because this was about her daughter, and she had to be sure that she wasn't going to make it about herself. But she'd been lost in a whirlwind that was Katie coming to her, wanting reconciliation in their relationship, and fighting against the insatiable hope that maybe this time was different.

"Maybe," Chris whispered to herself as she stepped into the small room.

Chris stopped short just inside the door. Katie walked on ahead of her, sitting down in the only place that had two open seats, but Chris couldn't look at Katie. Her eyes were glued to the cute, young brunette who sat with her arms crossed over her chest in a protective stance with an empty seat next to her. The one empty seat Katie had left for Chris.

What the hell was Ash doing here?

Chris wanted to throw accusations. She wanted to lob them,

yell, scream, but she was eaten up by embarrassment in two seconds flat. Katie was there to share that night. She was there to talk about her experiences with Chris being an alcoholic and how that had affected her life, and she wanted Chris to shut up and listen. She wanted to do it in a safe place, where she knew she would have support, despite how unconventional it was.

Chris' heart hammered. She wanted to walk out, cry, and go find her own meeting. Some place she could burrow down, get what she needed and then hide away again because there was no way she knew how to face this. Face Ash.

"Mom?" Katie called from across the room, beckoning her over with a single look.

Chris balked. She managed to get her feet unrooted from the doorway and sliding them one after the other across the short blue, stained carpet. She held her breath as she slid into the seat next to Ash and gripped onto the arms of the forty-year-old chairs that had lost all their padding throughout the years. She couldn't speak.

Every word she might have had was caught in her throat, and she couldn't even manage to shift a hello to Ash and apologize ahead of time for what was about to come out because she knew... Chris knew how bad this was going to look. She was a shit parent as a drunk. There was no doubt of that, and she fully admitted it too. And Katie was about to lay that bare in front of this entire room.

"Hey," Ash whispered.

Chris nodded at her, words still caught in her throat. A cold clammy sweat broke across her back and in her pits. This was going to be it. Ash was going to see the real her, and there was no hope of any future with them.

And she had to focus on Katie. Katie was the whole reason she was there. Connect with her daughter. Understand what her kid had been through for years. Make amends now that she knew where the damage was and just how much there was. Help Katie heal.

But fuck, what was Ash doing there?

Who was the drunk in Ash's life?

Chris closed her eyes and drew in slow deep breaths to steady her racing nerves. She missed the opening of the meeting while she worked through the new techniques her therapist had taught her that were barely working because what the hell was Ash doing there?

Katie spoke up, her voice quivering. "Hi, I'm Katie. And my mom is an alcoholic."

Chris breathed out what she swore was her last breath. She couldn't look at Ash. She couldn't even look at Katie. She clenched her jaw tightly, tears brimming in her eyes. She'd done this all wrong. She should have told Ash before, but they'd barely even started an actual relationship before all of this had happened, and timing was never in her favor and—

"And she's been an alcoholic for the majority of my life." Katie's voice grew stronger as she continued her story. "I don't remember a time when she was sober, until recently."

At that, Chris opened her eyes and turned her head. She looked directly into Ash's bright blue eyes. Surprise. Hurt. Anger. Confusion. Chris willed herself to do something, anything, but she wasn't there for Ash. She was there for Katie. Shaking her head slightly, Chris mouthed the only thing she could think of, *I'm so sorry*.

"My mom's been sober for almost two years now, but it hasn't been easy. I don't think she'd tell you it was easy, but between the two of us, it's been really hard."

Chris closed her eyes again, centering herself. She had to focus on Katie. That was why she was there, after all. That was the entire purpose of being in this meeting.

Katie.

Looking at her daughter, her dark curly hair that was cut to her shoulders, her dark brown eyes, the strength in her shoulders and her stance even though Chris knew she was scared shitless to do this. Katie was amazing. She was the woman Chris had never been able to become, and she'd learned it all from Andry. Andry who had been the parent who was present, the one who was there when Katie hurt herself, the one who had taken the brunt of responsibilities.

"I don't know who my mom is." Katie's words stung.

Chris knew they had to. They were the truth. In the nearly two years since she'd been sober she hadn't had a chance to get to know Katie, and Katie hadn't had a chance to get to know her —not that Chris fully understood who she was when she was sober. Chris dashed her tongue across her lips and glanced back at Ash—Ash who stared directly at her.

Katie sniffled, and Chris whipped her attention back to her daughter. "Mom wasn't there when I was growing up. I mean she was there because she always came to every activity of mine that she could, but she wasn't there." Katie tapped her head. "Her mind was always somewhere else. On booze."

A double pang of guilt ate away at Chris. Here she was again, her attention divided and not where it should be. Taking another steadying breath like she'd been taught, Chris uncurled her fingers, determined to listen to every word of Katie's story.

"Mom was drunk all the time when I was growing up. None of us really realized just how bad it was. I mean, I just thought it was normal. That's who she was, honestly. A drunk. Her entire focus was about getting to her next drink, and she didn't care if it was at home or out late at night with her friends. It tore our family apart."

Chris hated that she'd done that. She was the cause of the breakup between her and Andry. She'd never had any doubt of that, and staring Andry in the face, looking her in the eye, and understanding just how much damage she had done was the hardest thing ever. But doing it again with Katie topped that. Andry had been gracious, like she always was with her words and her actions. Katie wouldn't do that. She was brutally honest, just like Chris.

"My parents split when I was fourteen, but they weren't

really together before then. Because all my mom cared about was drinking. It got really bad that year. I thought about killing myself several times."

Chris' chin jerked up at that. She wanted to wrap her arms around Katie's shoulders and hold her tight. But she didn't feel like she had that right anymore. While Katie still might be her only child, Chris wasn't a parent to her—not in the capacity that she should be.

"But I didn't, and I'm still here. I can honestly say I've never had a drop of alcohol, even being in college." Katie chuckled lightly. "I guess that's one *good* lesson Mom taught me." Her lips curled upward. "But in the last five years I haven't really talked to my mom much. She's been around, but I haven't gotten to know her. It's no fault of her own. Like I said, she's coming up on two years sober."

Chris' gaze was riveted to Katie. When had her daughter become so strong? When had Katie gotten her life together so much? A lump formed in Chris' throat, and she struggled to see the little girl that she always saw her daughter as. Katie wasn't that little five-year-old with pigtails anymore. She was a grown ass woman, and Chris had been the central cause of most of her trauma.

"I'm so proud of her." Katie sniffled, tears welling in her eyes and threatening to spill over. She bundled up the sleeves of her sweatshirt and wiped at her cheeks. Katie let out a wry laugh. "I told myself I wasn't going to cry."

"You've got this, girl," someone from across the room said.

Chris couldn't tear her gaze away. Katie was amazing. She had been through so much, and Chris had no doubt that she would come out on the right side of all of this. Katie wasn't strong because of the trauma she'd experienced, but she was strong because she was willing to deal with it. Chris breathed relief. Her heart warmed slightly, comfort settling into the pit of her belly. Katie would be okay.

"I'm so proud of my mom. Two years? I never thought it was

possible for her to even make it past a week. There were times when she tried getting sober, but she always failed. But this time..." Katie turned, looking directly at Chris.

Chris' breath caught.

Katie reached out, holding Chris' hand in her own and squeezing hard. "This time I think she might do it."

Chris cried. She couldn't hold it in anymore. She shook her head and wiped her own tears from her eyes.

"It's not been easy, that's for sure, and I still don't know who she is." Katie faced everyone else in the room. "I don't know how to get to know her. She's my mom. I should know who she is, right? But I don't. I don't know. But I want to."

That small piece of hope was all Chris needed. If it took years, decades, the rest of her life Chris was going to work on her relationship with Katie. Katie deserved it. And she deserved both her parents to be in her life as much as she was willing to let them be.

"So here we go. Step two of the rest of my life. Maybe someday I'll know what it's like to know who my mom is." Katie sat back heavily in her chair and finished wiping the tears from her eyes.

Chris snagged a couple tissues and shoved them into Katie's free hand before leaning over and kissing Katie's cheek. She didn't care in that moment if they were in a room full of people and this was her adult daughter. Katie had to know.

"I love you," Chris whispered. "I love you so much, and I'm so, so sorry."

"It's not okay, Mom, but we'll figure it out." Katie leaned her head on Chris' shoulder and closed her eyes.

Other people talked, but Chris barely heard what they had to say. She stayed focused on Katie as much as she could for the rest of the hour-long meeting. When it was time to go, they stood up and said their prayer. She kept a tight hold on Katie's hand, not willing to let her go just yet.

Ash stuttered in her step as she gathered her purse from the ground. Chris almost reached out, but Ash jerked her shoulder back and out of Chris' reach. The clear sign was *don't touch me*, and Chris was going to respect every second of that. She was just about to say something, when Ash shook her head, her eyes wide.

Chris collapsed. Ash backed away from her before turning around and practically running out of the room. Normally, Chris would have followed her. She would have run after to figure out just exactly what she had done, but she couldn't. Katie's hand in hers was a strong reminder of why she was there.

Amends.

With Katie. Not with Ash. Not with anyone else. This was about her family and righting the wrongs she had already done, when she was a drunk. Not the fuck ups she made this week or last week.

But why had Ash even been there? Chris was pretty sure it was her very presence that prevented Ash from sharing that night. Which was a pity. She'd obviously come there because she needed support. Just another notch of fuck ups to add to her belt. Chris couldn't win no matter what she did.

Katie looped her arm through Chris' as they walked down the long hallway to the end of the church building. "I hope we can talk more."

"I'll listen as often as you want to talk." Chris dropped a kiss into her daughter's hair. "I think we have a lot of talking and listening to do, respectively."

"Yeah," Katie murmured. "But not tonight. That took everything out of me."

"I get it."

They stepped outside into the freezing air in the dead of winter. Chris shuddered as she looked around the parking lot for her car. She hit the button on her key fob just as Katie stopped her with a tug to her arm.

"I didn't lie tonight, Mom. I am proud of you."

Chris was ready to break down again. She smiled at Katie. "You're amazing, in so many ways."

"So are you. I wish you'd believe that."

Parting her lips, Chris stuttered to find an answer. What was she supposed to say to that? Again Katie stole the words right out of her mouth. "I'm so sorry that I couldn't be who you needed me to be."

"There's still time, Mom."

Giving a small smile, Chris tugged Katie in for another hug. "Yeah. We'll get there."

CHAPTER
Twenty

"HOLY FUCK."

Ash swung into her car and slammed the door. She pulled out of the parking spot as fast as she could. She drove toward home, but stopped at Holliday Park. She couldn't go home yet. She couldn't walk into that house and reasonably look at her girls and think she could parent them.

Because holy fuck.

Chris was a drunk.

Everything clicked into place. Chris never drinking when they went out, the subtle questions about why Ash wasn't drinking, the closed-off feeling about her relationship with Katie and what she'd done to screw it up.

Ash's heart raced.

How had she not seen it before? It was just like it had been with Mari. She'd been completely oblivious to the fact that the woman she was with was a drunk. Ash fisted her hands and crashed them down against the steering wheel. The bolt of pain was exactly what she needed to shock her back into reality. She did it again and again.

Tears burned down her cheeks as she rested her forehead

against the steering wheel and covered her face with her arms. How come she didn't notice?

How come she kept falling for women with the same problems?

Ash dragged in a deep breath, her chest heaving as she tried to pull cold air into her lungs. She couldn't do this. There was no possible way she could put herself right back in the same situation as before, right? That had to be asinine and crazy. She would do more harm to her girls than she could possibly think, especially with Avonlee in the state that she was currently in.

"What the hell was I thinking?" Ash wiped her cheeks, the tears flowing freely down her cheeks, and she didn't even try to stop them.

The floodgates were opened, and she needed to let the demons wash through her. Mari had lied to her so many times in the years they had been married. It had become such a common thing for her to lie about how drunk she was, about how much liquor she had consumed, about how unstable she was.

Ash had asked. And then she had stopped asking. She'd given up. She'd avoided. She'd ignored. All the signs had been there, and they haunted her ever since. She should have been so much more observant. She should have known better than to trust a drunk. The question was, would she make the same mistake twice? Because she damn sure didn't want to.

Which meant she couldn't be with Chris.

It meant that she had to practice self-preservation instead of allowing her heart to run the conversation. She had to protect herself from going down the same path she did before. A cry ripped from her chest. It reverberated around the car, screaming back at her. It had been a long time since she'd heard such a horrific sound.

Since Mari died.

Ash withered.

She had to talk to Chris. She wasn't the asshole that was going to ghost her, but she really didn't want to have that conversation. She didn't want to explain the things that Chris didn't know. It would wound her too much—both of them. For Chris to know... Ash had to stop that line of thinking. It would devastate her to the point of no return.

Pulling back on the relationship was the only option she had.

But she would have to talk to Chris first. But not today. Today she needed to let this all sit with her, let her heart mend a little and build up her defenses because she knew she would need them. She couldn't be this raw. Chris would think it was all because she didn't want to be with another alcoholic, and while that was true, it was *another* part that was more true.

Ash allowed herself to cry for another ten minutes before she dragged her weary body, mind, and soul together. Her parents would be expecting her home already. She'd called them in a fit of panic last minute when she'd found the meeting and knew she had to attend. But she hadn't gotten what she needed out of it. She hadn't found support. She'd been too stupefied to even begin to find someone she could talk to about Avonlee.

Driving home was difficult, but Ash knew she had to do it. She needed to talk to Char about Chris, and she needed to be in her safe place just so she could think clearly again. The long drive home was one of the hardest she had ever made. She pulled up into her driveway, and her phone buzzed in the cupholder. Ash parked and picked it up to stare at the text message.

Chris 8:37 pm - Can we talk?

Ash's heart sank. She didn't want to talk. She didn't want to listen. She wanted to ignore the problem that had just landed in her lap. But she couldn't. She owed it to herself and to Chris to at least have one last conversation about what was going to happen next.

Ash 8:38 pm - Not tonight.

She slipped her phone into her back pocket as she turned off the engine to the car and got out. The last thing she needed was to be distracted by a conversation that she couldn't control and one she knew which direction it was going to take.

At least Chris was sober.

That was the only thing she could think of. The thought that kept spinning through her mind. Chris was sober. But she was still a drunk. Ash understood how these things worked. She'd been working with homeless families for a few months now, but she'd been there and done that before. She knew what alcoholism could do to a family. First hand.

It destroyed them.

Screams echoed through the door and the closed windows before she even stepped inside. Ash's shoulders pulled tight as she hesitated when she opened the door. Avonlee was in a deep rage. She should have known better than to leave her alone after the last few days. She'd held it together so far, and they had a few nice days of snuggles and calm conversations, but she also knew that the dam would break.

It seemed tonight was that night.

She should have planned better. She should have worked harder at keeping Avonlee safe from herself. Ash should have been a better parent. Because she needed to be. There was no one else who was going to be there for her girls. No one but her. Mari had made sure of that with her own stupid decisions.

Ash pushed open the front door to the house. Her dad stood with Rhubie clinging to his leg. Her mom had her hands up as if defending herself against the onslaught that was Avonlee. Ash sucked in a sharp breath and held it in her lungs. She couldn't let this get out of hand. She couldn't let Avonlee keep running their life with her tantrums.

She understood the pain and the anger. She felt it too. But that didn't mean Avonlee had to take it out on the rest of them. It didn't mean that she couldn't learn to express these things in healthy ways that stopped hurting the ones she loved the most.

"Stop it!" Ash shouted, catching the attention of the room.

Avonlee jerked with a start, her gaze locking on Ash. Now she had a new target for her anger.

Ash cut her hand across the air, silencing anything that Avonlee might have said. "You need to cut it out. I understand that you're hurt, that you're angry, but you need to take a deep breath and say it calmly. Stop screaming it."

"You're screaming now!"

"Enough!" Ash shouted back.

She couldn't take much more of this. Her soul was breaking every time Avonlee went into this kind of tantrum. All she wanted to do was hug her daughter, wrap her up in the love that she knew Mari felt for her. But it was impossible if Avonlee wouldn't accept it. And right now, she'd be lucky if Avonlee didn't storm off in another fit of rage.

"I want you to take a deep breath."

"No!"

"Then go get a pillow and scream into that."

"What?" The tension was thrown off. Ash pointed to the small square pillow on the couch. "Grab it. Scream into that. Shout at it like it's Mom. Tell her how mad you are at her."

Avonlee looked from Ash to her grandparents. They encouraged her. Avonlee hesitated, but she stepped toward the couch and grabbed the pillow. She awkwardly said in a tiny voice, "I'm mad at you, Mom."

"Say it like you mean it!" Ash raised her voice again. "Let her have it. She deserves to know how pissed you are!"

Avonlee shook her head.

Ash sighed heavily, dropped her jacket and her purse on the back of the couch and snatched the pillow from Avonlee's hands. She held it out in front of her before setting it back on the couch. "I don't deserve this, Mari. None of us do!"

Vibrations coursed through her body in seconds. The anger that she'd suppressed for years bubbled up, exploding out of her.

"*You* did this to us!"

"Mommy!" Avonlee screeched, her eyes wide.

Ash shook her head. "This isn't supposed to make sense, baby. This is to get off our chests what we're feeling. And you know what, I'm mad as hell that Mom isn't here. Aren't you?"

Avonlee's jaw dropped.

Ash turned back to the pillow. "You're missing everything you wanted! You're missing out on our babies growing up! On promotions, on graduations, on problems and laughs. You did this to us, Mari. No one else."

Avonlee clasped Ash's hand, but her gaze was locked on that damn brown pillow. Hope surged into Ash's chest. Was she actually going to do this?

"I'm so mad, Mom." Avonlee sounded way more confident this time. "I'm so mad at you. You left us."

Avonlee's voice broke right along with Ash's heart. This had been what they'd needed. Ash held her daughter's hand while she yelled at the pillow like it was Mari. She stood there, not stoically like she wanted, but feeling every punch Avonlee gave to her dead mother. The bottled up emotion of years past came rushing forth in a release. The dam finally broke.

When she was done, Ash held Avonlee in her arms and rocked her as she sobbed. She curled around her daughter, protecting her, dropping kisses into her hair and running soothing fingers over her arms as she held on with everything she had in her. Her parents put Rhubie to bed while Ash continued to hold her baby. She wasn't going to let go.

The explosion of emotion left her raw. Ash stroked Avonlee's hair, the long strands coming loose. Her heart rate calmed as the night slipped into melancholy. Her mom reached over and brushed her fingers along Avonlee's forehead, and Ash realized her baby was asleep in her arms, probably the first good night's sleep she had gotten in a while.

"Want me to put her down?" her mom asked.

Ash shook her head and buried her nose in Avonlee's hair. She sucked in a deep breath, calming herself with the scent. "I'll put her down in a bit. I just want to hold her right now." When had her voice vanished? She could barely make the words out.

"I can't blame you, honey." Her mom sat next to Ash on the couch, stroking Ash's arm back and forth. "What can we do for you?"

"Nothing, Mom." Ash closed her eyes. She felt awful, but that was expected. She was thrown through the ringer time and time again, and it was a struggle just to attempt to keep up with it all. Ash tightened her grip on Avonlee. "Thank you so much for being here tonight."

"Was the meeting helpful?"

Ash mulled that one over. She wasn't sure it was helpful at all. Looking her mother directly in the eye, Ash said the only honest thing she could. "It certainly brought a few things to light."

"The pillow thing was a really good idea."

"I had a therapist do that with me once. I was so shy at first, but once I got into it, it really worked for a while there." Ash shifted her leg down. "I'm going to go put her to bed."

"Want help?"

"No, I got it. Thanks."

Ash roused Avonlee into a half-sleep and walked her down the hall to her bedroom. While she laid down with her to get her back to sleep, Ash stared up at the dark ceiling. The front door closed as her parents left, and the house was cast into an easy and comfortable silence. Ash longed for more moments like these.

She must have fallen asleep, because she jerked with a start when Avonlee flopped over on top of her. Blinking her eyes, Ash dragged herself out of the twin bed and into the living room. She checked the doors and turned off the lights, snagging her phone from the kitchen table where she'd left it. She didn't even bother getting into pajamas. She stripped down naked and climbed into her cold bed.

Her phone lit up with a text. She almost put it down without reading it, but the name caught her attention. Ash slid her thumb along the screen, opening her phone. Her heart couldn't take much more of a beating that day. She was so weary. Reading the text, she dropped the phone onto her chest. Sliding it onto the charger, she turned onto her side and stared at the wall until she fell asleep.

Chris 8:40 pm - Just let me know when you want to talk.

CHAPTER
Twenty-One

CHRIS PRESSED her phone to her ear, the incessant ringing she knew wouldn't end until Ash's sweet voice came over the line with an, "Hi, you've reached Ashton Taylor. Please leave a message."

Day one she had expected it.

Day two she had still hoped Ash might pick up.

But now it was day nine, and she wasn't even sure why she was still calling. She sighed heavily as it went to voicemail and put her phone down. Ash hadn't answered any texts either. Not since that night. What happened that night between the two of them was a travesty. But Ash not talking to her at all was worse. Chris couldn't stand it. The silence was louder than anything, and she wasn't quite sure what to do with it.

Because she missed Ash.

She missed Ash's presence, her smile, the warmth that she brought into every room with it. But it really only proved just how much what she'd thought in the beginning was true. She was too fucked up for love. And the hope of that happening had been dashed the moment she had walked into that room in the basement of the church.

"What was I even thinking?" Chris put her phone into her

pocket and woke up her computer from its sleep. She had work to do.

She was just about to dive head first into a report when Ms. Linda shouted through the main office into hers. "Ms. Dunja needs you now. There's a fight."

"You're kidding me. Where?"

"In the hall."

"Shit," Chris mumbled under her breath as she booked it out of her office. With her radio clipped to her hip, she practically ran through the halls as fast as she could.

Esther stood in the hallway, Avonlee facing her on one side and another girl on the other. Chris couldn't make out who it was. But they weren't fighting currently. She had hope of resolving this without a suspension. Esther locked her eyes on Chris. She looked harried and panicked.

Chris could understand why, based on her past.

Straightening her shoulders, Chris moved to stand in between the girls and stared Avonlee down. "My office. Now."

"She started it!" Avonlee yelled.

Chris flipped her hand up in a stop motion. She didn't want to hear any more of this, not while they were standing in the middle of the hallway with classroom doors open. A fight wasn't something that the entire school needed to know about.

"Enough, Avonlee." Chris put more force into her tone than usual. "We'll discuss this in my office."

Avonlee pouted, but she spun on her toes and started walking down toward the office.

Chris sent a look over her shoulder at Esther, pointed at the other girl, and then followed Avonlee to make sure she arrived in her office. She sat her down in Chris' personal office and told Linda to watch her before she stalked back down to Esther. What was going on in her school?

It was like everything was falling apart around her and within her. She didn't have a moment to catch up. Chris steadied herself as she went. When she arrived, she found that the other girl was

Kelli. She'd suspected it, but had hoped it was someone else. Rubbing her temple, Chris glanced over her, finding her nose bleeding and her lip split. It seemed Avonlee had a decent right hook at least.

Chris beckoned Kelli toward her with the crook of her finger. Esther ran her hands through her hair, stress evident in the lines of her face. Chris would talk with her when she had a chance, after dealing with the girls. She took Kelli straight to the nurse before calling to talk to Esther.

"What happened?"

"I'm not sure. Avonlee was in the bathroom. Kelli insisted on going. The next thing I knew I heard them screaming and fighting in the hall. I haven't managed to get anything out of either of them." Esther sounded frantic.

Chris would give Mel a heads up so she could provide some extra support for Esther later that day. Chris sighed heavily, pressing the phone at her desk to her ear. She looked over Avonlee who had her head resting on her arms at the small desk in the corner of her office. It was rare for full on fights to break out in an elementary school, but it wasn't unheard of. But between girls?

"Had the issues between them calmed down before this?"

"Unfortunately, no."

"Esther, you should have told me sooner."

"I thought I had it handled."

Chris grimaced. That was a conversation for another day. Esther was slow to trust, and even though Chris had thought they'd made some strides in that direction, old habits were hard to break. She of all people knew that well. And the reminder from Ash and Katie was just as stark now as it was before. "You need to call me in sooner next time."

"I will." Devastation rang through Esther's voice.

"Good. I'm going to get their versions."

"Let me know what you find out."

"Always." Chris hung up and stared Avonlee down.

Anxiety swam in her own stomach because this would definitely involve a phone call to Ash, and she could only hope that Ash would actually answer this time. Because Avonlee was going to receive a suspension most likely. Kelli too, but at the moment, her focus was on the hurting young girl in front of her.

Chris sat down heavily next to Avonlee and crossed her ankle over her knee. "Want to tell me what happened?"

"No."

"Well, I need to know before I call your mom to come get you."

Avonlee snorted. "She's going to be pissed."

"Probably." Chris rubbed her palm over her knee. "So what happened?"

"Kelli is a bitch."

"Well, that's a pretty strong accusation. Care to share why?" Chris had to use every ounce of patience she had because from the way it looked right now, Avonlee was completely at fault. But then again, Chris had insider knowledge of the fact that Kelli was a bully and that she was the leader in a crew of bullies. They'd tried to separate them over the years, but with only two classes in each grade it was impossible. Junior high should help solve some of those problems.

"She won't leave me alone," Avonlee mumbled the words into her arm.

Frowning, Chris tried to ease into this vein of truth. "How is she not leaving you alone?"

"She followed me to the bathroom."

Chris pursed her lips, watching Avonlee closely. She glanced out the door to find Linda eyeing her and pointing toward the phone. Chris shook her head. She needed no interruptions for this.

"She hit me first."

"Did she?" That was new information that Chris was very interested in. It wasn't the first time Kelli had done that either. "Where did she hit you?"

"In my stomach." Avonlee flinched as if she was remembering the moment of the hit. "Because I wouldn't move out of her way."

"That's the only reason?"

Avonlee nodded. She slid her gaze upward slowly, eyeing Chris with a serious look. "I hit her back when she called my mom disgusting."

Chris cringed. She had wondered if that was where she was going. Kelli was known for making her viewpoints on things obvious, and one of those was that she was staunchly homophobic. Chris had dealt with it and her parents for years, and she wasn't looking forward to another conversation like this.

"I won't stand for that. She deserves so much better."

"I agree with you there." Chris trailed off, not quite sure what to say in response, but she understood Avonlee's outrage.

"My mom's been through enough, you know? She doesn't need people to throw it in her face."

"Losing your mom is hard on her. I know that. But it's also hard on you, and you don't need it thrown in your face, either."

Avonlee harrumphed. Crossing her arms, she eyed Chris seriously. "I'm glad Kelli doesn't know what really happened."

"What do you mean?" Chris listened carefully, wondering if she meant the real reason for the fight.

"Mom killed herself."

"What?" The hair on Chris' arms raised. "Your mom told me she died in a car accident."

Avonlee nodded. "She did. But she caused the accident. She and Mommy were out on a date, and Mom had been drinking. Mommy didn't know, and she crashed the car. Pops and Gram came out to stay with Rhubie and me because no one was home."

"What do you mean no one was home?" Chris tried to keep the panic out of her voice, but this was all new information. It was all something so very relevant to another part of her life. She flicked her gaze over at Linda, who kept giving her nervous glances.

"Mom and Mommy were in the hospital. Mommy came home after a week, but she couldn't drive for a long time. I don't remember how long because her leg was broken and her arm. But Mom never came home."

Chris remembered this from the story that Ash had shared with her. More pieces to the puzzle that was Ashton Taylor fell into place. "How did your mom cause the accident again?"

"She was drinking."

Cold washed through Chris. Ash was at the Al-Anon meeting because Mari was a drunk, and because Avonlee was struggling and she needed to know how to tell Avonlee the whole story. Chris was an idiot. She should have figured it out before now. She should have put two and two together.

"Avonlee, I'm so sorry." Chris reached out and touched Avonlee's hand lightly. "Alcoholism is something that affects so many people. I can only begin to imagine how you were affected by it."

Immediately thoughts of Katie, being that young—younger even—of the times Chris had driven drunk with her in the car, the times she'd shown up drunk at Katie's band concerts and debates, her eighth grade promotion dance that Chris had stupidly volunteered to chaperone. Katie had known every time that Chris had been drunk. She must have been afraid for her life.

"I'm so sorry," Chris repeated, but she wasn't only saying it to Avonlee. She was saying it to Katie. And she would say it a million times over.

"It's not okay, you know? She almost killed both my moms."

"She did." Chris wanted to cry. She blew out a breath and squeezed Avonlee's hand before leaning back. "But that doesn't mean you can punch Kelli."

"I know," Avonlee whispered. "But she made me so mad."

"Right." Chris rubbed her lips and flexed her fingers. "But you can't be fighting in this school."

Avonlee closed herself off. Chris watched it happen right in front of her. Avonlee's shoulders tensed, her eyes dropped to the tabletop in front of her, her cheeks reddened with embarrassment.

"Fighting isn't tolerated in the school."

"I know," she whispered again. "But I won't stand for someone bullying my family."

"I'll deal with Kelli. I promise you that she's not going to be without consequences either." Though the bloody nose and busted lip were certainly a pretty good consequence. No one had dared to take Kelli to town before. Chris wondered if it would curb her appetite for bullying or not. "Go sit out by Ms. Linda. I'm going to call your mother."

"No, please don't."

There was the reaction Chris had hoped for earlier. "I don't have a choice, Avonlee."

As soon as she was alone in her office, Chris snagged her office phone and dialed Ash's cell. Ash picked up on the second ring. "Hello?"

Chris shivered at her voice. She had longed to hear that tone. How was she supposed to talk now? Chris bit back the fear as she made her vocal chords work. "Ash, it's Chris, and before you get mad, I'm not calling about..." She paused. How would she even describe that? Gritting her teeth, Chris forced out more words. "...the meeting. It's about Avonlee."

"What happened?" Ash rushed out, but she sounded so weary.

Chris' heart went out to her, but there was nothing she could do from where she stood, and with what had happened at the meeting, and the information Chris now had in pocket, she wasn't sure anything could be done to rectify their budding relationship. It was doomed from the start.

"There was an altercation. Avonlee was involved in a fight."

"You're kidding me." Ash groaned.

"I wish I was." Chris flicked her gaze to the window in her

door, as if she could see Avonlee sitting outside in distress. "Avonlee caused some physical damage to the other student. I don't know yet if they'll file charges."

"Charges?" Ash squeaked.

"Avonlee hit the other student in the face, Ash. It's not looking good. I'll let you know more when you get here."

"I can't come right now. I have a huge meeting."

"Ash..." Chris trailed off, catching herself. "...this can't wait."

"It'll have to. I'll be there as soon as I'm done." Ash hung up.

Chris sighed heavily, pinching the bridge of her nose. She had another student to deal with, and her parents. She could try Ash again later if she didn't show up in the next hour. Chris had more than enough work on her hands for the day, and she wasn't looking forward to what was to come. She couldn't do anything right, no matter how hard she tried, except this. Her job was the one place she always excelled.

CHAPTER
Twenty~Two

ASH PUSHED her thumb hard into the doorbell at the school. She vibrated from nerves and frustration. She hadn't been able to focus during her meeting. She'd left as soon as she could and come right down here, more pissed than anything. She didn't have a full understanding of what had happened with Avonlee. But heads were going to roll as soon as she stepped inside Chris' office.

She stalked through the halls with fire on her heels. Chris was going to pay for taking out her own anguish over their breakup on Avonlee. Ash wouldn't stand for it. Marching into the office, she glared at Linda before flashing her gaze to Avonlee, who sat with her head to the ground in the corner of the office.

"Where's Chris?" Ash spat her name out like a curse.

Ms. Linda shot her head right up to Ash, giving her a look of surprise. "Dr. Murphey is in her office."

Chris showed up in a flash, arms crossed over her chest, pushing her breasts up, though Ash was pretty sure that wasn't the purpose of the look. She was coming out to protect those in her care from the rage that Ash brought with her.

"My office," Chris commanded.

Compelled, Ash walked toward Chris' office with a glance at her daughter. Her heart raced with anticipation from the upcoming confrontation. She wasn't sure if she wanted it or not. Ash pursed her lips as Chris shut the door behind them.

"Avonlee punched another student in the face, twice. She caused a bloody nose and a busted lip, though it doesn't seem as though stitches will be necessary." Chris' tone was sharp and curt.

Ash wanted to retch. She held her hand over her stomach tightly, staring wide-eyed at Chris. She hadn't realized it was that bad. She'd thought it was a push or a shove. But this? She plopped heavily into the chair. Chris stayed standing.

"I'm suspending her."

"You're not!" Ash jerked her chin up at Chris. "It was that Kelli girl, wasn't it? She's been bullying Avonlee since she started school here. She's the one who deserves to be suspended."

"I can't talk about other students, Ash, and you know that." Chris crossed her arms again, spreading her stance, ready for whatever shake down was coming her way. And she must have known it was coming. "I'm suspending her. She escalated quickly, and I'm worried about her."

"You're worried?" Ash's eyes went wide as her tone filled with disbelief. She straightened her shoulders, trying to find the energy to stand up and rage, but she couldn't. All she saw was the broken woman in front of her, the one who had sat next to her daughter in that meeting, riveted to Katie's story. "She's not your daughter, Chris."

"No, but she's my student." Chris' fists were clenched tight. Her jaw was set.

What was she thinking? Why couldn't Ash stop throwing these outrageous accusations at her?

"I know how you deal with students."

"That's a low blow, Ash, even for you." Chris put her hand up, stopping Ash from responding again. "We're here to talk about Avonlee. She can ask for a suspension hearing if she wants to argue for a lesser sentence, but I don't think she will. She was very clear about why she did it."

"And why is that?" Ash kept the anger right in front of her.

"There were disingenuous remarks made about your family."

Ash tightened instantly. She understood what that meant, even if Chris hadn't said the words. But she wanted to hear it. She knew Chris was walking a damn thin line in what she could share. But Ash wanted to push that. Didn't she deserve more than that? "Is she a homophobe?"

Chris' eyes watered when they locked on Ash's. She said nothing, which was as much as she could offer in that moment. Ash knew it was true. She collapsed into the chair. She never wanted her own sexuality to be a curse for her child, but she should have known better. She should have predicted this.

"What do we do?" Ash softened.

"Avonlee is going to be suspended for three days. She can come back on Monday, and we'll set up a behavioral plan for her in the meantime." Chris sounded confident, strong.

Ash wished she had some of that within herself, but she'd lost that when Mari had died. She'd never found it again, and she wasn't sure it existed for her either. She covered her face with her hands and dragged in a deep breath. "What am I going to do with her?"

"She's struggling, and in big ways." Chris finally sat down next to Ash, but she maintained a healthy distance between them.

She understood why Chris was being so distant. She had to be. Ash had ignored calls and texts since that fateful night. She'd done the very thing she hadn't wanted to do, and she'd ghosted Chris. But this was something they couldn't avoid, and she was stuck in Chris' office talking about her malcontent of a daughter.

"What do I do?"

"You need to focus on her." Chris looked at Ash directly. "Do what I wasn't ever able to do."

"What does that mean?" Ash's heart was in her throat, a pit

of guilt already eating away at her.

Chris sighed heavily, her lips pushed together. Ash wanted to reach out and touch her, soothe the discomfort she was obviously feeling, but she hesitated. They weren't really together anymore, but they also hadn't talked. Their focus was on Avonlee, but they still had so much more going on between them under the surface, things they couldn't resolve that day.

"It means be the parent to her that I couldn't be to Katie." Chris flicked her gaze up to Ash. "And I know that's personal and unprofessional, but I hope you understand. Avonlee is struggling right now, and what she needs is her mother's undivided attention."

Was this the breakup speech? Ash's stomach plummeted. She'd wanted to talk things out, not break up, right? "So you're suspending her to give me that time to focus on her?"

"No, I'm suspending her because she punched another student in the face twice."

"Because she was being bullied!" Ash's voice rose. She had to defend Avonlee. "It's not her fault."

"She punched another student," Chris repeated, calmly.

"I get that. But it was in self-defense." Every muscle in Ash was tight and ready to spring into action. Yet she couldn't get over the damn lump in her throat. "This is ridiculous, you know. You've always had it out for me."

"What?" The question rang through the air.

"Ever since I was a kid. You hated me." Why was she going this direction? Ash shook her head wildly as she was fraught with emotion. She had to pull herself back together. "So now you're taking it out on my kids? I expected more from you, Chris."

"If you're going to accuse me of that, you can call me Dr. Murphey." Chris stood up sharply and walked toward her desk. She rummaged around in some folders off to the side before pulling something out and slapping it onto the table. "And if you're going to accuse me of that, write up a formal complaint and send it to the district. I'm not going to take this bullshit from you."

Chris walked back to her desk, leaning against the edge of it with her arms crossed. Underneath the anger, Ash swore she saw the hurt behind the mask. She just couldn't focus on it. If she did, she knew she'd let her guard down too much and then she'd be putty in Chris' hands again. And she couldn't allow herself to trust a drunk—not again.

"And while you're at it," Chris added, "Why don't you throw in that I'm a drunk principal. That should really add to the ruin of my career, which I assume is your hope in this entire conversation."

Shock hit Ash full force. She should never have allowed herself to even think that this was a possibility. She'd been so stupid lately, blinded by the fact that she had hope. Well hope was a fickle thing, and she didn't want it anymore.

"When can Avonlee come back?"

"Monday. We'll have a meeting Monday to discuss her behavior plan we'll be creating while she's on suspension."

"And the other girl, Kelli?" Ash tightened again. She could keep this professional now. They'd lobbed accusations at each other multiple times already, and Ash would do the right thing now. She'd keep this about her kid.

"The other student is also going to be suspended, other than that I can't get into the details of the consequences for them."

Ash glared. "Why not?"

"Confidentiality. If there continues to be issues between Avonlee and this student, then I'll suggest a meeting with parents together, but it will be a last resort." Chris stood still by her desk, the distance between them widening like a chasm.

Ash could feel it, and she knew whatever had been between them was likely gone. She'd ensured that. "Why a last resort?"

"Because I don't think it's going to be productive, honestly. I know this family well, and I don't think their views and beliefs are going to change." Chris looked drained.

Ash could only imagine what a tough day it had been for her.

"I'll let you know if I find out if they'll be pressing charges or not. If they are, Avonlee might be facing more serious consequences than suspension because I won't be able to have them in the same school."

"Are you threatening expulsion?"

"I'm not threatening anything, Ash." Chris held her ground. "I'm telling you a possible outcome from this. They stopped before we needed to call the police, but if they were adults, Avonlee could be arrested for a felony. Any hit to the face is a felony."

Ash groused. Her jaw was tight. She could barely stand to sit there any longer. "Is that everything?"

"Yes. I'll have Ms. Dunja set up some assignments for Avonlee to do on her iPad so she can keep up from home."

Snorting, Ash stood sharply. "I can't believe you're doing this."

"Ash, what don't you believe? She physically attacked another student."

"She didn't instigate the fight!"

"How do you even know that? You didn't even stop to talk to her or start with the whole story when you walked in here."

Ash glared because she'd been caught in being angry for anger's sake. She was acting like the teenager she had been when they'd met, and she hated herself all the more for it. "Fine. What happened?"

Chris blew out a breath. "Avonlee is being bullied for a number of things by one student in particular. But that doesn't excuse what she did either. She can't be punching people in the face."

Ash knew that. She agreed with it. But that didn't mean she wanted to say that out loud to Chris. "So she defended herself."

"And you," Chris added. "But she should have reported the bullying, which she hasn't done."

"Avonlee doesn't exactly trust people."

"I thought we had worked on that some." Chris squared her shoulders, a point of pride coursing through her.

They had. Avonlee hadn't had a bad word to say about Chris. In fact, the small moments that Avonlee had actually talked to Ash about school, Chris had been the subject of a lot of those conversations. Not that Ash was going to share that now.

"Can I take her home?"

"Yes. I'll talk to you Monday about the behavior plan." Chris looked Ash directly in the eye. "Please answer the phone when I call for that."

"Of course I will." Ash stood up and shrugged her jacket onto her shoulders. "This is about my daughter."

Walking out of the office, Ash collected Avonlee. She didn't want to look back at Chris, but as soon as she stepped out of the main office, she glanced over her shoulder. Chris stood, devastated, watching as they walked away. That look hurt. Ash wanted to run up to her and beg for forgiveness. She'd let the bitch come out of her in the worst possible way.

If all she'd been doing was protecting her heart and her daughter, then why did she feel like she needed to send Chris apology flowers?

Oh right, she'd been a bitch.

Still, she knew better than to believe in love again because when she let her guard down, Chris was nothing more than a bully. Ash would get the full story out of Avonlee when they got home, but she had no doubts that Chris was overreacting to a simple incident.

Getting into the car, Ash started the engine and blew out a breath. She had to get herself under control. Because she had to figure out just what she was going to be doing with her daughter for the next three days. Holding back her cry, Ash drove toward home. She hated this. She hated feeling vulnerable and split open. She hated that Chris had that power over her, and Ash wasn't going to give it to her again. She should have known better. People don't change.

CHAPTER
Twenty-Three

"YOU READY?" Chris asked Esther as she stepped into the fifth-grade classroom.

She'd been in that classroom far more than she should have that quarter, but if she could support Esther with her difficult class, she would. But today was the end of the day on a Friday, and Chris would rather be anywhere but here. It had been a long week, and all she wanted was to go to a meeting, get her head on straight, and spend some time on the phone with Katie like she'd promised to do.

"Yes," Esther answered.

Chris sat down at one of the classroom tables with her. Esther pulled out a file of paper that she'd printed off and set it between them. Chris skimmed over it to see how the behavior plan was done up for Avonlee. They'd already had the meeting for Kelli, and it had gone about as well as Chris expected it to—which was not.

"I like this." Chris pointed to a portion of the paper. "I meant to tell you that when you emailed it to me."

"It was a last minute add, but I've noticed Avonlee really responds to firmer structure and rules, so I was hoping this would help."

"If only Kelli was the same." Chris stretched back in the chair as they waited. The bell had rung ten minutes ago, and they were still waiting on Avonlee and Ash to show up for the meeting.

"She's in a tough situation."

Chris agreed, but she also thought it was mostly because she put herself there. "I think we need to give you the easy class next year."

Esther chuckled. "A class where I didn't have to break up fights would be appreciated."

"I'll get right to work on that. How is everything else going?" Chris had meant to check in with Esther over the last few weeks about the custody hearing that was fast coming up, but she hadn't found time yet. She hated that she'd avoided it too because she was usually the first person to offer support.

"My lawyer says it's open and shut."

"But it's Skip."

"Yeah, it's Skip." They shared a knowing look. "I can't help but wonder what bomb he's going to throw next."

"Hopefully none." Chris heard Ash's voice down the hall. She glanced at the door, waiting for them to come in, her heart in her throat. Why was she so keen on seeing Ash? Especially with the way they had left everything earlier that week.

Esther must have heard them too, because she faced the door as well. All personal conversation ceased. Avonlee stepped into the room first, and she didn't look happy, but neither did her mother. Ash was still gorgeous, just as the day Chris had met her again, but she looked harried. Her hair didn't look like it had been washed in days, and the dark rings under her eyes were deep and purple. Concern flashed through Chris, but she couldn't comment on it. She knew where they stood, and the fact that she wanted it verbally said didn't mean anything.

"Come in, sit down," Esther said. Chris was thankful Esther spoke because her voice had lodged in her throat and refused to work.

Ash sat across from Chris and Avonlee across from Esther. Chris would let Esther do most of the talking since this was her show. Chris was there as an administrative presence and to guarantee that the behavior plan was going to be enforced.

The meeting went well, and quickly. Ash and Avonlee agreed to everything, and Ash kept sending her daughter furtive glances like she was going to blow up again. Chris could only hope that this was the wake up call Avonlee needed to start controlling herself a bit better. She was lucky Kelli's family decided not to file charges, though that was probably because of the history of bullying she had at the school.

Throughout the entire meeting, all Chris wanted was to snag five minutes alone with Ash and talk to her. Just talk like they used to, get some things out in the open and on the floor so they could maybe find some peace with this. Especially since they'd be seeing a lot of each other for the next five years until Rhubie went to junior high.

"Ms. Dunja, can I ask you about the science homework?" Avonlee sounded so small. "I've tried a couple times to do it, but I just don't understand it."

"Sure."

Chris nodded toward Ash. "Want to talk in my office for a minute?"

"Not really, no." Even though she'd answered in the negative, Ash stood up and started toward the door.

Chris took that as her sign and stood to follow. They walked side by side down the hall in complete silence, the tension in her chest rising, and she realized belatedly that Ash might think this was related to Avonlee. She stopped sharply and touched Ash's arm lightly to get her attention. "I'm sorry, I didn't make it clear that this wasn't about school stuff."

Ash's lips parted in surprise, and Chris knew she'd been right to realize Ash's assumption. Ash glanced back toward the classroom, her shoulders stiff. "I guess now is as good a time as any."

Chris disagreed with that. A week and a half ago would have

been preferable, but since that hadn't happened, this was better than nothing. They continued to walk, the silence strained between them. When they reached Chris' office, she shut the door and closed her eyes briefly to center herself. She could do this. She'd thought about exactly what she would say for days now, and it needed to be said.

"I'm so sorry that I didn't tell you before the meeting." Chris couldn't look at Ash. She was slowly being eaten by embarrassment and shame, and while she knew she shouldn't be ashamed of her drinking problem, she was. Especially after learning about Mari. "I should have told you much sooner."

"You should have." Ash's tone was terse.

Finally, Chris turned around. She looked directly into Ash's eyes and the hurt she had stored in them. Chris felt that hurt viscerally in her own body. She wanted to make it vanish, disappear. But that was the problem with being a drunk—that pain never went away. She should have known better.

"I didn't know how to tell you," Chris murmured. "And quite honestly, I didn't think one night was going to become anything else."

"No, I understand that night. But after that?"

"After that I was a principal and you were a parent." Chris crossed her arms, so uncomfortable with the conversation and knowing that it was one they needed to have. "To tell you then would be to jeopardize my career."

"But after that," Ash pushed. She stepped in closer to Chris, close enough that they could reach out and touch each other.

Oh, how Chris longed for that. She missed Ash's arms wrapped around her, she missed the tender touches and soft kisses. But she held her ground. They weren't there to touch or reconcile. They were there to hash this out, get the hurt feelings off their chests, and move forward in their separate directions.

"After that, yes, we should have talked. It's my fault for not doing that." Chris also wanted to add in that Ash had withheld as well, but she didn't. That wouldn't help the situation any. "I should have told you. But Ash, I was so scared."

"Scared of what?"

"Because I know what you think of me." Chris did. That had been why Ash ran out of that meeting, why she'd refused to have this conversation. Ash understood deeply just how fucked up Chris was and exactly what her addiction would do to someone and the people surrounding them. She was well within her right to protect herself. "I was scared because I knew what would happen as soon as you found out."

There. She'd said it. That took more courage than anything Chris had done other than getting sober and talking to Katie. She put her hands out to her sides and looked Ash directly in the eye.

"I'm a drunk, Ash. I've been an alcoholic for about half my life, and I finally got sober almost two years ago. Two years next month. But that's not a long time in the scheme of things." Chris twisted her hands together. "I should have known better than to think something could work between us, and for that I truly apologize."

Ash stilled. Chris wasn't sure what was going through her mind. She wished she did, but it was hard enough to know what the tension was in the room. It was there, but she couldn't name it.

"That's all I wanted to say."

"Yeah?" Ash said sharply. "Because I haven't talked yet."

"Then the floor is open." Chris waved her hand out in front of her, but she tensed, waiting for the other shoe to drop. She'd known it would. Now was the time for Ash to let loose that anger.

"You're an idiot, you know that?"

"Yup." Chris squared her shoulders. She was so glad she'd shut the door so that no one could just accidentally walk in on them. "I do know that."

Ash shook her head slowly, stepping in closer. Why was she

standing so close? Chris needed her to back up and put some space between them. "You deserve to find happiness, Chris. Andry told you that, right?"

She had. Chris regretted sharing that information with Ash now. She swallowed hard, ready to refute that argument.

"Stop. You do deserve to find happiness, and two years sober is a damn good thing to be proud of. That's not what the issue is."

Chris furrowed her brow, confused now. "If the issue isn't that, then what is it?"

Ash sighed, moving in even closer. They now stood nearly toe to toe. Chris had to tilt her chin up to look into Ash's eyes. It was like Ash was going to lean in and kiss her, but that couldn't be right, could it? They were fighting. They were breaking up. What was going on?

Reaching out, Ash touched the side of Chris' face. She flitted her fingers over her cheek, and then over her lips. "Chris, you deserve the world, but I can't give it to you."

"I don't understand."

"I know." Ash gave a sad smile. "I know you don't, and that's okay. Because you can't possibly understand. You can't possibly know why."

Chris' stomach sank. She did know. Avonlee had told her, and again, it only confirmed what she'd been thinking all along. Ash couldn't be with a drunk, not someone who could have so easily made the same mistakes Mari had. Chris had done that. She'd driven drunk more times than she could count. She'd hidden her drinking for years and no one knew. She was exactly the woman Ash had left behind, and she knew she was the woman Ash would never want in her life again.

"I don't want to hurt you," Ash whispered.

"I don't want to hurt *you*," Chris repeated, hoping that her words would sink in. "I never meant to hurt you."

"I know." Ash's look saddened. "I guess it's just the way it's supposed to be, don't you think?"

"Unfortunately."

Ash leaned in, her head tilting down and her lips parting. Was Ash going to kiss her? Chris' heart caught in her throat. Her brain told her to move back, but her heart told her to lean in. As a result, she was left frozen to the spot, unmoving and waiting to see what Ash was going to do next. Ash looked at her directly in the eye.

"You're so beautiful." Her words were nothing more than a murmur, and if she hadn't been standing so close, Chris was sure that she would have missed them.

But as it was, Ash slid forward. Their lips brushed. Just a tender rub one against the other. Chris sucked in a sharp breath, her eyelids fluttering shut. Was this meant as a goodbye or torture? She wasn't sure which. Reaching out, she grasped Ash's elbows to steady herself and whatever was going to come next.

"Stunning," Ash said as she moved in to press their mouths together again.

Chris barely responded, but as Ash continued to touch her, kiss her, Chris finally relented. This had been what she'd wanted since the moment they'd found each other again, and it wasn't something she wanted to give up. Even if she understood why it had to happen. She hummed as she dashed her tongue out, tracing Ash's lower lip before nipping at it.

Ash's lips curled upward in a smile, the feel of them moving against Chris' mouth was one of the most tantalizing things she had ever felt. Was this true vulnerability? It didn't feel scary. In fact, it was utterly empowering. Surging forward, Chris tangled her fingers into Ash's hair and held on tight, the embrace deepening as she lost herself in this one moment.

There was nothing around her except Ash. Nothing was distracting her at this moment. Whatever this moment was. She didn't care because it felt amazing. Heart, mind, soul, and body were all attuned and open to Ash for the taking. She had nothing to hide anymore. Nothing to fear. Chris groaned and lost herself.

She had no idea how long they stood there, making out like

teenagers before they had to go home. But when Ash pulled away, breaking the kiss, that smile forever on her lips accompanied with the sad look in her eyes, Chris knew.

This was goodbye.

A cold crept over her skin. She shivered. She was in tears when she brought her fist up to her mouth and bit into her finger to center herself. She had known better than to think she deserved love. She really had. Because when she let her guard down, no matter how amazing it felt in the moment, no one wanted to stick around. She was too screwed up, a drunk without recourse. No one would ever love her back.

"Maybe someday you can find that happiness, Chris." Ash cupped her cheeks and pressed a sweet nothing to her lips. "You do deserve it."

CHAPTER
Twenty-Four

THE HALL WASN'T empty today. Not like it had been the last time she'd walked down it. Kids ran in and out from place to place, and Ash had to watch her step for fear of crashing into one of them. But they'd be gone soon, because the bell had just rung to send them on their way home.

Ash was miserable. Her thoughts ricocheted from Mari to Chris to Avonlee and Rhubie and right back to Chris and that damn kiss.

What the hell had that been?

She couldn't even explain it. She couldn't even begin to logic her way through why she'd done that, but she had definitely been the one to instigate. Chris had stood there, defenseless, vulnerable, and Ash had taken advantage of the entire situation. She'd taken advantage of Chris.

Every time she walked down the hall of the school, she was reminded of that long walk they'd taken to Chris' office, and of the incredibly long walk she'd taken back when she'd gone to find Avonlee. In the two weeks since it had happened, she hadn't seen Chris. Avonlee hadn't gotten in trouble. And there hadn't been any late night phone calls or random text messages.

Though Ash had definitely read all the old texts they'd sent to each other.

She'd read them so many times that she nearly had them memorized. But it wasn't just that. Ash had found herself at her computer several times over the last few weeks—typing. Words. To a new story. She almost couldn't believe it. She didn't want to—not yet. And she damn well wasn't telling anyone.

But was this her getting her passion back?

It couldn't be. She loved to explore feelings through the words and characters and that wasn't something that she was ever willing to give up. This book, while fiction, didn't need to be for publication. It just had to be for her, and that thought made it so much better.

Ash walked into Avonlee's classroom first, finding Ms. Dunja sitting at her desk. They'd arranged this meeting to check in on Avonlee's progress. Ms. Dunja smiled at her.

"I'm just going to start with there has been quite the change in Avonlee in the last few weeks."

"That's good to hear." Ash let out a breath, the anxiety in her chest more than she'd expected.

"It really is. It gives me a lot of hope. And the other student has been doing better as well."

"So Avonlee has said." Ash had noticed the same changes, but she was glad that Ms. Dunja was saying them as well. She and Avonlee had found time in the last two weeks just to be together and talk. It was easier with family around because they could give one kid attention while she lavished on the other. She hadn't expected that to be one of the advantages of moving there.

"She's still struggling with reading a bit."

"Still?" Ash blinked. When had Avonlee ever struggled with reading? Science, yes, but reading? Biting the inside of her cheek, Ash looked Ms. Dunja over. "What's she struggling with?"

Was it an insult to injury that Ash was a published author?

Or that writing and reading were her passions? Only if Avonlee was doing this on purpose, which was still in question.

"I think she might be dyslexic."

"You're kidding me." Ash plopped down into a hard plastic chair. "She's never been evaluated for anything before."

"Really?" Ms. Dunja frowned. "I'd like to have her evaluated for it, if you don't mind. There are some things she does when writing that tip me off to it."

"I just...no one's ever said anything about it before." And Ash had completely missed it. Not that she would know what to look for. That wasn't something she struggled with, and she wasn't aware of everything that was involved in a diagnosis. Though she definitely knew that the internet searches were going to be her friend as soon as she got home and had a minute.

"She's very good at hiding it." Ms. Dunja shifted in her seat. "I think she's embarrassed by it."

"Well, I can see why." Ash rubbed her temple. "So what do we do about it?"

"Let's get her evaluated and take it one step at a time. If she's been able to hide it for this long, it might not be that bad, or I could be completely wrong."

Except Ms. Dunja was a teacher, and she understood these things far better than Ash did. She saw them more often and would know what to do. Ash, on the other hand, felt completely in the dark.

"Sounds like a plan," Ash choked out.

"Good. Other than that, Avonlee is doing amazingly well. I'm pleased with her progress on her behavior."

Ash nodded, her heart sinking with the last bit of news. She was going to have to work doubly hard to make sure that Avonlee didn't feel awful about herself if she did have dyslexia. She talked with Ms. Dunja for a couple more minutes before leaving the room. Her girls were outside playing on the equipment like they'd discussed in the morning. She could see them through the window.

She was just about to step outside, when she saw Ms. Walsh walk out of the main office. Ash canted her hand to the side. That was Chris' ex-wife's new fiancée. It was such a small world here, and she was struggling to keep up with all of it.

"Do you have a minute?"

Ms. Walsh stopped. "Yeah, what's up?"

"I just wanted to check in on Rhubie. She's my quiet kid, but while I was here, I figured it couldn't hurt."

Ms. Walsh smiled, softening instantly. "Want to go to the classroom?"

"Sure." Ash followed her back toward the second grade classroom. It was decorated differently than Avonlee's. Less formal and filled with hand drawn pictures all over the walls. "Wow."

"Yeah, I keep it all until the end of the year, then I let the kids pick one piece they want me to keep. The rest go in the trash."

"I don't know how you manage to get it all up there."

Ms. Walsh shrugged. "It takes some special attention to detail sometimes, but that is, fortunately, something I'm really good at."

"So how's Rhubie doing?"

"She's doing great." Ms. Walsh sat down at her desk. "She's such a sweet kid, always willing to help me out."

Ash smiled at that. She found the same at home too. She was the calm one in the eye of the storm. "I'm glad to hear that."

"She's talked a bit about why you moved here."

Sucking in a breath, Ash cringed. She'd expected this. But at the same time, she had hoped to fly under the radar a little bit.

"I think it's helped her to talk about it."

"We've been talking about it a lot at home, mostly Avonlee and me. Rhubie's the stoic silent type."

Ms. Walsh chuckled lightly. "So was I."

Ash raised an eyebrow at that.

"My dad died in a car accident when I was a kid too. Freak sort of thing, really, but I understand what both your girls are going through, and you a bit. My stepmother raised us, and it took a while for me to understand her point of view, but I finally know what she went through."

"A while?" Ash had to hope that it wouldn't take too much longer. The amount of anger that Avonlee tossed her way was starting to consume her and overwhelm her.

"A long time." Ms. Walsh frowned. "Like...decades long."

Ash hissed.

"I don't think it'll take you that long. I had other issues to deal with." Ms. Walsh reached over and covered Ash's hand. "It's hard, I know, to go through something like that. Devastating in ways we never anticipated, and horrific all at the same time. It's natural for the girls to be mad, you too for that matter."

"I know," Ash muttered. She'd heard it all before from the therapists—hers and Avonlee's.

"What I'm saying is that forgiveness is key to moving forward. And sometimes it takes a bit to get there."

Ash jerked her chin up. Why was she thinking about Chris? She wasn't thinking about Mari and forgiving her dead wife. She was thinking about Chris, and the strong way she'd stood in front of Ash and confessed everything—how scared she was, how alone she was, how she felt so screwed up. Ash had taken it in stride, but at the same time, she'd finally seen the true Chris standing in front of her, probably for the first time ever.

"Forgiveness?" Ash repeated, not quite sure what else to say.

"Yeah. Everyone needs to forgive everyone. It takes time, believe me I know it, but it's worth it in the end."

Ash pursed her lips, looking Ms. Walsh over. "Can I ask a frank question?"

"Sure, go ahead."

"About Chris."

Ms. Walsh stilled, her eyes widening. "Is this a personal question?"

Nodding, Ash folded her hands together, trying to figure out how to word everything that was rocking around in her brain.

She didn't want to come off as insensitive, but this woman—someone who was so interconnected and disconnected—might just be exactly who Ash needed to talk to.

"I'm going to reserve the right not to answer depending on the question."

"That's fair," Ash murmured. She took another second before gathering her courage to ask, "Is Chris a good person?"

"One of the best," Isla answered honestly.

Ash could see it in her gaze.

"I wouldn't be working here without her. Andry was my principal, and Chris took a risk and hired me mid-year, which if you don't know anything about teaching, that's unheard of. She did it for Andry, so we could be together without the complication of Andry being my boss."

Ash's eyes widened. "I didn't know that."

"I don't think she talks about Andry much."

"Not in that way," Ash answered. "Usually just in how much she screwed everything up."

Isla blew out a breath. She glanced toward the door. "I'm going to shut that."

When she returned to her seat, Ash was waiting for the rest of the story, and she wanted to ask questions, but she wasn't sure what to ask.

"Chris protects everyone, you have to understand that, and what she protects them from the most is her."

Ash furrowed her brow. "What do you mean?"

"Her goal is to protect people from herself because she sees herself as always doing more harm than good. I've seen her do it with other teachers and students, with Andry, and with Katie. She'll sacrifice herself if she thinks there will ever be any harm from her. That's the real reason I ended up with this job. I took it, selfishly, but she didn't offer it selflessly. She was trying to make up for the damage she'd already done."

That made absolute sense. Everything that Ash had seen over the last few months pointed straight to that. It was probably so much of an ingrained habit that Chris didn't even know she was doing it.

"For the record, she's miserable right now."

Ash had also figured that was true. She didn't even need to see Chris in person to know that was true. She'd guessed that would happen as soon as she'd left her office the last time, the bittersweet nature of that kiss, so passionate, but with an end in mind for both of them.

"I've never seen her like this before," Isla continued.

"What do you mean?" Ash asked.

"Chris is one of the strongest people I know, and her feet have been dragging these last few weeks. I'm not entirely sure what's happened, just hearsay with what she's shared with Andry and me, but Ash..." Isla trailed off, looking Ash directly in the eye. "She's hurting."

"I am too."

Isla squeezed her hand tightly, the compassion in her gaze absolute. "I know I have a bit of an odd relationship with Chris because of the circumstances, but she is one of the strongest women I know. She truly has an amazing heart."

Ash loved hearing about this side of Chris. It gave her so much more to think about, but she still wasn't sure it would change anything. Ash settled into the quiet between them, the last question mulling through her mind. She hadn't come in here to ask these things or to put her heart and mind at ease.

"I feel like you want to ask something else." Isla's smile was so kind and gentle.

Ash's eyes watered, and she wasn't sure why. She wanted to be stronger than this, stoic. But she couldn't be. "Can I trust her?"

"I trust Chris with anything I need. She is one of the most trustworthy people I know, despite what she's been through and what she's done in the past. She's always looking out for everyone else." Isla paused for a strong effect, her gaze hitting Ash's with a full force of honesty. "What she really needs is someone to take care of her."

That hit different than Ash expected. Her heart thudded wildly. "Thank you."

"Anytime." Isla squeezed Ash's hand again. "But Rhubie is doing amazing. I love having her in my classroom."

"Thanks." Ash smiled again, her mind pulled back toward her kids. "I appreciate it."

As she walked out into the hallway again, Ash almost went to the office. Her feet almost took her directly to Chris, and she had to force herself to turn toward the playground. Ms. Walsh's words rang through her head, not words said as a teacher but as a person who had experienced so much. Forgiveness. But who exactly did Ash need to forgive?

CHAPTER
Twenty-Five

"STOP TALKING SHIT ABOUT YOURSELF."

This wasn't what Chris expected. She was sitting with her ex-wife directly across from her and her best friend next to her at her favorite restaurant. It wasn't something she'd ever thought would happen again, but here she was. The nickel-brushed high top chair was hard under her ass as she sipped the sweet tea she'd ordered.

Mel stared at her hard, like the words she was saying would seep into Chris' very soul. "You think I don't know what you're telling yourself after all this drama."

"I'm telling myself a lot of things," Chris muttered into her poutine. It was her favorite thing to order here, and she wasn't going to let it go to waste despite what they were here to talk about. She needed to suck down the food before she lost her appetite.

Mel sighed heavily, and Chris caught the look that she shared with Andry. Since when had the two of them started talking again? Chris understood they lived in a medium sized town and queer-folk were hard to come by, but Mel hadn't even realized she liked women until last year.

"Whose idea was this?" Chris pointed her fork first at Andry and then at Mel. "Because I'm not sure I'm liking this idea anymore."

Andry gave her a small but pleading smile. "It's taken us years to be able to have civil conversation, don't you want to continue in that direction?"

Chris narrowed her gaze. "I'm not sure yet."

Andry laughed lightly as she grabbed her soda. "I think you secretly do."

"Why would you say that?"

"Because outside of Mel, I'm your only friend."

"How sad is it that my ex-wife is my second best friend?" Chris pouted and shoved another bite of fries and gravy into her mouth.

"At least I'm second. I'm not sure anyone could replace Mel." Andry winked at the woman in question before diving into the plate in front of her.

Chris rolled her shoulders and tried to brush off the awkward tension that settled into her chest. There was a purpose to this so-called meeting between the three of them, leaving Esther and Isla behind, and Chris wanted to know what that purpose was. She'd just been told when and where to show up, and that her food would be paid for.

Mel jumped in with a huge wink. "I'm just glad I'm number one."

"What are you two going on about? Seriously." Chris straightened her shoulders and pinned each of them with a serious look. "I'm not dying or something, am I?"

"No." Andry softened her gaze. "But we are concerned about you."

"Oh, fuck this." Chris groaned and shoved another forkful of food into her mouth. This was definitely not a conversation she wanted to be in the center of. "I'm fine."

"Are you, really?" Mel pushed.

"Don't you two have other people to bug now?"

Mel chuckled and shook her head. "They both told us to deal with you, actually."

"Are you serious?" Chris' mood hadn't been that bad, had it? She'd tried her best to hold her own and keep her crap mood out of the school, but if everyone around her knew it, then she wasn't as good at hiding it as she thought she was.

"Yeah, I am." Mel took a slow sip of her drink, eyeing Chris over the rim. "I don't think anyone but those closest to you have noticed. We have special insider knowledge to who you are."

"Perfect," Chris muttered. "So is this an intervention?"

"Of sorts," Andry jumped in. She brushed her long brown hair over her shoulder as she watched Chris carefully.

Chris knew she was being observed and judged. And she appreciated that they were paying attention—she was glad they were. It warmed her to think that someone cared, that someone she had hurt so much could possibly care about her still. It was probably because of Katie, but if that was the only reason Andry still talked to her, then she would take it.

How pathetic was that?

Chris cringed at the trail of her own thoughts. She should be better than this by now, shouldn't she? Her therapist had told her that it took time, but she still wanted it to happen instantly.

"So, are you going to tell me about her? You gave me a brief summary, but from what Mel filled me in on, I don't have the whole story." Andry set her drink down, her pointed look serious.

"I don't know why you care. And I don't mean that in a mean way. I meant that honestly. I don't understand why you care."

Andry's face softened, the lines around her eyes and her lips smoothing out. "Because I love you, Chris, despite your best efforts to make me not love you."

Chris pouted.

Andry shook her head. "You can't deny that you tried."

"I did, on occasion," Chris muttered, her chest heaving from being called out. She hated this feeling. It was like someone had shone a light on her and all of the dirt under her rug.

"Now that we've settled that," Andry said with a smile. "We're concerned about you."

"Concerned about what?"

"Ash," Mel said. "You haven't really told me what happened."

"It's nothing. It's going to be nothing. That's all that happened." Chris' cheeks burned. She didn't want to go through this conversation again. She'd had it in her head with herself so many times over that she couldn't stand to do it in front of them. Not the two people she trusted most in this world. The two people who had consistently stood by her through all her drunk shenanigans.

"Chris," Andry's smooth voice reached her ears. "Talk about it."

"There's nothing to talk about, that's what I'm saying. It was really nice while it lasted, which wasn't long, and that's that. Nothing more."

Andry reached over and touched Chris' hand. When had she started trembling?

"Look, I'm fucked up, okay?" Chris dropped her fork, and pointed at Andry. "Do you know how stupid I was with you? Not just my life, but I really screwed up yours. And Katie?" Blowing out a breath, Chris shook her head. "I know I've only just started to figure out how fucked up Katie is because of me. I can't even imagine what else she hasn't shared."

"Are you done yet?" Andry broke in, her tone sharp.

Chris couldn't fathom why she was angry. She should be happy that Chris was finally willing to admit all the wrongs she'd done over the last twenty plus years of knowing each other.

"No, I'm not," Chris started in again. "It's a good thing Ash figured it out before it was too late. She was smart to leave when she did."

"Did she leave? Or did you just assume she would?" Mel's questions rang through the air, sending a chill down Chris' spine.

"She left. She gave me the kiss of a lifetime and then walked out after saying goodbye and that she hoped I'd find happiness some day. But you know what? I found it. All right? I found it with her, and I don't really want to go looking for it again."

"Oh Chris." Andry touched Chris' arm again, curling her fingers around Chris' wrist in a tight grasp. "I don't think you should give up just because one person wasn't willing to accept you."

"It's not just one person." Chris slid Andry a look of *you've got to be kidding me* and held it. She of all people should understand what Chris had gone through.

"Chris, you can't compare what happened with us to what happened between you and Ash." Andry's eyes widened.

"Why the hell not?"

"Because you're sober now," Mel jumped in, causing Chris to look at her with wide eyes. "You've been sober for two years, and you've never managed that long before."

"It's not *that* long," Chris refuted.

"Quit being so damn hard on yourself," Mel scolded. "I'm tired of this pity party."

"She's right," Andry added. "You've worked so hard on changing those bad things about yourself. Stop selling yourself so short. I'm tired of it."

Chris wanted to throw her little pity party. It wasn't like she had invited Mel or Andry to it. They'd crashed it. And all for what? To try and drag her away from her own party? No. This was her time, and she wanted to sit in the shit feeling she'd found.

"And the Katie thing, I can understand. But she has a lot of her own stuff that she needs to work through too as she gets older, and that's what she's doing. You should be glad that she's trying to work on that with you instead of pushing you away. I honestly feared that she would take you out of her life for a while. I'm so happy that she's not."

"Me too." The weight of what Andry shared sat squarely on

Chris' shoulders. She didn't want to give that up, the connection to her only daughter. "And I'm going to work with her on it as long as she'll let me."

"Good. And what about Ash?"

Chris groaned. "Just drop it already."

"Here's the thing, Chris, and I think Mel can attest to this. You are an amazing person. That's why I still love you. I'm not in love with you. I think we might have always been better off as friends, but we jumped head first into a relationship and creating a family, and I love you all the more for it. You're stubborn, you're amazingly strong, and you fight for those you love no matter what they've done to you."

Chris opened her mouth to protest, but Andry put her hand up.

"You hired Isla so that I could be happy." Andry's eyes watered. "I'm not sure you could have done anything else to tell me that you loved me still."

"Andry," Chris whispered. "I don't know what to say to that."

"Because it's true. You have a heart of gold, Chris. It just got buried there for a bit and only in some ways."

That didn't quite help Chris feel any better about herself, except that she knew without a doubt that Andry was telling her the truth.

"We came out tonight to tell you to stop being so hard on yourself. You've been going through a lot of changes in the last few years. Enjoy the benefits of those changes, please. You deserve to."

"I don't." Chris couldn't allow herself to believe what they were saying. It had been too damn long and she'd made too many damn mistakes.

"You can't keep punishing yourself for what you've done in the past." Mel snagged one of Chris' gravy covered cheese curds. "Because that's when you start to really annoy me."

"Perfect." Chris started eating again, her appetite coming back slowly. "Ash broke up with me—if we can even call it that because it wasn't like we were actually dating—as soon as she found out I was a drunk. I get it. Her wife died because she was a drunk. Why would she want to be with someone so similar to her wife?"

Mel's jaw dropped. Andry stared at Chris wide-eyed, her lower lip quivering. Chris cringed. She shouldn't have said that. She should have kept her mouth shut on that front.

"Her late wife was an alcoholic?"

Nodding, Chris shared what she knew of the story, skimming some of the details because it really wasn't her story to tell. "So I can fully understand why I'm too screwed up for her to want to be with me. It's fine. I accept that."

"Don't give up, Chris." Andry was back with that smooth tone. The one that she used when she was trying to convince Chris of something she didn't want to do—like go to the doctor for a routine check up. "You've worked so hard on yourself in these past few years. I've seen it. Don't give up just because your first time out in the dating world in years didn't work out. Have some hope. And have some belief in who you've become."

Chris wanted so desperately to believe Andry. She always had a way with words like that, and Chris longed to hear it on a regular basis, but that wasn't her role anymore.

"I agree." Mel shared that same quality of tone. "Give yourself a break, Chris. I'm tired of seeing you drag yourself down."

"I'll try." Was she only agreeing just to get them to stop talking about this? She wasn't sure, but if it worked, she'd take it.

"I know you'll find happiness someday."

"Yeah," Chris muttered. Andry was forgetting what she'd said. Chris had found that happiness with Ash, someone she had been truly herself with, vulnerable with, for the first time in years. And that was gone in a flash. "Maybe."

CHAPTER
Twenty-Six

"THERE'S no one to stay the night again." Jack stepped into her office doorway and cringed.

Ash was tired of their staff calling out. It hadn't just been because of illness, she was sure some of it was the transition and them not liking her style of leadership, but she was getting really tired of it.

"Who is it this time?" She almost hated asking, because if it was Steven, then she'd have to fire him. He'd called out so many times in the last few months, and she couldn't keep finding backup.

"Steven," Jack muttered. "I know this isn't his passion to work here as a house parent, but he's barely showing up for the shifts he should be."

"I'll talk to him. Can anyone else cover?"

Jack shook his head. "I would, but Amy has an early morning appointment for the twins in Denver. I need to be there for it."

"I understand." Ash rubbed the tension in the back of her neck. She would love for that tension to ease, but it hadn't in days. Well, really weeks, if she were honest. It hadn't gotten better since she and Chris had last talked, since they'd kissed, and ultimately, this could be the perfect opportunity to see Chris again.

All she had to do was get on that phone and call Chris.

"Thanks, Jack," Ash mumbled and stared at the black desk phone in front of her.

"Do you want me to try some of our backups?"

Ash shook her head. It took her a minute to look up at him, making eye contact. "I'll make the calls."

Jack left, but Ash was left still staring at the phone. Could she do this? Could she do it and not long to see Chris more than what she was there for? There were other backups she could call, but she knew Chris would come. Without a doubt, Ash knew that Chris would drop everything to come to the house and stay the night.

Reaching forward, Ash snagged the desk phone and her cell phone, pulling up Chris' name and number. She dialed into the work phone and held it to her ear. Her heart raced. Was she crazy for doing this? There was something about Chris that she longed for, and she couldn't put her finger on what. Even after putting distance between them, she still desired Chris.

She wanted Chris' arms around her. Fingers inside her. But more than that, she wanted Chris to sit with her, stand with her, just look at her. What kind of sappy romantic had she turned into? She'd sworn after Mari that she would never fall in love again. She had the love of her life. She didn't need that again. Mari was enough.

"Jack, you caught me just before a meeting. What's up?"

Startled, Ash pulled the phone away from her ear and stared down at it. She'd called from the office line, so of course Chris would assume it was the person who normally called her.

"Jack?"

"It's me." Ash's voice cracked, and she cleared her throat to repeat herself. "It's me, Chris."

"Oh."

That single syllable said a whole lot. Ash had longed to hear

Chris' voice directed at her. She'd heard her from across the playground at pick up, or in the halls when she'd checked in with Ms. Dunja for Avonlee. But this was so different. To have all that energy charged directly at her took her breath away.

"How are you?" Chris asked, slowly.

Because Ash wasn't talking. She couldn't get her brain to work alongside her mouth. She stuttered, "Uh...uh...good."

"That's good." Chris sucked in a deep breath.

Ash knew she had to get to the point of this call. Chris was likely busy with school things, and Ash should stop wasting her time. "Are you busy tonight?"

"I'm going to need a little more detail than that, Ash."

Right. Ash was messing this up way more than she expected she would. Chris shouldn't have this kind of power over her still. Ash had broken it off. She'd told her no, that they couldn't do this. Ash had been the one to draw the hard line in the sand, and Chris had respected that ever since. Which Ash had appreciated, but that didn't stop the longing in the center of her chest.

"I need someone to stay the night. Tonight. Steven called in, again."

"All right."

Ash could hear the clicking of a computer keyboard in the background. She held her breath, hoping that Chris would be available because she really didn't want to call another backup. Ash wanted to see her, even if she couldn't have her.

"I have a seven o'clock meeting. I can be there when I'm done."

"So eight-thirty?"

"Yes."

"Is this..." How did Ash ask this discreetly? It wasn't any of her business, but she wanted to know that the little conversation in Chris' office all those weeks ago didn't throw her back into a state of drinking.

"Is it *that* kind of meeting?" Ash dropped her voice, masking the word. She had to remember that she was probably still at the school and wouldn't openly say where she was going. She should have known better.

"Yes, it's *that* kind of meeting, Ash."

Ash didn't miss the bite in her words, and she hated that she'd been the cause of it. She shouldn't have asked. She should have just let it go and let her curiosity burn in the pit of hell that she'd put herself into. "I shouldn't have—"

"You're right. You shouldn't have. Do you still want me to come or not?"

"Yes." Ash wavered on the word. She wanted to say so much more, but she bit her tongue. "I'll see you when you get here."

Ash hung up as quickly as she could. She needed to stop acting so stupid in front of Chris. They were going to have to deal with each other for years to come, not just at the school but here, and she really had to figure out exactly how to talk to Chris without making it such a big deal.

Calling her parents to see if they could pick up the girls was easier than she thought. She'd never believed she'd rely on them so much, but when they offered to have the girls overnight because it'd be easier, she readily agreed. Having family nearby had definitely been the better decision, even if it was hard to leave the home she'd brought her kids to when they were born. And where she'd buried Mari.

She really should bring them out there some time so they could visit her. There was never a doubt in her life that Mari was the one and only love that she'd have. She wouldn't allow anyone else to take that spot. Brushing her fingers through her hair, Ash stared at her cellphone.

What she would give to be able to text Mari right now and ask for advice.

Wouldn't that be odd, though? Asking her wife for advice on someone she had a massive crush on? She smiled at that. Mari would find it absolutely amusing. She'd probably giggle and tell Ash to go after her. She was the light of Ash's life, always smiling and laughing—the sunshine to Ash's grumpy.

She should remember Mari like that more often, the good times. She should work harder and move away from the terror and anger that she felt still at Mari's passing. It was so much easier said than done. Especially when Avonlee was struggling so much.

She finished out her day and waited until everyone was upstairs making dinner for the night. She was going to have to stay until Chris arrived, which meant she had another three hours at least to wait. It would be quiet, but she could either decide to get more work done to get ahead or she could work on something else.

Something that seemed far more interesting at the moment.

Ash sat at her desk and pulled out her laptop that she'd brought from home. She bit her lip and looked out the door to see if anyone was down there or if all the families were upstairs. Ash didn't see anyone, so she opened the last document she had been working on.

The words flowed out of her. She closed her eyes and let the story move from her brain to her fingertips in seconds. She wasn't even sure how this was happening. It had been so long since something was this easy, and it felt amazing.

She completely lost track of time, and it wasn't until her phone dinged with a text message that she pulled herself out of the story. Three hours already? Ash picked up her phone and frowned at the text. Chris. She swiped her thumb across the screen to read it.

Chris 8:26 pm - I'm leaving now. I should be there soon.

Excitement coursed through Ash's veins. How was that even possible? Or was it just nerves masquerading as excitement. Ash bit her lip and stared at the text. Should she even respond? It would be courteous even if Chris didn't read it until after she got there.

Ash 8:28 pm - Okay. See you soon.

That didn't sound too hopeful did it? What was with her? Ash stood up and walked around her office. What was wrong with her? She couldn't even begin to form a coherent sentence. She didn't want to like Chris. She wanted to find that calm place she'd had with Mari, the place where she knew she was beholden.

Oh! That was a good word. She should add it to her story.

Smiling, Ash bent over a sticky note and wrote that word down. She hesitated before she sat in her desk chair again only to immediately stand up. The energy coursing through her was uncontrollable. That wasn't something she was used to.

She walked through the house, the kids getting ready for bed while the adults yelled at them to listen just like any normal family would do. She smiled at it. Ash shoved her hands into her pockets and walked back down the stairs to her office. She couldn't sit still.

The minutes ticked by like hours as she waited for Chris to arrive. She needed to know what was going to happen. But what did she want to happen? Ash honestly had no idea. If she went with her gut, then there was no reason she should be like this. They'd had sex, twice, and that was it. They'd thought about dating, learned more about each other, and then realized this was a mistake so they'd stopped.

Ash blew out a breath and crossed her arms. She flopped down in her chair just before she tensed. Chris' voice boomed through the upstairs. Ash could only make out muffled sounds, but it was there. The families had let her in already. Ash's heart was in her throat. She had barely been able to form words on the phone. How was this going to work seeing Chris in person?

She stayed put. Chris would come down there. She knew she would. Ash held her breath. She fiddled with anything she could reach. She closed her personal laptop and shoved it back into her bag.

Oh my god, I'm nervous!

Ash couldn't even figure out how to place that feeling. She shuddered as she straightened her shoulders and started to log out of her work things. She was ready to go home, and it was probably better that she do that sooner rather than later. She was just finishing up with her work things when she was startled by a presence in her office.

Looking up, Ash met Chris' eyes. She was as stunning as ever. Her long hair was around her shoulders in waves. The shirt she wore today was tight across her breasts, and the light blues in it matched the jacket she wore over it. Chris leaned against the frame of the door, her hands on either side as she pushed in but didn't step inside Ash's oasis.

Ash's breath caught in her throat, her heart skipping a beat. She couldn't, could she? Mari was the love of her life, her one and only. There wasn't any room for anyone else, was there? Not for the first time, she started to question herself. Dragging her gaze all the way down Chris's body to her chucks that she always seemed to wear and straight back up over her hips, the curves of her body, her breasts, to her lips—the damn kissable lips—Ash locked their gazes together.

She was dumbstruck. She couldn't speak.

Chris continued to look at her, probably wondering why Ash was being so weird. But Ash literally couldn't form words. Where had that ability from twenty minutes ago gone? Chris canted her head to the side, her tight curls falling to one side. Ash clenched her fists at her sides. She had to say something. She had to speak. But just as she tried to form words, Chris finally shook her head, a pitiful look crossing her gaze. Her voice was so firm and confident when she spoke.

"Well, I'm here."

CHAPTER
Twenty-Seven

"I SEE THAT," Ash's voice was smooth.

Chris was checking in, like she would with anyone when she arrived. They had tasks for her to do, usually they would tell her about who was there, though one of the families was the same as the last time she'd stayed. But she hadn't expected Ash to look so worn down and like she was on the verge of tears.

She wasn't sure she'd be able to walk away without making sure that Ash was okay and that it wasn't her very presence that was causing the issues to begin with. But how to check in with her without causing any more harm? Chris was stuck between a rock and hard place, not knowing what to do.

"Thank you for coming tonight."

"Anytime," Chris breathed out the word. Again she was caught in what to say. "Do you mind if we talk?"

Ash's eyes lit up, a smile curling on her lips more beautiful than anything Chris had seen before. She wanted to rush in and wrap her arms around Ash, figure out what was going on between them, but she stopped herself because she knew. She knew there was nothing left between them except the last tendrils of arousal and connection. Something that they were surely to break with some time apart.

"Yes. Please."

Satisfaction rolled through Chris. She stepped inside the office and shut the door behind her. Leaning against it, the knob still pressed against the palm of her hand, Chris let out a long breath. "I never really got to apologize to you."

"For what?" Ash stood up slowly when Chris didn't come closer.

Chris held her breath, clenching her jaw. She ran her gaze all over Ash's body, from her head to her toes and back up again. Chris still hadn't gotten used to Ash catching her breath like that. It was amazing. But she held her ground, knowing that nothing more was going to come of this conversation than amends.

"For not telling you sooner. I should have."

"Probably." Ash crossed her arms and leaned against the desk, her butt on the edge of it. "But it's hard to share what we're ashamed of, isn't it?"

"Always." Chris let out a nervous chuckle. "I've been a drunk more of my life than I've been sober. And it really wasn't until I hit rock bottom, until I brought alcohol into the school building for the first time and the last time, until I really understood that I would lose everything, that I committed to getting sober. It was bad."

"I imagine." Ash looked her directly in the eye. "I've seen others go through it."

"Yeah, me too. But when you're in the midst of it yourself, it's a whole different experience." Chris put her shoulders against the door, needed it to center herself so she didn't step any closer to Ash, because that was what she really wanted to do. "With-drawal was awful."

"That I can't imagine, thankfully." Ash's smile turned wry and vanished before Chris' eyes. "Mari was an alcoholic." Ash kept her eyes glued to the floor in front of her.

Chris decided to let her talk. She could tell Ash that she knew, but it was more important that Ash share now that she was ready. Holding her ground, Chris listened with an open heart.

"That night...when she died...she was driving. I was in the car with her, and I didn't..." Ash's voice snapped. She looked up at the ceiling, her eyes watering. "I didn't know she was drinking. She'd told me she was sober. I couldn't smell it on her. I'd just started to relax about it because it had been long enough, but it wasn't. And she nearly killed both of us."

"Oh Ash." Chris longed to reach out and touch her, hold her, comfort her. But she stayed put, the permissions not given for her to come closer.

"She didn't. She's lucky for that, but the alcohol is what killed her. She was so drunk, Chris. She was so over the limit. And she was so torn up from the accident. They tried everything they could to keep her alive, but it wasn't enough. It wasn't...enough," Ash trailed off, full tears streaking down her cheeks. "I should have known better, but I didn't."

"Ash, if she didn't want you to know, she would have hidden it. Take it from someone who was damn good at hiding it. My best friend, Mel, didn't even know until I came clean to her one night. She helped me through a brutal detox." Chris would forever love Mel for that. She shouldn't have done it. She should have forced Chris to go to the hospital or a rehabilitation center, but she didn't.

"I know. I know." Ash looked up, her eyes still watery. "It doesn't make it easier. I loved her so much."

"I imagine you always will. Great love like that doesn't die."

Ash looked at her sharply, eyes wide. Chris stared back, concerned she'd overstepped, but Ash didn't elaborate on what that look was for.

"She's the love of my life, Chris. The mother of my children. She'll always be a part of me."

"She will," Chris agreed. "I wouldn't wish for it another way."

Ash nodded. She cupped her cheek with her hand, her eyes

lighting up as she shook her head at Chris. "I don't drink because of her."

"I figured as much. I kept meaning to ask you why you didn't drink, but I didn't have the guts. It would too easily lead into why I don't drink." Chris mulled that one over, the realization hitting her as soon as the words were out of her mouth. "I guess I chickened out on the easiest way to tell you that one, didn't I?"

"We're all allowed to be afraid of sharing our shame."

Wasn't that the truth? Chris looked at Ash across the small office, seeing her fully for the first time. Just as broken as Chris was but in such a different way. Were they really kindred spirits? What Chris had told Andry and Mel came back to haunt her. She'd found happiness in this broken spirit, a way to perhaps mend, but that had been shot down in seconds flat. She wasn't sure she was willing to risk it again.

"Anyway, I just wanted to apologize for not telling you sooner. I really should have."

"There's a lot of complications to our relationship, Chris. Keeping that secret close to your chest isn't something I blame you for."

"It's not?" That surprised Chris. Her heart thudded steadily. She was sure Ash blamed her for it, blamed her for being a drunk who thought she could get away without the world knowing.

"It's not." Once again, Ash gave her a beautiful smile. "We don't know each other that well. And like I said earlier, there are a lot of complications in our relationship."

"Like me being the principal of your nightmares."

Ash snorted lightly, pushing to stand up. She wrapped an arm around her middle, holding the other one. "Definitely not my nightmares."

"Like our one night stand that turned into two nights?" Chris lowered her voice in case anyone was outside listening, though she had her doubts. All the families were busy doing what they do before bed time. Her cheeks were red though, thinking about what they'd done and how she'd like to do it again. Maybe against the desk.

Nope!

Have to stop thinking like that.

This wasn't the time or place. That had been taken out of her hands, and Chris was okay with that decision. She stayed right where she was, watching carefully as Ash stepped closer, one foot in front of the other.

"Yeah, that. Those texts were hot, though. I haven't sexted anyone in years."

Chris choked. "I've never done that. I've taught way too many classes on why that is the worst idea on the planet."

"Makes sense why you were so hesitant then." Ash's tone lowered, a huskiness to it that wasn't there before.

What was happening? Chris couldn't keep up with these shifts in Ash's mood. Her heart raced as Ash took yet another step closer. She wanted to hope, she really did, but she wasn't here for hope. She was here to apologize—make amends—somehow find a way to move forward.

"You know," Ash started, "I didn't find you remotely sexy when I was in high school."

"Thank god for that," Chris breathed out, relief washing through her. She hadn't thought that Ash had, but to have it confirmed was that much better. Chris continued to grip onto the doorknob, making it her lifeline. "Ash, what are you doing?"

Ash shook her head, stopping in her tracks. Her eyes widened, and her gaze flirted all over Chris' body and centered on her lips, remaining there. "I don't know."

"We shouldn't be doing this," Chris whispered.

"We shouldn't be doing anything." Ash listed forward, raising up on her toes before dropping back down. But she didn't take another step closer. Chris was grateful for that.

"I came here to tell you that I'm sorry."

"You did. And I accept your apology." Ash flashed her a cocky grin. "Why do we keep ending up in the same circles? It's been a decade and a half of this, and still, I can't *not* find you somewhere in my life."

Chris frowned at that. What was she saying? Chris hadn't been in her life since that class back in high school. She was just about to ask, when Ash held up her hand.

"It's a long story, but remember I told you when I couldn't get your voice out of my head?"

Chris nodded.

"Well, that's what I mean, for the most part."

"What do you mean *for the most part?*"

"It's a long story." Ash's arms tightened around her middle. "Now isn't the time for that conversation."

"All right." Chris would accept that. She wouldn't ever force anyone to talk if they didn't want to. "Well, I guess I should go get ready for bed." Chris turned toward the door.

"Chris."

"What?" Spinning around, Chris froze.

Ash was standing right in front of her. When did that happen? When had she moved so swiftly and quietly? They couldn't be doing this. Chris wasn't sure that she could take another dose of what had happened in her office. She'd been left longing and bruised and broken after that. While her meal with Mel and Andry had helped ease the sting a bit, it was still there. She didn't have to dig too hard for it.

"Thank you for sharing with me, finally," Ash said, reaching out and wrapping those long fingers around Chris' wrist.

That touch was amazing. Chris had never thought it would happen again, and even now she struggled to believe it herself. While she wanted it to, she knew it couldn't happen. She was too damaged for Ash. They shared too much of a similar past, Chris on one side and Ash on the other. She couldn't bring herself to let Ash fall into her trap of destruction because that was exactly who she was. Chris took things and destroyed them.

"I really appreciate it."

"Same," Chris forced the word out of her throat. "Thank you

for telling me about Mari. It helps me understand you and your girls better."

Ash gave her a sad nod. "I didn't tell Avonlee until recently. I wanted to protect her."

"I understand that." Chris chuckled. "I always want to protect everyone."

"So I've heard," Ash murmured, her fingers tightening again. Ash raised her chin up, locking her gaze directly onto Chris.

She'd heard? Who had she heard that from? Or was she just surmising because of their interactions. Chris needed to know if Ash had been talking about her to someone. Who would even share that kind of information with her?

"Stop panicking," Ash said. "It's not a bad thing, but like you said earlier, it helps me understand you better."

"There isn't much to understand. I'm a pretty simple person."

"No one is simple. You should know that," Ash countered.

Chris knew, of course, that she was right, but she wasn't entirely sure that she wanted to admit it. "Ash, I really should get ready for bed."

"I know. I just wanted to talk to you a bit longer."

"Talk about what?"

"Anything, honestly." Was that longing in her tone?

Chris hesitated to see it there, hear it, but she felt the same. To spend just five minutes with Ash would be worth the pain of walking away—at least she was pretty sure that was the case. She wanted it to be anyway. But was she just setting herself up for torment later?

"We did talk," Chris made her tone sharp, terse. She needed to put those walls back up. They shouldn't be doing this, and if Ash called again for an overnight, Chris knew she was going to have to decline the opportunity. "I'll see you around, Ash."

Without another word, Chris twisted the knob in her hand and pulled open the door. She walked out of Ash's office and straight into the small bedroom they kept for house parents. As soon as she was closed inside, Chris blew out a breath and closed her eyes. She had to get herself under control.

Even if Ash was the one, she had made it very clear that nothing could happen between them again. Chris bit her lip. It hurt to think that, to know that because of her past that she might never find happiness. It was one of the worst hurts she'd felt in a long time, and it seared its way through her chest in a sharp stab.

What was she doing?

This was insanity, and she had to find the way out. Now.

"MAMA!" Avonlee raced into Ash's arms, wrapping them around her waist in a tight squeeze.

It was the Friday before spring break, and Ash was so ready for it. She didn't have the week off, but her whole family was taking turns caring for the girls. Ash was sure they could all use the break from routine.

Whatever that night had been with Chris last week still stuck in her mind. And every time Ash picked up the girls from school, her eyes were peeled for Chris. Where was she? What was she doing? Was she smiling? What was she wearing today? Would her looks still have that intensity to them?

She couldn't stop the questions from rolling through her brain, and it wasn't until Avonlee tugged on her arm and said her name again that Ash finally dragged all her attention back to her daughter. "What is it, baby?"

"I got a golden ticket today!"

Ash furrowed her brow, a shiver running through her. She had absolutely no idea what Avonlee was talking about. Rhubie ran over to her next, wrapping arms around her in a tight hug too before snagging her sister and hugging Avonlee.

"What's a golden ticket?"

"You get them for doing something really good." Avonlee's eyes lit up, the blue such a reminder of Mari and what she looked like when she was excited even though Avonlee was a dead ringer for Ash.

"Oh, that's cool!"

"It's awesome." Avonlee grinned. "I've been doing so much better this month. Ms. Dunja even said so, that's why she gave me the golden ticket."

"Well, I'm proud of you." Ash straightened her back, swiveling her head from side to side as she tried to look for Chris. What was she doing? She should be focused on her kids. They were her everything.

So why did she want to see Chris so much?

That was the question she wasn't quite sure she wanted to answer. Not yet anyway. That night in her office, something snapped. Ash's heart had been full and warm and like they were right back in Chris' office and Ash was asking her out. But she didn't want that. She wanted to remember Mari and the pain and be the grieving widow. She wanted to know that her wife wouldn't ever be forgotten. But anytime Chris was nearby, it was like Ash forgot the real woman she'd fallen in love with all those years ago.

Chris was so honest, almost to a fault. And Ash couldn't feel bad if she wanted to keep some of who she was a secret, especially since they hadn't really even started dating.

"Mom, can we play?" Rhubie asked, pulling on Ash's hand.

Ash glanced over at the playground set that swarmed with children. She looked at both the girls and gave a slight shrug. This was what they needed, some time together as a family, doing something fun. "Sure, why not?"

They took off, leaving their backpacks at Ash's feet. She picked them up and stalked over to one of the few benches in the playground and sat down. Ash watched her daughters play and run, but she also looked around for Chris. She should be here, shouldn't she?

Ash let the girls play for twenty minutes before the chill settled into her chest and she called them so they could get home. She wanted to get started on dinner and have some time with her kids as a family, which they rarely seemed to do anymore. She walked between them as they went to her car. Just as she was passing through the parking lot, Ash caught sight of Chris.

Chris's hair was pulled into a ponytail, long down her back. Ash's breath caught in her throat, and she faltered in her step. Chris hadn't seen her yet. Ash clenched her fists and was about to call out, when Chris turned by the doors to the school and made eye contact with them. She nodded, her lips thin and jaw set. She did nothing else as she ducked into the school and vanished from Ash's sight.

What was that about?

Rhubie tugged on Ash's hand. "What's for dinner?"

"Oh, I don't know, baby." Ash was barely able to tear her gaze from the door that Chris had disappeared into. Were they at that point now? Not talking. Barely acknowledging each other's existence?

On the one hand that was probably a good thing. But on the other, Ash hated it. This wasn't what she wanted. Was it? Longing settled into her chest in a way it hadn't been there in ages. It ached. Ash reached up and rubbed the center of her chest as she stepped off the sidewalk and crossed the street to her car.

They loaded inside, and she made the quick drive home. Instead of sending the girls to do their homework immediately, Ash put on a movie and made some popcorn. She sprinkled salt and some dry dill into it, Rhubie's favorite, and sat down with them. She only half paid attention as the girls jumped around, moved from place to place, watched the movie, and generally just relaxed.

Maybe she wouldn't even cook dinner that night. Maybe she would order something, and they would dine on the excitement of a break. Ash smiled at that and whipped out her phone. It didn't take her long to put in an order to their favorite take-out and just wait for it to arrive. She would make this a good night, even if she still couldn't get Chris off her mind.

Her phone rang.

Ash stared down at it, the number popping up from the school. Frowning, Ash maneuvered off the couch and walked to her bedroom. Her stomach sank. Every time she got a call from the school, something was wrong, usually with Avonlee.

"Hello?" Ash answered, waiting for Ms. Dunja to come over the line.

"This is Dr. Murphey calling from Irving Elementary. Is this Ashton Taylor?"

Ash's stomach twisted hard. What was happening? Chris had never been this formal with her before. Never ever. The lump in her throat swelled, and tears burned in her eyes. What had she done?

"Yeah, Chris, it's me." Ash choked back the pain in her voice, at least she hoped she did. She didn't want Chris to think there was anything wrong.

"I was calling because Avonlee got a golden ticket today. Her teacher, Ms. Dunja, gave it to her for excellence in academics and for helping her reading buddy in the first grade class with reading."

The tears that had been in Ash's eyes flowed down her cheeks. It wasn't because of Chris, though. This was all because of Avonlee. Her baby who had been struggling so much was finally honored for doing something good, something well. Her heart thudded with pride.

"So Ms. Dunja gave her a golden ticket, which is a great honor, and both Ms. Dunja and I are really proud of her and the progress she's made in the last few weeks. Avonlee has proven that she can work hard."

"Chris," Ash's voice broke on her name. What was she hoping for?

"That's all I'm calling for Ash." That was Chris, broken. "I'll see the girls when they get back from break."

With that, Chris hung up.

Ash stared at her phone in her hand, her heart racing wildly. What was wrong with her? Immediately she called Char.

"Come over, please."

Char groaned. "What if I had a date tonight?"

Ash snorted. "Your dates come over late and leave early. Tinder can wait until tomorrow."

"You're mean."

"Come over, please."

"You were just a jerk to me. What makes you think I'd want to come over after that?"

Ash pressed her lips together hard, curling her feet up under her as she leaned into the pillows on her bed. "I don't know what to do."

Something must have shone through Ash's voice because Char stuttered in her silence. It wasn't much longer until she said quickly, "I'll be right there. Give me ten."

Ash hung up and curled onto her side on the bed in the fetal position. Her mind was so clouded with thoughts and confusion that she wasn't sure which direction to turn or go or what to think or feel. It was all just circling around in her brain like a garbage disposal.

"Mama," Avonlee said as she stepped into Ash's bedroom. "What's wrong?"

"Oh, nothing, baby." Ash forced a smile onto her face. She held her arms out for Avonlee to come cuddle against her and hug her. "Dr. Murphey just called. She told me all about your golden ticket."

Ash brushed her fingers through Avonlee's hair, curling the loose strands around her ear.

"I'm so proud of you, baby."

Tears threatened to spill over her eyes again. She had been doing way too damn much of that lately. Ash tugged Avonlee in closer and wrapped her tightly in a hug. She held on, drawing in her scent and settling into the familiarity. She needed this more than anything.

Rhubie rounded the corner, canting her head at them. Ash grinned and moved her arm to hold it out for her other daughter. She wormed her way into Ash's embrace, settling her head on Ash's shoulder with a smile. This was perfect and exactly what she needed. They stayed there until there was a loud knock on the front door.

The girls jerked, but Ash laughed lightly. "It's Auntie."

"Oh!" They raced toward the door to open it.

Char came in with bags in her hands. "I got the good stuff."

"What good stuff?" Ash wrapped her arm around her middle and leaned against the entry into the living room.

"Ice cream, Funyuns, and whatever chocolate bars I could grab."

Laughing, Ash walked toward the kitchen table as Char set everything down. "You're an idiot, but I love you."

"Love you too. Now go get us some bowls and spoons."

"Yes, ma'am."

It wasn't long before the adults were sitting at the table and the kids were on the couch watching a new movie. Char kept sending Ash sidelong glances. Ash knew she was going to have to give in and tell her why she'd called her to come here, but at the same time, she struggled to find words for it to make sense in her head. As soon as she said it out loud it wouldn't make any sense.

"I was lonely, okay?"

Char raised an eyebrow at her, as if she wasn't quite believing Ash. Which was fine. Ash didn't quite believe it herself either. Though loneliness had become her constant companion in the last few years. Since moving here, she hadn't felt it nearly as often as before. Why was that?

"What's the real reason?"

Ash narrowed her eyes and sighed. "I don't know how to explain it."

"So start with what you do know."

"I miss her." Ash moved her spoon around her ice cream bowl. What had she been thinking? Char was probably the last person she should call because Char would lay on thick exactly what she thought and most likely what Ash needed to hear. Still, Ash wasn't sure she wanted to hear it.

"That's natural."

"Yeah, but I don't want to miss her. I want to just live my life, raise my kids, and go on from there." Ash shoved a giant spoonful of the Bunny Tracks ice cream into her mouth. This one was her favorite, and she'd taken the Funyuns and crunched them up to sprinkle on top to add texture and flavor to it. She'd figured out this combination when she'd been pregnant the second time—with the baby they'd lost—and she'd kept on doing it to keep that memory fresh. She was such a nostalgic granny at heart.

"Ash, I think this is normal. Her birthday was last week."

Jerking with a start, Ash looked at Char surprised. They were talking about two different women, the two women in Ash's life. And while she'd thought about Mari on her birthday this year, it hadn't been a big deal. Not like the last two, and the girls had barely mentioned it as well.

Char studied her curiously, her gaze flitting all over Ash's face. "You weren't talking about Mari."

"I wasn't," Ash whispered. "I wasn't even thinking about her."

"Chris?" Char whispered back.

Ash nodded, giving confirmation, but she really didn't want the girls to hear her. This wasn't something they needed to know. Ash slowly picked up her spoon and took another bite. "It's probably just because I started my period or something."

"I've known you your entire life." Char gave her a steady, firm look. "You don't do raging weird hormones. Ever. Except when pregnant."

"Now who's being mean?" Ash settled into the moment, her heart easing with the distress that had been caused. What was she supposed to do about all of this? She could barely even talk about it. Still, having this one-on-one time with Char had been exactly what she needed. "I don't know what to do about it."

"What's your gut telling you?"

"I don't know." Ash cringed. That was the problem, really. She had no idea what the next step was.

"What do you want?" Char pinned her with every ounce of seriousness she had.

Ash sighed. She ran her fingers through her hair and closed her eyes. She tried to pull words and thoughts and feelings from the center of her body to some place where it would make sense. But she just couldn't. She ended up just shaking her head and saying the only thing that came to mind. "I just want one night of happiness."

"What would that look like?"

"So many different things." Ash gave Char a sad smile. "Mari back, here, with us, even if it was just for one day. Someone new. The girls just smiling and laughing. So many things, Char."

"Come here." Char leaned over and wrapped her arms around Ash's shoulders and tugged her in for a tight hug. "We'll find you some happiness, okay? It might not be today, but it will be someday."

"Yeah," Ash whispered. "Someday."

CHAPTER
Twenty-Nine

"MEL, I need to talk to you." Chris leaned into Mel's empty classroom. She was going to demand this moment from her friend, whether she had the time or not. Because Chris was torn.

Mel looked up, meeting her eyes, and nodded her agreement. "Shut the door."

"God, yes." Chris stepped into the classroom and closed the door behind her. "How's your class going now that we're back from break? Has the crazy calmed down in them yet?"

Mel's eyes crinkled as she smiled. "It's taken the full two weeks since coming back I think, but they're calming."

It was mid-April, and the end of the school year was closing in faster than Chris wanted to admit. While she appreciated the calm of the summers, she also hated how quiet they could get. It meant way more temptations than she was ready for, but maybe this summer would be better. Maybe it wouldn't be so hard. Last year had been the worst.

"That's good. I feel the energy leaving the school, that after-break energy. We're getting back into routines."

"We are." Mel was still watching her, as if she could really tell what was going through Chris' mind at the moment.

Sometimes having friends that close was a curse and a blessing. But she had come here for a reason either way. Chris plopped down into one of the chairs and crossed her arms. Then she shifted her legs and uncrossed her arms. She stared out the window. Where to begin with this one?

"Avonlee, Ash's oldest, earned pizza with the principal."

"Oh, that's great! She was having all those issues, right?"

Chris hummed and nodded. It was a good thing. It took a lot in order to earn that, but they'd all agreed to let her in on it since she'd had such an amazing turnaround in the last few months. Except there was still the problem of Ash, and Chris wasn't sure how to navigate that one. She'd kept as much distance as she could, reverting back to complete professionalism. She had to stop letting Ash get under her skin in that way.

And Chris had taken great pains to put more distance between them, including not staying the night at the house anymore. She needed the space to protect herself more than anything. Chris shuddered, mulling through her thoughts. How was she going to approach this one? The problem was she was too close to the situation, which was why she'd sought out Mel. She needed the outside observer.

"I don't want Ash to think I'm playing favorites. That's what got me into trouble with her when she was my student."

Mel whipped her head up. "What do you mean?"

"I favored her as a student." Chris frowned at that. She hadn't wanted to admit it for years, but after teaching for so long she understood there were often favorites, those students who left a sizable impact on her life. Ash was one of them. "She had such potential with writing, and so I gave her more attention than others. She thought it was bullying."

"No way."

"I'm not the most personable teacher out there." Chris let out a wry snort.

"No, you're not. But that's part of your charm." Mel grinned broadly.

Chris rolled her eyes dramatically. Mel was always looking on the brighter side of life, wasn't she? Still that hadn't been what Chris had come there for that day. "So I don't want her to think I'm doing the same with Avonlee."

"But Avonlee earned this privilege, I assume."

"She did. Esther is the one who suggested her for it, actually."

"Not bad then. Follow that up with a paper trail and you'll be fine."

Chris narrowed her eyes. "I don't think that's how it works anymore." At least not with Ash. They always seemed to be at odds, not quite understanding each other or where they were coming from. Nothing of that had changed in the last seventeen years, despite what Chris had thought there for a moment. It would be best for Chris to slide through this as much as she possibly could. She didn't want to make any more waves for Ash. She wanted to be the best principal that she could be for the girls, but that was it. She was done.

Ash wouldn't want her no matter what.

Which was a good thing.

Because Chris didn't deserve it.

She would fuck it up as soon as she hit the ground running.

Sighing, Chris leaned back in the chair and looked out the window again at the kids playing outside. It was a sunny day, one of the first few they'd had since winter eased into spring. Shuddering Chris turned to Mel again.

"Tell me I won't screw this up."

Mel's face fell. She leaned forward, her hands folded as her elbows hit the desk. "Chris, you're not going to screw this up."

"I'm not convinced."

"You are by far the best principal I've ever worked with."

Chris narrowed her eyes. "I've been your principal for the last twelve years. And before that you only worked under Josh. That doesn't exactly leave me with many warm feelings."

Mel waved her off. "You are the best principal I've seen out there. And I think a lot of that is because you think you aren't, so you're always working at being better. You have to accept that you were made for this."

Chris had accepted that, but she still wasn't sure about the first part of what Mel had said. She always felt as though she was failing somewhere, and since she'd sobered up that had really only turned into being hard on herself because she'd been drunk for so long. A functional drunk, but that was only a small concession.

"I'm not the best principal out there."

"I didn't say you were." Mel winked. "But you are one of the better ones. You've got this, Chris. Stop second guessing yourself. You need to get yourself together and stop being so hard on yourself. You're brilliant, you're amazing, and those kids deserve everything."

"They do," Chris agreed. "All of them do."

Leaning forward, Chris stared at her folded hands. Mel was right. She had to stop second guessing herself. Avonlee deserved this. She checked her watch and cocked her head at Mel. "Well, it's pizza time."

"Wait, what? You waited until now to ask me this?"

Chris shrugged. "Avonlee was a last minute addition to the party, and I just needed someone to talk to."

Mel grinned at her. "I'm always here to listen. You know that."

"Of course I do. Why do you think I'm here?"

Chris was lighter as she went back to her office to check on the pizza order. They were going to eat it in her office since there were only six students from the fifth and sixth grade classes who would be joining her. It would just be a matter of time before she had to deal with Ash again. She knew it. And she needed to steel herself for when that moment came.

～

Chris stepped out into the sunshine, needing the warm rays on her face. It had been a long quarter and an even longer year. The second year sober was harder than the first in some ways. In others it was easier, but it still wasn't anything she would wish on anyone. She shoved her hands into her pockets, the lanyard jingling around her neck as she walked.

Kids already raced by her as they ran to their parents. The older kids left the school without really giving her a second glance. Chris smiled as she watched them go. The sixth graders were ready for seventh, and to leave her school to go to the next. She sighed. Most of them were ready, anyway. Not all of them. That was going to be baptism by fire for those few. But they'd get there eventually. Sink or swim.

The noise was what Chris craved. The energy that was pure joy and happiness. She longed for that every day, which was what made the summers so long to begin with. As much as she needed the break, some days, she needed this more.

The breeze was wonderful against her cheeks. Anthony spotted her from his door and ran over, wrapping his arms around her hips in one of the biggest hugs he had given her to date. She ruffled his hair before glancing over at his mother and smiling. "What's happening, Anthony?"

"Nothing! Mom says we're going to go to Denver this weekend."

"Oh?" Chris raised an eyebrow at him. "What are you doing in Denver?"

"Aquarium! I've never been there before." His eyes grew wide as saucers.

"I have. You'll love it."

He nodded voraciously before running to the playground. He usually stuck around there until his mother was ready to leave and then she'd collect him.

When had spring crept up on her? She'd just been in the throes of winter a few days ago, wasn't she? Walking over to where Mel stood with her class, waiting for straggler parents to arrive, Chris doled out more hugs and praises for her students.

Mel waved at her and came to stand closer, wrapping her arms against her body to protect her from the chill that was still in the air. Chris wasn't bothered by it. She rarely was.

"How did pizza with the principal go?"

"Good." Chris smiled. "Like always."

Mel rolled her eyes. "And Ash?"

Chris shrugged. "Haven't seen her yet."

"Uh huh, and you're not out here for any particular reason... like looking for her?"

Shooting Mel a dirty look, Chris paused. "No, why would I be doing that?"

"Because I know you. And you like to play with fire."

"Ha. Ha." Chris looked across the playground. "Saw Anthony. He said he was going to Denver this weekend."

"Hmm. He is." Mel frowned a little more than Chris expected. "Hearing is coming up, and Esther wants to spend as much fun time with him as she possibly can. In case it goes sideways."

Nerves hit Chris squarely. "I can understand that one."

"Yeah, I think everyone can."

"Dr. Murphey!" Rhubie raced toward her, wrapping arms around her much like Anthony had.

Chris hugged her back. She was about to step away from her when Avonlee came up to her, shyly. If she was younger or more demure, she probably would be scuffing her foot against the gravel.

"Thank you," Avonlee said, her voice muffled, but Chris heard it.

She would hear it anywhere. "For what?"

"For the pizza."

Chris grinned broadly. She bent down a little to make sure that Avonlee saw her eyes. "You deserved it, kid. That's why you were chosen to join in the party and the reward today. I promise you. I didn't pick your name for it. Ms. Dunja did."

Avonlee's eyes widened, and she looked up to Chris with a brilliant grin, one that was easy. Chris imagined she didn't do that often, and she was so glad to witness it now.

"You earned it, Avonlee. I'm so proud of you for it, too. You've done amazing changing your behavior this quarter. It's like you're a whole new kid." Chris straightened back up, looking around for Ash. When would she ever stop doing that?

"One you like?"

Chris had to pause and remember what she'd said before she answered. She gave Avonlee a serious look and nodded. "Yeah, a kid I like for sure. You're now one of my top kids going into sixth grade next year. That's exciting. I know I can count on you for things like morning announcements and helping out in the office if you want."

"You sure?"

"Yeah, if you want." Chris put her hands on her hips. "Of course, I'd want you to help out."

"That'd be awesome!" Avonlee bounced in her shoes.

"There you are." Ash's cool tones reached Chris' ears. Immediately, every nerve in her body was ready for whatever was going to come her way. Chris clenched her jaw and turned to look for Mel as a distraction and a way out of this conversation, but Mel had already gone back inside, leaving Chris alone with Avonlee, Rhubie, and Ash.

What the hell was she doing?

"I had pizza with Dr. Murphey today!" Avonlee proudly proclaimed.

Chris cringed. She hadn't wanted to be around for this conversation and unlike with the golden tickets, she didn't make calls home to families for this one. She sucked in a breath and rolled up on her toes. How could she get out of this conversation?

"Did you?" Ash asked. "Why's that?"

But Ash wasn't looking at Avonlee. She was staring directly at Chris.

"I earned it!"

"She did." Chris added. "It's a reward for kids who have made improvements during the last quarter. Avonlee was one of six students who earned it."

"Interesting." Ash hadn't dropped her gaze from Chris. Her eyes were direct and curious, as if she had a question on the tip of her tongue and wasn't willing to let the words loose.

"Not really. I do them once a quarter for the first three quarters of the year." Chris shrugged. "It was good seeing you, Ash."

Chris ducked her chin and turned on her toes. She headed straight for the closest door, swiping her badge to get inside. As soon as she was safely in the hall with the door closed behind her, Chris made her way to her office. That had gone way better than she'd expected it to. Now if she could only manage to keep it like that for the next four and a half years. It would get easier, right?

CHAPTER
Thirty

"WHAT AM I DOING?"

Ash sat in her car outside of Chris' apartment. She should have called or texted first. She should have done anything to alert Chris to the fact that she wanted to talk. Instead, she was sitting outside like some crazy stalker or something. Chris would turn her away in seconds flat.

As she should.

So what was she doing there?

Ash still hadn't fully answered that question for herself except that she wanted to see Chris again, and that she wanted to specifically see her outside of any work environment. Chris had been giving her the cold shoulder, not that she was mean or cruel, but she'd been completely professional. She talked to Ash like they hadn't formed any kind of relationship.

But they had.

And over the past weeks, Ash realized that she wanted that back in her life. She wasn't sure how it all was going to work out in the end, but she missed the close connection they shared. It was as if someone from her past understood where she was coming from, someone other than her family. Dragging in a deep breath, Ash forced herself out of her car.

She walked slowly to Chris' door, and when she knocked, she held her breath. What was she doing? This was crazy talk. She never would have thought about this happening before, ever. She'd been adamant for the last two years that there was no one out there for her other than Mari and that was how it was going to be.

It had been a poor decision to close herself off from possibilities.

Her knuckles were cold and ached when she rapped them against the steel door. Ash had spent the better part of the last four weeks finishing a novel she swore she'd never write. But it was done, and she knew what she was going to do now. This had to work. Just like everything in her novel had wrapped up, she needed a conclusion to this. One that was far more satisfying than what they'd found.

The doorknob turned. Ash's heart moved into her throat, her entire body poised and ready for the insanity that was her plan. She could do this. The door creaked open, and Chris' beautiful and confused face peered out from the crack. She opened it wider, and relief flooded through Ash.

One step at a time.

"Hi," Ash said awkwardly. This part she should have planned better. Words were where she thrived, but it was written words, not verbal. "Um...do you have a minute?"

"A minute?" Chris squared her shoulders, looking past Ash before locking eyes on her again. She didn't open the door wider, and she didn't step back from it. "What's going on?"

"I just wanted to talk."

"We don't have anything to talk about," Chris countered.

Ash knew that. They'd made it very clear where the boundaries were, and once again, she was the one forcing their hands into talking about something Chris was resistant to. But Ash had to know—was she only resistant because Ash had told her no?

"I know." Ash rubbed her lips together, flexing her fingers as she tried to find words. "I know I put that boundary up. I was wondering if we could take it down. If only for the rest of today."

Chris' eyes widened. Her thin lips parted, and her chest rose as she took a deep breath. Ash was prepared to be told off because this was insanity. She knew it. They were playing tug of war with whatever was between them, but Ash was here to surrender. She was here to let both of them win—at least she hoped that's how this conversation went.

But with the look on Chris' face, Ash started to doubt this was as mutual as she had hoped. Once again, nerves bloomed into her chest, and she was left standing on the other side of the door like an idiot. She should have called or texted. She should have done something to warn Chris that she wanted to have this talk or give Chris the chance to tell her *no, now's not a good time.*

"Why are you here, Ash?" Chris finally asked, her tone strong and forceful.

Ash was about to balk and back away, but when she looked into Chris' eyes, she saw pain and hurt. She'd caused that. She knew it without a doubt, and she wanted to assuage it. "I was wrong."

"You were wrong?"

Ash nodded. "I thought I was right, but I wasn't, and I know that I hurt both of us with that choice. Moving here was a hard decision to make, but I realize now how much better it was for me and the girls. I need to be here."

Ash was making a mess of this conversation. Her eyes prickled with tears as she struggled to find any words that made sense.

"I need to be here because I have support here, and I have hope here. I have hope." That was what she'd been looking for. "I have hope because you showed me that love isn't in the past for me, and I can have that again. I'm not just a grieving widow."

"You were never just a grieving widow."

"I know, but I wanted to be." Ash held her ground. She didn't move closer to Chris or farther away. She looked Chris directly in the eye when she spoke next. "I wanted to be stuck."

"And now?"

"Now I've changed my mind."

Chris pursed her lips, her gaze dragging down and up Ash's body, making her shiver in the intensity. Ash held her breath until suddenly Chris stepped back from the door and let Ash inside. They moved to the couch, the same place they'd first had sex. The connection wasn't lost on Ash. She was tense as she sat down, her shoulders tight and her chest heavy as though a weight rested on it.

"What have you changed your mind about?" Chris asked slowly, staring down at something on the floor.

Ash pulled her lip between her teeth. Now she really had to find the right words for this. "For a relationship."

"With me? Or in general?"

Ash's jaw dropped. She reached over and touched Chris' hands, drawing her attention up. "With you."

"But I'm a drunk, Ash. I don't keep that a secret."

"Yeah." Ash blinked slowly. "You're a sober drunk."

"Two years last month. That's it."

"That's nothing small. That's huge. Two years..." Ash stared at Chris dumbfounded. "Do you not see how amazing that is?"

"Ash, it was very clear that you didn't want to be in a relationship because of my drinking. So I need to know why now—all of a sudden—you're changing your mind."

Holding onto Chris' hand was her lifeline. Chris' skin was smooth and warm against her own, and Ash didn't want to let go. That was just the thing. She didn't want to walk out of here without taking a risk on happiness.

"I found happiness with you that I wasn't ever expecting to find again."

"You can find it somewhere else."

"I might. I might be able to." Ash looked directly into Chris' eyes, her heart in her throat when she said the next few words.

"But I don't want to look anywhere else. I'm choosing to look only at you."

"I don't think this is a good idea."

"Why?"

"Because I'm a drunk, Ash, and I know what that means. And with Mari also being a drunk and not just that, but the circumstances surrounding her death, I can't understand why you would want to take that risk with someone like me."

The air was sucked right out of Ash's lungs. She squeezed Chris' hand tightly, scared she was going to stand up and kick her out, right when they were getting to the meat of the conversation. "Because you're worth it."

"I'm not."

"Shut up and listen to what I'm saying. You're worth it, Chris. You have done a whole lot of work to get to where you are right now, and I don't get any sense that you're willing to let yourself slide backward. You aren't Mari in so many ways, and I'm choosing to focus on that because it's impossible not to see." Ash lifted Chris' hand to her lips, pressing a small kiss to the top of her hand.

"I screw things up. You don't want to be with me."

"I do. That's the thing." Ash turned Chris' chin so they were facing each other. She needed to look into Chris' eyes when she said this. She needed Chris to see the honesty in her gaze. "I do want to be with you."

"You don't."

Ash chuckled. "You can tell me all day what you think I want, but you're not me. And I do want you."

"I'm going to mess this up."

"We're both going to mess up. That's just part of being human. What matters is how you fix it and move forward."

Chris dragged in a slow, deep breath and shook her head. "I've worked so hard to keep a distance from you, and do you know what I've learned?"

"What?" Ash felt Chris soften instantly, as if the resistance that she'd opened the door with was completely gone. Elation burned through Ash. Was this actually happening?

"It's impossible to resist you."

Ash grinned, her entire body warming with hope. "So what does that mean?"

"I don't know." Chris flipped her hand over and laced their fingers. "Would I like this? Yes. But there are so many complications, and so much already between us. I'm not sure we can work through that."

"Can we try?" Ash held on to the flimsy hope that she had, needing it to exist in her life in what little way was possible. Without it, she wasn't sure what her life would look like going forward. Now that she'd found that flutter of happiness, she didn't want to give it up.

"What does that mean for you?"

"Starting to do something different tonight. It means we set apart time for each other. We text and call and do relationship things." Ash furrowed her brow, not quite understanding why Chris wasn't getting this. A relationship wasn't that hard, was it?

"And when it doesn't go well?"

"Then we talk to each other, and we listen to each other. Look, I don't expect this to be perfect, nor do I expect you to be perfect. This is us just trying to navigate every moment together." Ash squeezed Chris' hand, and then she waited. This was Chris' time to figure everything out. And all Ash could do was listen for what Chris was thinking and feeling.

"I don't think this is going to go well."

Ash understood Chris' hesitation. She tended toward the fatalistic even if she didn't always share that was her viewpoint. Waiting again to see if Chris was going to continue, Ash gave in when the silence continued between them. "Are you willing to risk that it might actually go well?"

Chris slowly turned to look Ash in the eye, directly. Her lips parted, her breath coming in long slow drags. Ash was entranced by Chris' mouth, the shape of her lips, the small little lines around the edges, the pale pink natural color.

"Yeah," Chris answered. "Yeah, I think I am."

Ash grinned. She leaned in, tenderly pressing their mouths together in a light kiss. "I'm so sorry I didn't figure this out sooner and that I hurt you in the process. I didn't intend to."

"I know," Chris murmured back. "You were protecting yourself."

"And you were protecting me from you." Ash winked. "But now that we're on the same page, what do you want to do?"

Chris cocked her head to the side. "I suppose we should go on a proper date."

"One where you don't get called away?"

"Right." Chris frowned. "Katie and I are working on things. Slowly but surely."

"That's better than nothing." Ash ran her hand along the inside of Chris' arm, holding onto her tightly. She squeezed lightly and leaned in more, resting her head on Chris' shoulder.

"It is." Chris kissed Ash's head. "Where are the girls?"

"My parents' house for the night. They've been taking them every other weekend for one night. I'm getting used to sleeping alone even if I don't like it."

Chris hummed, silence filling the air between them, but it was comfortable. Ash didn't care what they did that night so long as she got to spend some time like this with Chris. She wanted to get to know her again. The start and stop of their relationship had been tough, but here they were, back at the beginning again.

"Do you want to Netflix and chill?"

Ash gurgled with laughter. "Do you even know what that means?"

"Yes!" Chris' cheeks were a bright red.

Ash kissed her lips lightly. "You're adorable. Oh! I wanted to give you this."

Reaching into her pocket, Ash pulled out a flash drive. She

held it out for Chris to take, but Chris wouldn't lift her hand up and instead just stared at the drive like it was some odd object.

"What is it?"

"It's a book. I don't know if you have a computer that uses flash drives, I know they're becoming few and far between, but I didn't know how else to give it to you."

"A book?" Chris eyed it carefully and plucked the flash drive up with her free hand. She continued to stare at it.

"I told you that your voice has always been in my head, every time I write." Ash chuckled a little. "No matter how hard I tried to get you out of my brain, I couldn't. But I stopped writing when Mari died, reasonably so. But in the last month, I started again."

"Really?" Chris' eyes widened, and she clasped the flash drive like it was a precious stone. "So this is the story?"

"The second draft, yes."

"Are you going to publish it?"

"I don't know." Ash gave her a sad smile. "I haven't decided yet. I thought that part of my life was done and over with. But this..." Ash tapped Chris' hand "...might just prove that theory wrong."

"It might." Chris' lips curled upward. "So do I get to read it?"

"Yes."

"Now?"

"Only if you want to." Excitement coursed through her. "But I might have a better idea of what we can do."

"What's that?"

Ash raised up and swung her body around so she straddled Chris' legs. "I believe Netflix and chill was an option on the table."

"Really?" Chris looked up at her. "Because I don't want to rush into anything."

"I think we're beyond the rushing portion of our relationship." She was so fucking happy. Ash bent down, cementing their lips together in a gentle embrace. "Besides, I only get one night every two weeks without the girls. Do you really want to waste that precious time?"

Chris chuckled. "Why do I keep finding you in my lap?"

"Well, it's a pretty good lap to sit on." Ash smiled down at her. "So is your face."

"Ash!"

"What?" Ash blushed, but she was smiling. Happiness coursed through her, and she wanted to ride that wave for as long as possible. "It's true. I'd sit on your face any time. You're wicked with your tongue."

"To be fair, Ash, so are you."

Ash's body was on fire. She wanted Chris to touch her everywhere at the same time. Plopping her full weight down on Chris' legs, Ash bent her head and captured Chris' lips. Immediately, the kiss deepened. Happiness built in her chest, a warm gentle kind of happiness, the kind that she could easily surrender to if she wanted.

"I love your tongue," Ash murmured before diving in for another, longer kiss. One where their tongues tangled together, where their lips became moist, where their breathing was a struggle because all they wanted was mouth against mouth.

Every thought of what Chris could do with her tongue on Ash's body flitted through her mind in a millisecond. And she nearly overloaded from the possible sensations. Chris skimmed one fist and one palm down Ash's sides to her hips, holding on.

"So what are we doing during this session of Netflix and chill?"

Giggling, Ash pressed kisses down Chris' neck and over her chest. "You're going to drop that damn flash drive."

"I don't know about that. This is a never read before bona fide Ash Taylor novel. I'm the first to read it. I'm not sure I can give that up."

"You don't have to." Ash kissed her cheek. "It's all yours."

"I can't believe you wrote another book."

"Me either." Ash pulled Chris' shirt up. "But if you're going to touch me, you're going to have to put that thing down."

Chris whined in the back of her throat. "I'm not sure I can."

"Oh my god. Fangirl much?"

"I won't lie and say I didn't go buy every single one of your books as soon as I found out you were published."

Ash paused. She flicked her gaze up to Chris' eyes. A slow smile bloomed on her lips. "You did?"

"Of course I did. And I read them all."

"You're an idiot."

"So people keep telling me."

Ash reached for Chris' hand and took the flash drive from her fingers. She tossed it onto the coffee table and then jerked Chris' shirt up and over her breasts. She didn't care if she got it off or not, as soon as she could see Chris' bra she started feasting. She slid her tongue under the edge of the fabric and swiped her nipple.

This had been what she'd wanted, almost exactly. Chris sucked in a sharp breath and put her hand on the back of Ash's head, guiding her as she continued to lick and taste and kiss. "That feels good."

Ash smiled, trailing her tongue across the top of Chris' breasts. Then she sat back and pulled her shirt off, tossing it onto the floor. "So if we get one night every two weeks, does that mean I don't have to sleep alone anymore?"

"I guess it does if that's what you want."

"It is." Ash bent down and kissed Chris again. "I also really want to taste you."

"It's my pleasure to have your tongue between my legs."

CHAPTER
Thirty-One

CHRIS' mind was blown. She'd never expected Ash to show up tonight. It was almost dream worthy. And if she wasn't trying to get her pants down her hips and off her body, she would be pinching herself to see if this was real. To have Ash back at her apartment for this? But not just sex, this was so much more. This was what she had dreamed of, dared to hope for, and now it was reality.

Ash got down on her knees as soon as Chris had her pants pushed to her ankles. She skimmed her fingers down Chris' legs, over the short stubbly hair since it had been a while since she'd shaved. There hadn't been a reason for it, and since this was unexpected—she didn't think Ash would care. Chris didn't care. She just wanted Ash's promised tongue against her clit as fast as possible.

Holding her pants, Ash looked up and waited for Chris to step out of the circle of the leg of her pants, holding onto Ash's head for balance while she did it. It was a precarious position for her to be in, but to look down and see Ash's bright blue eyes shining up at her, like she wanted this. Like she was waiting for Chris to move just enough so that she could get between her legs and pleasure both of them.

"One more," Ash crooned, helping Chris focus on getting out of her pants completely.

Reaching behind her, Chris flicked the clasp on her bra so she was completely naked standing before a clothed Ash. She'd never done that with anyone before. She'd always thought it was fair for her partners and her to undress at the same time. This stripped her bare of any protections she might have.

And it was damn sexy.

Ash's fingers trailed up the back of her thighs and down again. Chris wondered if Ash salivated in anticipation. She knew she would be if their situations were reversed. Hesitating only for a moment, Chris reached down and pressed her fingers between her legs. She flicked them over her clit and nearly jolted at how sensitive it was. Her curls were damp.

"Ash," Chris whispered, a call to the wild she knew was about to come.

They both needed this. They both wanted it desperately. She could see it in Ash's eyes as they locked on her face, as they dropped down to where Chris' fingers were, in the dash of Ash's pink tongue against her lips. She wanted everything in this moment. They both did.

"Touch me already." Chris dipped her fingers between her legs and then moved them away, wet with her own juices.

Ash snagged her hand and pulled Chris' fingers to her mouth, covering them with her lips and sucking on them. She twirled her tongue in a circle, cleaning her off. The rough part of Ash's tongue on the pads of Chris' fingers sending waves of pleasure straight between her legs. Heat pooled again. Chris could only imagine the flavor, but she knew what Ash tasted like, that sweet mixed with a hint of salt. Dragging in a deep breath, Chris smelled nothing but her own arousal.

This was the sexiest thing on the planet.

"Let me watch you for a second." Ash's voice was breathy. She was entranced.

"Ash," Chris' voice was a whine. "I want you, not my fingers."

"You'll get me. I promise. No way I can resist that."

Chris frowned, but she moved her hand back between her legs. If this was what Ash wanted, then it's what she would do. She wetted her fingers again, moving them to her clit. Chris started a slow slide of her fingers, large circles to start. She kept the pressure light because she was still sensitive as fuck. She hadn't touched herself in so long. She had wanted to stop thinking about Ash every time she wanted something sexual, and when she'd been unable to turn her mind in a different direction, she'd just forced herself to stop all together.

"Ash, I can't do this for very long."

Reaching up, Ash gripped the back of Chris' thighs to help hold her still. "You'll get my mouth on you in a minute, don't worry."

Groaning, Chris closed her eyes. Her entire body became wobbly, and she was unsure of her footing, but with Ash keeping hold of her tightly, Chris knew she wouldn't fall. Even if she came hard, Ash would catch her. That was why she was there, wasn't it? Releasing those tensions, Chris focused on the feel of her fingers between her legs, on the sparks of pleasure as they ran through her. If she did this much longer, Ash would have to get second best.

"I'm not sure..." Chris trailed off, having to work overtime to keep herself focused on words. "...I'm going to last much longer."

"Don't hold back." Ash sounded so sure, so confident.

Chris loved when she did that. When she was pure strength in her vulnerabilities.

"Keep going," Ash encouraged. "Come apart for me."

Chris clenched her eyes tight. She focused on her body and what it was telling her, which was so different than anything before. She focused only on the sensations coursing through her, on Ash's hands against her, on the sound of her breathing in the still quiet room, on the scent of her arousal. All of it consumed her. There was nothing else.

Moving swiftly, Chris reached for Ash's head as her hips

jerked with a start. She rolled her fingers around again. The last few pulses of her body were pooling together, and there wouldn't be an end to it. She tightened her grasp on Ash's head, clenching her jaw. She didn't want this. She wanted Ash's mouth right where her fingers were. She wanted Ash.

But it was too late.

Chris crashed through her orgasm, her body jerking with a start. She released her fingers from her body and cringed as she tried to hold back. Ash pressed her mouth right against Chris' clit, sucking and twirling her tongue wildly. Chris gasped, heat searing through her. She was up on her toes, holding onto Ash's head, her shoulders, anywhere she could grasp onto.

Ash didn't slow down. She dove in, her mouth pressed tightly between Chris' legs as she teased her. Chris barely had a chance to breathe, her chest so tight from the force of her body trying to tightly control everything about this moment. Chris keened, her voice leaving her lips in a wild cry of pleasure. Still, Ash didn't stop.

She was going to combust. Chris swore it would happen. Her legs shook, barely holding her up. Ash dug her fingers in tightly because Chris was sure that she was rocking her entire body in some scary way like she'd topple over any moment.

"Ash," Chris cried, her voice breaking.

Staying true, Ash continued to tease her, suck her, bring her closer. Chris was so screwed. She dug her nails into Ash's scalp as she careened through another orgasm. Her knees gave out, and Ash jerked quickly, grabbing onto Chris' hips to help ease her down to the couch. Chris landed with a thud.

She threw her arm over her face. Her heart raced so fast she was worried it'd come out of her chest or cause a heart attack. Chris took deep breaths to slow it down. Her legs were numb—jelly—and she wasn't sure she'd be able to stand and support herself again. She giggled. Then she laughed, the full belly sound of it erupting from her chest and through her throat and out her mouth.

"What the hell, Ash?"

"Wicked tongues and all that." Ash sounded so damn pleased with herself.

Chris didn't have the wherewithal to move her arm and look Ash in the face, but she imagined the satisfied look. It would be beautiful. Finally Chris moved her arm away and turned her head to find Ash grinning like the Cheshire cat.

"Good?"

"Yes." Chris nodded, her own lips moving to match Ash's grin.

"I'd love to try that in your office."

"Oh my god. No!"

"A girl can dream, can't she? You might find some of that in there." Ash pointed at the flash drive on the table. "But you'll have to wait to read it."

"It's not another YA novel?"

"Oh. Now." Ash's cheeks flushed.

Chris loved it. She chuckled lowly. She covered her face again, rubbing her hands up and down her cheeks. "Your office might be better."

"Oh no. That house is never empty."

"We're not having sex at work," Chris reiterated.

"Like I said, a girl can dream. Now." Ash moved upward and walked her fingers over Chris' stomach to her breast, flicking her nipple in the process, before landing on Chris' lips. "Where is the strap?"

"You want the strap-on after that?"

"Oh yes, most definitely." Ash's voice sounded so husky, absolutely filled with desire.

Chris wasn't sure how, but she was ready to go again. Not that she thought she could sit up even. And putting that thing on for Ash was going to be a different story entirely. Ash would have to sit on her. That would be how it'd go.

"Chris...?"

"Top drawer of the nightstand. It's already cleaned and ready."

Ash raised an eyebrow at her.

Chris shrugged. "I don't like dirty toys."

"Good for us, then."

"You get it. I'm going to meld myself with this couch for a little longer."

"Perfect," Ash purred.

Chris relaxed while Ash disappeared. She couldn't believe this. Ash actually wanted her. And it wasn't just because she was convenient like when they'd gone to The Office. Ash had shown up, came and found her, and poured out her heart. Chris couldn't stop smiling. This was what she had hoped for. This was everything she could have wanted.

"I figured I could just let you lay there, legs spread, and sexy as hell."

"Huh?" Chris turned her head up to find Ash, naked, with the strap on around her hips, the cock jutting from her. "Fuck."

"Hmmm." Ash smirked. "Yes, exactly."

"D-did you lube that?" Chris stuttered. "Because it's been a long time since I've taken one."

"Of course. You don't think I'm a jerk, do you?" Ash moved to kneel between Chris' legs. "But this way you don't have to move at all."

"Fuck," Chris whispered again. Words had completely left her.

"Exactly," Ash repeated, laughing lightly.

She bent forward, using her tongue to lick Chris straight up. Chris shivered as she hummed her pleasure. She was completely enthralled with everything Ash did.

"You ready?"

"Not sure I'll ever be." But Chris widened her knees and threw her hands over her head. She gripped onto the pillow and waited for Ash to begin.

It was slow at first. Ash would push in and then pull back

slightly. She'd push in more and then pull back. As soon as she got the tip in, Chris felt so full, but she knew there was more to come. She raised her hips up to meet Ash's gentle probing. Instinctively, Chris knew Ash was going slow for her benefit, and she appreciated it. She hadn't lied when she'd said it had been a while. Andry had never been too fond of it.

Chris groaned, biting her lip as she pushed her shoulders into the couch. This was sensational. Ash leaned over her, kissing her lips before pushing the toy in even more. Chris gasped.

"Is that all right?"

"Yes," Chris hissed back. "Yes, slow and steady."

Ash didn't answer as she moved again. She pressed kisses to Chris' neck, to the tops of her breasts, then back up her neck to her lips again. Chris deepened the kiss, drawing Ash's tongue out to tangle with her own.

Pulling back slightly, Chris murmured, "don't stop" before diving back in for another kiss.

Willingly, Chris surrendered to this moment. She laid herself bare in front of Ash and let Ash be in control, something that she struggled with every moment of her life. She held on to Ash's hips as she rocked them, starting a slow and steady rhythm just like Chris had requested. She never sped up. Chris moved her hand down, swiping her fingers over her engorged clit.

"Damn that's sexy," Ash stated, as she leaned on her hands and looked down at their bodies, her hair falling over her shoulder to curtain Chris' view.

It was sexy. Chris had never felt so connected with someone before. Or at least it had been a really long time since it had happened. She loved it. "Keep going."

"I'm not stopping," Ash answered.

Chris could feel herself once again pulling together toward orgasm. This would have to be it though, at least until she rested. She needed to catch her breath and her bearings, and as much as Ash had suggested it in jest, Chris wanted to sleep with her. Not sex. Not teasing like this. Chris just wanted to hold Ash against her chest, curled around her in slumber.

"I'm close." Chris held her breath. Her stomach tightened. She looked up into Ash's eyes as she was awash with a smooth kind of pleasure. The kind she'd longed years for and never wanted to give up.

"Don't hold back."

"I'm not," Chris whispered. She couldn't break eye contact with Ash. Not this time. Looking up into those bright blue eyes, the happiness reflected in them, the joy, the simplicity but also the complications of this moment, Chris allowed herself to feel. "Come up here and take that damn thing off."

Ash laughed, and the smile never left her face as she pulled out and divested herself of the strap. She set it on the coffee table and then moved to straddle Chris again.

"Uh uh. Up here."

Ash's grin faltered for only a moment before she started to move. Chris stayed put as she waited for Ash to hover just above her head. This was what she'd been waiting for.

"One tongue for another?" Chris teased.

"Get to it," Ash answered.

"Yes, ma'am."

Chris dove in. She licked Ash firmly, savoring that familiar sweet and savory flavor. She hummed and closed her eyes at the pureness of it all. She twirled her tongue around Ash's clit before diving her tongue as far into her as she could. Ash was so wet. Her juices coated Chris' chin and cheeks.

Chris put everything she had into this moment. She played it like it was the last chance she was going to get with Ash. It probably wasn't, but with the way her life was, she couldn't be sure. She wrapped her arms around Ash's thighs and held onto her creamy smooth skin.

Crying out on top of her, Ash rutted against Chris' mouth wildly. Chris almost didn't have to do anything except hold her mouth in one spot. Sucking a little harder, Chris gave everything she had in that moment to Ash. Her body ached, her muscles bone tired from the long week she'd had, but she couldn't let this opportunity pass up. Despite how many times she told herself she wouldn't let Ash back into her heart, she'd jumped at the first chance she had.

And she didn't regret it.

"Chris," Ash's voice cracked.

Looking straight up at Ash's face peeking through the movement of her breasts, Chris watched as she crumbled. Her entire body shook with pleasure. More juices slicked against Chris' skin, but she didn't move away, not yet, not until she knew Ash needed her to.

It wasn't much longer until Ash shifted off Chris and sat precariously on the edge of the couch. Chris ran her fingers up and down her arm as they looked at each other in quiet reverence.

"I'm so glad I showed up tonight. I was almost a chickenshit and left."

"I'm happy you didn't," Chris responded. "I'm so happy you didn't."

Her heart filled, that old sense of hope tugging at her again. Was this really what she wanted? Chris was pretty sure it was, at least for now. She could handle this for now. It was when she started to think about someday that she struggled, that she started to self-sabotage, that her nerves kicked into high gear and she lost control over herself.

"Can we go lay in bed?" Chris asked suddenly, needing to be so much closer to Ash. Anything that would help silence the fears rambling around inside her. "I just want to hold you."

Ash's smile was brilliant. "Yeah, of course. That can be the chill part of our Netflix and chill."

"Jesus." Chris smacked her forehead and rolled her eyes. She was an idiot to the core, and she wasn't sure how she'd ever get over her own awkwardness.

Pulling herself to sit up, Chris shook her head. She couldn't believe that she'd said that. It had worked, but she could scarcely believe it.

"Come on." Snagging Ash's hand, Chris wove their fingers together.

They walked comfortably toward Chris' bedroom. She slipped onto the mattress and settled with Ash next to her, arms wrapped around each other. This was what Chris had longed for the few times they'd been together. The tender touch, the closeness, the connection between them—it was what she craved. And this was how she got intimacy, far more than sex. Chris had forgotten that about relationships. It'd been so long since she'd been in one where it was present.

Kissing just under Ash's ear, Chris didn't stop there. She pressed sweet kisses anywhere she could reach on Ash's body. She wouldn't give this up for the world if she could avoid it. She just had to keep on the path that she was working toward— sober, vulnerable, and strong.

CHAPTER
Thirty-Two

THIS TIME the drive to their chosen date night location wasn't filled to the brim with apprehension. The air felt clear and bright. Ash got out of her car and met Chris at the front, wrapping their fingers together tightly. She didn't want to let go. Last time there had been something that had held her back, and when Chris had left unexpectedly, she'd been devastated yes, but also somewhat relieved.

This time came without all that baggage.

Ash and Chris sat down, and ordered their drinks and food. Ash couldn't stop looking at Chris. She nearly couldn't believe that they were finally on a date. That she was seeing someone who wasn't Mari, that she was willingly throwing herself into another relationship.

"What?" Chris asked, a hint of disbelief in her tone.

Shaking her head, Ash leaned back in her chair and smiled. "Nothing."

"There's not *nothing* in that look," Chris accused.

"Fine. I was just thinking about how happy I am. Honestly," Ash added at Chris' deepened look of disbelief. "I never thought I'd be in a relationship again."

"You like to pine, don't you?" Chris narrowed her eyes at Ash.

"Sometimes." Ash giggled lightly. "You would too if you were me."

"If I had found the love of my life you mean?" Chris' words weren't said in anger, but Ash detected the note of sadness in them.

Reaching forward, Ash snagged Chris' hand with her own. She didn't want to let go ever. She traced her thumb over the smooth skin she found. "That's not what I said."

"I love Andry, but I'll agree that she wasn't the love of my life. It's very clear that we didn't have what you and Mari had." Chris tensed. Ash could feel it in her muscles from across the table.

Frowning, Ash did the only thing she could think of. She let go of Chris' hand and moved around the table to sit next to her. She dropped a hand onto Chris' thigh and squeezed her knee. The sides of their bodies pressed together snuggly. Ash looked into Chris' deep brown eyes, into the hurt that still lingered there, the shame at her past and her failed marriage. Ash kissed her cheek. Then her other cheek.

"Sometimes our hearts are bigger than we expect them to be."

"How did you get so wise? Seriously? I met you as a snarky teenager who wanted nothing to do with any authority figure. You wanted nothing to do with me, and I only marginally wanted anything to do with you. And here we are, seventeen years later, holding hands, kissing—I don't know how we got here."

"Kismet?" Ash asked. "Fate? Desire? Second chances?"

"Second chances implies there was a first chance, and no thank you to sixteen year old you. That was..." Chris shuddered "...just no thank you."

Ash giggled. "Good, I'm glad we're agreed on that. No attraction until this year."

"None at all on my part. Trust me. That was the height of my relationship with Andry. We were doing so well then." Chris covered Ash's hand with her own, curling her fingers. "You didn't have a crush on me back then?"

"Hell no."

Chris snorted lightly. "I don't think many students had crushes on me."

"You might be surprised." Ash leaned in more. "This former student definitely has a crush on you now."

Chris turned, and Ash stole her lips. The kiss was brief but deep. Ash didn't want to tempt herself too much since the girls would be home that night and they only had a few hours for dinner. She'd much prefer for Chris to stay the night with her, but that was impossible right now.

"That's just weird," Chris murmured. "I'm not sure I'll ever get used to that one."

"Do you just ignore that part of our connection?"

"When your mouth is on mine...or elsewhere? Yeah, I do just ignore that part of things."

Ash chuckled, her voice low in her throat, aiming for seduction. "Oh Dr. Murphey, how very vanilla of you."

Chris blushed hard. Her entire face turned red. Ash took Chris' hand and slid it into her lap, pressing their clasped hands between her legs.

"I never would have pegged you—oh wait, did that."

"Ash," Chris hissed. "Are you serious right now?"

"Serious as a doorknob." Ash kissed Chris' cheek again. "But if you want me to stop, I will."

Chris groaned. Her eyelids fluttered shut, and she rested her forehead on Ash's shoulder. Ash reached up with her free hand and threaded her fingers into Chris' hair, massaging the back of her neck and the base of her skull. She had so many damn knots in her muscles. Ash really needed to pay more attention to those.

"Don't stop," Chris whispered.

"Don't stop massaging or don't stop the raunchy flirting?"

A giggle bubbled up from Chris, her body shaking against Ash's as they held each other.

"Don't stop either," Chris answered confidently. She lifted her head and kissed Ash's lips lightly. "But do stop when the waitress comes back."

"Fine." Ash gave her a mock pout. "But back to what I was saying, I never would have pegged you for being so vanilla."

Chris shrugged. "I live a very boring life, what can I say?"

"Say we can spice it up."

"I think you've already accomplished that."

"This?" Ash moved their hands more firmly between her legs, flattening Chris' against her crotch and hoping she would do something about it. "This is nothing."

Chris rolled her fingers twice before pushing in and increasing the pressure. She didn't let up. Ash's clit pulsed with pleasure, and she hummed as she pressed a kiss just under Chris' ear.

"If I could take you home right now, I would." Ash flicked her tongue against the lobe on Chris' ear. "And I'd take you."

"You're not going to make tonight by myself easy, are you?"

"There's always the phone."

Chris groaned. "You know how much I hate phone sex."

"Ah, but my dear Dr. Murphey, there might not be another option."

Ash pulled away slightly when their waitress appeared with their food just as Chris had requested, but she stayed sitting next to Chris instead of moving back to where she had been. She liked this better. They could touch this way and with far more subtlety.

"I did want to talk to you about something, though." Apprehension filled her now. It wasn't that she thought Chris would disagree with her. It was more she was scared what it would mean for both of them moving forward.

"Sure." Chris cut into her steak. "What about?"

"Avonlee and Rhubie."

"Yes, can you tell me why you named your daughter, Rhubarb?"

Ash's jaw dropped, her cheeks heating from embarrassment. "Mari chose her name. Mari being short for Marigold, and she always said marigolds and rhubarb go hand in hand. I don't know, I'm not a gardener. That was her thing."

Chris chuckled, her nose wrinkling. "Both are certainly odd names for people."

"I'm sure you've seen your fair share of odd names."

"I have," Chris agreed.

"Anyway, about the girls, I'm not sure I'm ready for them to know yet."

"About us you mean?" Chris always was direct, but her tone didn't harbor any bad feelings that Ash could detect.

"Yeah, about us. Avonlee is finally calming down. I don't really want to upset her again and send her back down in a new spiral of chaos."

"I understand." Chris reached for Ash's hand, twining their fingers. "I really do. I would like to tell Katie, but she won't tell anyone. She kept Isla and Andry a secret, not that she was asked to, she just did it."

"She did?" For some reason, that surprised Ash. Katie was older for sure, but that was her mom.

"She knew what it would mean if it got out that her mom was dating her teacher."

"I'm sorry, say that again?" Ash already knew, but she was curious if Chris was willing to admit it.

"Oh." Chris pursed her lips. "Isla used to work for Andry. When they started dating, Isla applied for a job and I hired her."

"Why?"

"So they could be together."

"You really are just one big teddy bear under all that hard exterior, aren't you?"

Chris raised a shoulder and dropped it, focusing on her food. "I take care of the people I love."

"That you do." Ash kissed Chris' knuckles. "I'm just not ready for that fallout yet."

"You're not sure if we're ready for it."

Ash's lips parted in surprise. Again, Chris' directness took her. "A little of both, actually. Until we know where this is going, for sure, I don't see a need to tell them."

"Are we going to talk about my job at all in this conversation?" Chris took a sip of her drink, but that same tension that was there before was back.

Ash hated that she was the reason for it. "We probably should."

"I can land in some serious hot water for this."

"It can't be unheard of for a teacher to date a parent."

"It's not unheard of, no." Chris pursed her lips. "But for a principal...we're on a whole different level in some ways. And I've made some enemies in the last year by standing up for those people that I love."

"Have you?" Ash raised an eyebrow. "I feel there's a story here."

"That story is for another day and another time, and in a lot of ways, isn't my story to tell. But I don't have as much pull or as many friends in the district as I used to." Chris leaned back in her chair. "It does worry me to date a parent."

"I'd hate to transfer the kids to another school simply because we're dating."

"I'm not sure it'd be wise for Avonlee. She's got one year left at Irving, and then she'll be in junior high. Think we can keep it a secret that long?" Chris pulled her lower lip into her mouth and sucked on it.

Was she nervous about all this as well?

Ash slowly shook her head. "No. No, I don't think we can. I don't want to. And let's face it, we were practically making out in the middle of a restaurant. I'm not sure either of us wants that."

"Good." Chris grinned. "I don't either."

"But I do want this to last," Ash whispered that part. It was the first time she'd said it out loud, and she wasn't willing to go back on it now. "I want us to last."

"Then keep up that delicious flirting you were doing." Chris winked.

"I'm serious."

"I am, too."

"Be careful what you ask for. Because if you're going to keep this up, I'm going to demand phone sex later."

"Done and done." Chris winked, then she went back to eating her steak like nothing had ever happened.

Taking a risk, Ash slid her hand under the table and right against Chris' crotch. Chris radiated heat from between her legs. Ash stroked slowly, first one finger and then two. Could she make Chris orgasm right here in the restaurant? Probably. But would Chris let her take it that far? Probably not. Still, Ash could tease with the best of them.

"Are we ever going to try that desk thing?"

Chris choked. Ash watched as she coughed and spluttered, reaching for her drink to chug a few good sips from it before glaring at Ash. "We're not at the school."

"My office then. Come on, we can fantasize, can't we?"

"Oh sweet Jesus."

"Call out to him all you want, Chris, but when my face is between your legs I'm pretty sure I'm your master." Ash pushed her fingers in hard, wishing that her hand was underneath Chris' clothes, but this would have to do. She nuzzled her face against Chris' neck, drawing in her scent.

Chris squeaked. She turned slowly to face Ash and gave her best glare.

"So, what are we going to master tonight?"

"Ash," Chris hissed.

"You do know that using that principal voice on me is only making this way worse for both of us, right?" Ash fought back the laugh that wanted to erupt from her. She really couldn't help herself.

Chris moved in suddenly, capturing Ash's lips in a deep kiss. She reached up and cupped Ash's cheeks, holding her in place.

Their tongues tangled, and Ash could taste the saltiness from the steak, the garlic from the mash. She hummed her satisfaction as she pushed into Chris, giving as much as she received.

Ash honestly couldn't have asked for more than this. Chris was so understanding, so protective, and so very present in this moment. It was all she could have ever wanted in a relationship. Nipping at Chris' lower lip, Ash pulled back.

"As much as I would like to eat something other than what's on my plate, we should probably focus on dinner. Especially since I know I won't get to eat anything else tonight." She sent Chris a sorrowful look, but one that had enough tease in it that she hoped Chris understood where she was coming from.

"Fuck, Ash."

"Does that mean a yes to phone sex tonight?"

Chris narrowed her eyes before closing them and nodding. "But you're going to have to be patient with me."

"I can always learn something new if you can."

"I don't know what to do with you half the time."

"I will honestly tell you that anything you do with me will be perfect. So long as you're there, Chris, that's all I need." Ash meant it too. She leaned in with one more kiss and then eased up on her flirting. She had pushed the lines a lot that night, and she was going to get what she wanted. Which was Chris and sex in the same sentence, even if it was over a video call. Oh, she should probably not mention the video part just yet. Plying Chris with more kisses first would be best for that.

CHAPTER
Thirty-Three

"I LOVE HER," Chris murmured out loud to herself.

She'd been thinking it for weeks now, but she hadn't dared say it out loud. And even now, she was only saying it to herself in the mirror of her bathroom as she leaned over the sink. What was she thinking? This couldn't possibly be love, could it?

Chris had worked so hard to put herself back together. She was sober now for two years, three months and three days. Had anyone asked her two years ago, she'd have said it was impossible. She still didn't believe it most days. But here she was, still sober. Still trucking along attending meetings and taking everything one day at a time so she didn't screw anyone else up in the process.

And now she was in love?

This wasn't part of the plan. Chris wasn't sure she could handle it either. She and Ash had found a nice balance the last month and a half. They had a date every week, and every two weeks they would stay the night together. The phone sex was off the hook, and Chris had learned how to enjoy it when she could. Every once in a while, she'd snuck over in the middle of the night and snuck out before morning so the girls wouldn't see her. But did she really want more than that?

Was she ready for it?

She'd also been asking herself that for the last six weeks. She'd decided she was ready for more than a quick night in the sheets with Ash, but saying those three little words would change a lot. There was no getting out of that. Still, saying them out loud to herself made her nervous enough. She had one failed marriage under her belt, she didn't need another.

What would Andry do in this situation?

That was a really good question because when they'd dated, they had dove in with both feet and didn't look back until it was too late. Chris wouldn't make the same mistake twice. At least not that one. Other mistakes she made more times than she dared to count.

Sighing, Chris pushed away from the mirror and walked out into her living room. Mel and Andry sat on the couch, waiting for her to return. When they had started doing these regular friends dates again, she wasn't sure about it, but she liked them. Even with all the history between her and Andry, they had found an easy friendship together, close to what they used to have. Chris had longed for that connection again.

Plopping onto the couch, Chris snagged the candied bacon wrapped little smoky and popped it whole into her mouth. She tried to fade into the background of the conversation going on between Mel and Andry because she didn't want them to figure her out. Not that they wouldn't anyway. She'd known them far too long to avoid that. But maybe if she kept to herself, then she could—

"Chris!" Mel called. "Are you back from outer space yet?"

"With that sad look upon my face?" Chris fired back, a crooked grin on her lips. Yup, she could steer this conversation in a direction she wanted it to go and away from where she didn't want it to go.

"Funny, funny. Har har." Mel rolled her eyes. "But seriously, are you paying attention?"

"Of course," Chris lied. Then she backtracked and shook her

head. "No, I was distracted. These really are my favorites." Chris leaned forward to grab another snack.

They'd opted to stay in her apartment instead of going out. In part because Chris was so edgy, but also because she wanted the comfort of her own home. For some reason she wanted the quiet tonight, unlike what she usually needed to calm herself.

"Chris?" Andry pushed.

Chris lifted her gaze to meet Andry's. "What?"

"What's going on?"

"Nothing."

"As you have said to me many times over the years...where's the poop, Chris?"

"There is no poop. I don't know what you're talking about." Her defenses were coming in two-fold. Chris cringed at that thought and shoved it into the back of her mind. She hated that she'd been caught off-guard by how astute they were.

"Oh, this is going to be good." Mel snagged the bowl of chips and leaned back in her chair like she was about to watch the game. "Take it away, Andry."

Chris narrowed her eyes at both of them. What was this? Some sort of mind fuck they were doing on her? Chris wasn't going to have any of it.

"How's Ash?" Andry poked her nose into the business Chris had been steadily avoiding.

She was screwed if they were starting there. Chris clenched her jaw and crossed her arms over her chest in a deep frown. Why couldn't they just leave well enough alone already. She sighed heavily and refused to make eye contact with either of them.

"You two are still...dating, right?"

"Yes," Chris mumbled, knowing she wasn't getting out of this any time soon. She was going to have to suffer through the inquisition and hope that she made it to the other side in one piece, and without revealing more than she wanted to.

"And how is that going?" Andry asked nicely, like she wasn't prying into Chris' personal life.

Chris pouted. She considered Andry more of a friend now than her ex-wife, but that still didn't mean she wanted to talk about this. Even with Mel she would hesitate. Wrinkling her nose, Chris closed her eyes. Her cheeks heated even though she didn't want them to.

"That well, I see," Andry added with a slight chuckle.

"Oh come on," Chris whined. "You don't have to know everything."

"No, but I do want the end to this one. You kind of promised it to me that day when you called me."

"What day?" Chris focused on Andry, confused as to what she could possibly be talking about.

"That morning when you figured out who Ash was, well, the first time. You held back on telling me she was a former student."

Damn it. Chris had called Andry, because Andry had seen her out with Ash that night and so there would be very little explanation about everything that had gone on. Chris' cheeks flushed with heat, embarrassment sweeping through her and taking over her entire being. What she would do without close friends, she wasn't sure, but sometimes she wished they would mind their own damn business.

"Oh, that day."

"Yes, *that* day." Andry was laughing again as she grabbed some more snacks.

"So, how's Ash doing?"

"She's good," Chris choked out. She flicked her gaze to Mel to see what she was doing. Mel sat comfortably in her chair, eating chips and keeping her eyes directly on Chris. Whelp, there was no escaping this now.

"Just good?" Mel pushed in more.

The tension in Chris' chest tightened. She'd been texting Ash on and off throughout the whole night, keeping in touch with her. She'd only stopped when both Mel and Andry had commented about her being on her phone way too much for their little get together. Chris hadn't even noticed, and normally she would be the first one to.

"Yup. She's good," Chris repeated. Why was she holding back on telling them so much? It could be because she thought Ash was the first who deserved to know, but that didn't really strike Chris as the reason. No, this was something else. Something that tugged deep inside her that she couldn't put words to no matter how hard she wanted to.

"Just good." Mel nodded slowly. "What does that mean?"

"It means she's doing good. Avonlee is doing good. Rhubie is doing good. We're all doing good."

"We?" Andry jumped right in on that one.

"Ugh. Yes. We. All of us. The whole lot of us." Chris bristled. Why was she letting this get to her so much? "We haven't told Avonlee and Rhubie that we're dating yet."

"I think that's wise," Andry commented, sipping her Shirley Temple. "They're pretty young to be sharing that with them so early into a relationship."

Their relationship felt as though it had been going on a whole lot longer than six official weeks. To be fair, it was closer to six months of figuring this out. They were about to head full force into summer, and Chris had no idea what that meant for their relationship or how they might possibly find more time with the girls being around even more than they were before.

"Right, so we're not telling them yet."

"But you will soon?" Mel asked.

Chris shrugged. "Someday, I suppose."

"So when does this move from being on the down low to being something you can shout about?" Mel was so direct sometimes.

Chris nearly choked again, but she stopped herself. She stared wide-eyed at Mel, wondering how she could choose her words carefully enough to get through this one. Chris swallowed the lump forming in her throat. She didn't want to lie to them, ever, so she wouldn't. But she also didn't feel as though she could say that she didn't want to talk about it and have them drop the subject.

"We don't hide our relationship, except when at the school and in front of the girls. I think that's reasonable."

"It is." Andry shot Mel a dirty look.

Was there something going on between them that Chris was missing? She hated not understanding everything in the silent communications that seemed to plague every verbal conversation. She was usually quite adept at reading those.

"But maybe at the end of the summer?" Andry followed up Mel's question with one of her own.

Chris sighed heavily. "Why do you want to know so much?"

"We're curious. You talk about her all the time. You text her all the time." Mel winked. "I may very well call you head over heels in love."

Chris blanched. The color drained from her face as a cold clammy feeling came over her. This had been what she wanted to avoid. Damn them for being so good at this. She hated that she couldn't control her reactions better. She would have reached for another little smoky, but she knew her hands would shake. It would only be another tell that Mel had hit the nail on her head that had fallen straight over her heels in love.

She was screwed.

"Chris?" Andry asked, her tone much softer and more concerned. "Are you okay?"

Quick. She had to say something, anything. Chris had to come up with some kind of excuse or reason as to why she was behaving and reacting this way. Something that would be better than Mel was right. She was completely in love with Ash. She hadn't thought of much else in the past few weeks, and she wasn't ready for that to be processed yet.

"Chris," Andry tried again. "You just had a whole conversation in your head. Do you want to let us in on it?"

"Not really," Chris mumbled. She clenched her eyes. Then she rubbed her hands up and down her cheeks roughly. She had to get a hold of herself.

Silence permeated the room for the first time that night. Guilt racked through Chris because it was her fault. Both Mel and Andry stared at her like she was going to snap. She had to assuage them, tell them she was fine. But she wasn't, not really. She was sitting on this giant revelation that she'd barely had real time to process.

"You love her, don't you," Mel said, her voice gentle this time, all of the teasing washed out of it.

Chris nodded, her lips pressed together hard. "But I don't know anything else."

"Oh, Chris." Andry moved to sit next to Chris on the couch and wrapped an arm around her shoulders. "Stop freaking out."

Chris snorted and shook her head. "Easier said than done."

"You remember freaking out when you told me that you loved me?" Andry ran her hand down Chris' arm. "You stuttered so hard you couldn't make the words out."

Chris glared at her. "Yeah, well, my idiocy reigns supreme."

Andry smiled. "I thought it was adorable. Still do."

Mel moved in on the other side. "Have you told her yet?"

"No, and I don't plan to."

They shared a look over Chris. She wasn't exactly happy about what she read in that look, but it would have to do for now because she wasn't going to poke the two bears surrounding her. Chris clenched her jaw.

"I think I'll keep things exactly as they are."

"Are you sure about that?" Andry asked.

"Are you scared she doesn't love you back?"

Chris froze. She hadn't even considered that. She'd been so caught up in her own drama and feelings that she hadn't even begun to wonder if Ash felt the same or different.

Mel frowned. "Shit, I didn't mean to bring that up."

Was she seriously this easy for them to read? Chris pinched

the bridge of her nose and sighed. "Look, I don't know how she feels. I have no desire to find out how she feels. All I know is that the way things are going right now are good, and I don't want to fuck that up."

"Chris," Andry said her name so calmly. "Love doesn't screw things up."

Chris sent her a flat look. "Oh really, Ms. Murphey?"

Andry paled and a slight frown formed on her lips. Chris knew it was a dirty move to make, but she did have a point with it.

"Sorry," Chris said immediately. "That was...uncalled for. But the point being, love does screw things up."

"Love doesn't," Andry defended. "People love, but they aren't love themselves. People are humans, and all humans make mistakes."

"I still don't understand how you could forgive me for half the shit I did."

"I've forgiven most of it." Andry shifted on the couch, moving a bit farther away. "It wasn't easy, Chris, but I'm glad we're at where we're at now. Aren't you?"

Mulling through that one, Chris had to agree. She nodded and snagged Andry's hand and squeezed lightly. "Yeah, I am. And I'm so happy you've got Isla."

Andry's cheeks pinked. "I am too."

"Which reminds me." Chris turned on Mel. "How did Esther's hearing go?"

Mel grinned broadly. "She won. She won full custody, and they increased his child support and spousal support, not that he'll ever pay that, but it's court ordered now. He'll struggle to run for office again if he doesn't."

"I'm so glad!" Chris leaned in to give Mel a hug. "Why aren't you out celebrating with her?"

"We did." Mel winked. "We definitely celebrated."

"Good." Chris pushed herself off the couch, mostly to escape more questions about Ash. She went to the kitchen to get another drink. As soon as she was alone, she let out a breath. She was in love, there was no doubt of that. The only question that remained was what she was going to do about that. And for now, the answer was simple.

Nothing.

Thirty-Four

"I WANT TO TELL THE KIDS." Ash rubbed her palms over her thighs, trying to dispel the clamminess. She was so nervous bringing this up. All summer they had fallen into an amazing pattern for their relationship, but she wanted so much more. And she couldn't shake the nerves that rolled around in her body.

"Tell the kids what?" Chris said, wrapping her arm over Ash's shoulders and tugging her into her side as they watched something on the television.

Ash wasn't even paying attention to whatever it was. She just wanted this quiet time with Chris to have a serious conversation about potentially moving their relationship forward. It was a big step for both of them, but Ash was sure they were ready. Steadying herself, Ash turned toward Chris to see her reaction. "That we're dating."

"Why would you want to do that?" Chris' tone was sharp.

It tore Ash's hope down a notch or two. If this really wasn't something that Chris wanted, then Ash was about to find out. She'd have to figure out where to go from there. Well, they'd have to figure it out together because she definitely wanted more than this.

"So I can see you more," Ash retorted, her defenses already coming up more than she anticipated. Didn't Chris want that, too? Or had Ash let everything slide into too much comfort that they wouldn't take any more steps forward.

"Well, I'd love that." Chris gave her half-cocky grin, locking their eyes together. Then she stopped smiling. She must have seen something in Ash's gaze, something that Ash herself was unaware of. Because Chris' demeanor changed in an instant. She became serious. Chris covered Ash's hand and tightened her grasp. "You want that, right?"

"Of course I do," Ash whispered. "I'm the one who brought it up."

"Right." Chris frowned. She glanced at the television one last time, but then she focused entirely on Ash.

It was unnerving to be in the center of Chris' gaze sometimes. Ash had to prepare herself again to dive into the conversation. She could easily bow out of it if she wanted, but she didn't. Canting her head to the side, Ash smiled. "I want to tell the girls about you."

"I'm really not sure that's a good idea." Chris shifted uncomfortably.

A weight settled onto Ash's chest. What was Chris' hesitation? They'd had a great five months together in a relationship. Certainly this was a natural progression of a relationship. She'd told her girls she was dating someone, but she hadn't told them who. They were curious and excited. They were happy. Avonlee had been wary at first, but when she'd gotten used to it, that calmed down. Ash suspected it would be the same when it was revealed who she was dating.

"Why wouldn't it be a good idea?"

"We could wait until Avonlee goes to junior high."

"You want to wait a whole year?" Shock stole through Ash. She hadn't expected that answer.

Chris shrugged.

"Do you think we won't be together in a year?"

"No, no, I don't think that at all." Chris rushed to snag Ash's hand again, holding her tight. "I want to be with you in a year."

"What aren't you saying, Chris?" Ash needed to know. She couldn't keep this inside her anymore. "Because I want to be with you, and I want to share you with my family."

"I just...I don't think it's a good idea. Not yet."

"Why not?" Ash pushed. Chris was still skirting around the issue, and it was bugging her. Why wouldn't Chris just say what she meant?

"We haven't even told each other that we love each other yet, and you want to tell the girls that we're dating?"

Ash stilled. She lifted her chin, replaying all the memories she had readily at her access. Surely they had said it, hadn't they? She pressed her lips together hard, trying to come up with a specific moment in time and frowned. She couldn't bring up one instance where they'd exchanged those words.

"You know what, you're right," Ash started. She scooted back into the couch, putting some space between them. "I guess we shouldn't tell the girls if we don't love each other."

"What?" Chris straightened her back. She reached for Ash.

"Well, if we don't love each other, then you're entirely right. We shouldn't tell them." Ash stopped, looking deep into Chris' eyes. "But I do love you. I thought it was pretty obvious by this point."

"Obvious?" Chris choked on the word, her voice vanishing at the end of it.

"Yeah. I mean, we spend all our free time texting and calling. And if we can get together, we do." Ash shrugged, knowing this was probably a bit of a mean way to have this conversation, but had Chris really thought that she didn't care? "But I guess if it's nothing more than that, like I thought it was, then yeah, we shouldn't tell the girls."

"I'm confused." Chris narrowed her gaze, the dark brown of her eyes hard to see. "Are you saying you don't want to tell them now?"

"I'm saying that I love you, Chris. I've already said it once, but I'll say it as many times as you need to hear what I'm saying. I love you."

"I..." Chris paused, her eyes flashing with realization. "You love me?"

"Yeah, I thought it was pretty obvious. Sorry. I would have said it sooner if I'd been paying attention. Yes, I love you," Ash repeated again just to make herself completely clear.

"I didn't know."

"I assumed you did." Ash cupped Chris' cheek. "I'm sorry I didn't say it before. But let's make it as clear as possible, okay?"

Chris nodded.

"I love you. You're stunning, you're amazing, you have a heart of gold, you're strong, and I don't know if it's possible that I could have fallen in love with anyone else. You're the one for me." Ash smiled, the full truth of her words hitting her at once, and she leaned in, kissing Chris on the lips. Everything she had said was true.

"I love you," Chris whispered, a smile blossoming. "For so many reasons."

"Really?" Ash couldn't stop grinning. Her heart swelled with hearing those words. She hadn't realized how necessary they were.

"Yeah. So let's tell them. I'd prefer to wait until Avonlee was out of my school, but I don't really want to wait another year."

"Then let's tell them." Ash moved in swiftly, covering Chris' mouth with her own. She deepened the kiss immediately.

Chris moved her hands up to cup Ash's cheeks and then slid them around the back of her neck, tugging her in closer and keeping a steady hold of her. Ash loved this. The power, the control that Chris used on her every time they were intimate. It made her feel like her place in Chris' life was solidified.

They stayed there for minutes on end, Ash completely losing herself in the kiss. She loved how Chris could rile her up in one look, in one touch, and tonight was no different. With the barriers down, with their emotions laid out for each other, it was all that much more intense. Ash shifted, leaning into Chris and nipping on her lip, speeding up the kiss, intensifying it in every way she knew how.

"I love you," she whispered, and she pushed Chris back. "Fuck, I love you. I never thought I'd say that to anyone again."

Chris hummed her approval, her eyes fluttering closed. "Me either."

"But it feels so damn good to say it." Ash kissed her way down Chris' neck to her chest, pulling at the buttons on her shirt. "Let me touch you."

"Touch me everywhere," Chris responded. Chris moved her hands between them, pulling at Ash's belt and then the button on her pants.

Ash kept herself raised up, knowing exactly what Chris was after and willing to give everything to her. Soon Chris had her hand in Ash's pants, the gentle slide of fingers against her slit. This felt amazing. Ash shivered in anticipation of what she knew was going to come, but Chris stopped. She removed her hand and pulled at Ash's shirt.

Removing the shirt, Ash dumped the rest of her clothes onto the floor while Chris watched. When she was done, she put her hands on her hips and eyed Chris seriously. "I don't think it's quite fair that you're completely dressed and I'm not. Join the fun, Chris."

"All right." Chris stood up.

Ash watched voraciously as Chris undressed in probably the most practical manner that she could. Ash loved it. This was exactly who Chris was, straight and to the point, blunt and beautiful. She shoved her crumpled clothes with her toe, moving them to the pile that Ash had made with hers. Chuckling lightly, Ash stepped forward and wrapped her arms around Chris' body, tugging her in close.

She wanted nothing more than to be close to this woman as often as she possibly could. And Ash was going to take every opportunity that was present to her. Hopefully, she had more of those in the future. Their mouths connected, their bodies touching. Ash walked Chris backward, smoothing her fingers over her curves, teasing her nipples into hard little nubs, and directing her straight into Ash's bedroom.

They landed on the bed, and Ash crawled to cover Chris, trying to keep as much of their bodies connected as possible. She was absolutely in love. She wasn't quite sure when it happened. There wasn't a singular moment that Ash could point to and say this was it. It was more of a slow dawning of realization over the past weeks and months. Chris had become her everything, the person she relied on, someone she trusted, and someone she knew was a strength for her. Ash wished she were the same for Chris, that their relationship went both ways.

"I love you," Chris whispered again, holding on to Ash's hips. "I want to do this at the same time."

"Okay." Ash smiled. "How are we doing that?"

"Sit in between my legs." Chris guided her now. She put one leg over Ash's, and Ash's other leg over hers. Then she tugged Ash closer until their bodies were inches apart. "Perfect."

Ash kissed Chris again. She closed her eyes, feeling the wholeness that settled into her chest. This had been what she was missing, even if she couldn't name it before. She loved Mari with everything that was her, but Chris added so much more to her life. She brought light into her again. Ash squeaked when Chris pressed a hand between her legs and slid the backs of two of her fingers down her slit.

"Wasn't expecting that?" Chris asked.

"No." Her breathing came in short rasps. Ash's pussy clenched, already anticipating what was going to happen. She wanted Chris' fingers inside her, against her, pushing, thrusting, rubbing ruthlessly. This was passion in its purest sense, and she wanted all of that with the backbone of love. "Touch me."

"Yes," Chris answered. She slid one finger in, straight to her knuckle.

Ash sighed, closing her eyes and resting her forehead on Chris' shoulder as she waited for the next move, as she waited for Chris' thumb, another finger, anything. But nothing happened. She wiggled, trying to get Chris to move, but she wouldn't. Frustrated, Ash pulled back and narrowed her gaze in Chris' direction.

"I told you, Ashton. I want this to happen at the same time."

She shivered at the use of her proper name. Chris had become more prone to using her given name while they were making love, and each time a rush of wetness pooled between her legs. It was honestly probably why Chris did it. She loved the rise she got out of Ash from it.

"Touch me, Ashton." Chris' demand was clear.

Ash's heart skipped a beat as she moved her hand between Chris' legs. She found Chris' lips swollen, hot, and wet. Sliding her fingers through Chris' folds, Ash dampened her fingers before sliding one and then another into her. "Like this?"

"Yes," Chris hissed. "Just like this."

Ash locked her eyes on Chris' face, not willing to look away from her. She slowly pumped her fingers, starting a tenuous pattern that she knew would be a slow rise to Chris' orgasm. Chris stared back at her, doing exactly the same. They matched patterns. Ash's lips parted as she focused not on her own body but on Chris.

"You're sexy as hell when you're in control like this."

Chris' cheeks tinged pink, and it made it that much sexier.

"I'm serious. I love when you take control, when you demand, when you know exactly what we're doing and how we're doing it." Ash added her thumb into the mix. She started with a broad circle.

Chris moaned, the sound sweet to Ash's ears. Chris mimicked the move. She reached up with her free hand and wrapped her finger around the side of Ash's neck, her thumb pressed into her pulse point. Ash waited, hoping that Chris would drag her forward, that she would tighten her grasp, that they would kiss each other into oblivion.

She wasn't disappointed.

Pulling her forward, Chris tightened her thumb. Their mouths connected, teeth scraping against lips, tongues tangling, breathing coming in quick rasps taken in desperate attempts to keep oxygen in their lungs. Ash lost herself in the moment. This was going to live in her brain for all of eternity. She would never lose the moment when she finally became the teacher's pet.

"Chris," Ash murmured. "I'm so close."

"Don't come. Not yet."

Ash had to concentrate now. Chris wasn't as close as she was, and she needed to fix the gap. She pressed her fingers harder and sped up the swipe of her thumb. Biting her cheek, she held herself back as much as she could, but when Chris hit her clit again, she was gone. Ash gasped. Her entire body rocked forward as she clenched against Chris' fingers.

She held on while Chris dragged her orgasm out, extending it as long as possible. When she finally had her wits about her, Ash resumed her pace. Chris would come. They would do this together. Ash held onto Chris' side, keeping her close as she tried to lean back. Ash understood exactly what was going through Chris. The closeness, the angle of their bodies, the vulnerability and connection that ran between them in this moment made everything intense.

"I love you," Ash repeated. She was determined to say it every opportune moment now. She never wanted Chris to miss it. "I love you."

Chris cried out, her body shaking as she held onto Ash's arms to keep as upright as possible. Ash continued to pleasure her, to draw out Chris' orgasm just like Chris drew out hers. Eventually, Chris straightened, her body still lax with energy spent as she leaned in and gave Ash a sloppy kiss.

"I really do love you."

CHAPTER
Thirty-Five

"I BROUGHT STUFF FOR S'MORES," Chris said as soon as the door opened.

Ash stood on the other side of it, Rhubie clinging to her leg and Avonlee glaring from the couch.

Oooof. This was going to be an interesting evening.

She anticipated it would have its good moments and its bad moments. She'd never been more nervous in her life. Andry had shared about Katie's first dinner with Isla as a date rather than a teacher, which Chris had relayed to Ash. Chris expected this would go about the same, except with a little more extreme behavior, all things considered. Avonlee was much younger than Katie, and she'd proven to be a bit of a loose cannon. At least Chris understood her and already had a bit of a good reputation in her life.

Still, there was only a week before school started, and Chris really should be focused on that. Instead she was here, because Ash had asked her to come and told her this was the night. Six months they'd basically been dating, and Chris still wasn't sure she was ready for tonight. Not that she'd ever be.

"That sounds amazing!" Ash took the bag and stepped backward.

Rhubie didn't break her hold.

Chris sent her a smile, but she was afraid it was a bit more like a grimace. She had to pull her shit together. Swallowing down her own discomfort, Chris bent down to Rhubie's level and made eye contact. "This is all a bit weird, isn't it?"

Rhubie nodded.

"Yeah, I get that. Let's just let it be weird for now, okay?"

"It's more than weird!" Avonlee called from the couch. "Are you going to make me call you Mommy at school now?"

"No." Chris stood up and put her hands on her hips. She looked Avonlee over. "Are you going to give your new teacher as hard a time as you gave Ms. Dunja?"

Avonlee paled. "Who is my new teacher?"

"Wouldn't you like to know?" Chris winked. When she glanced at Ash, she couldn't tell if she'd made a massive misstep or done the right thing. Ash seemed affronted, but she clutched the bag of groceries tightly to her chest.

"Maybe we should start the s'mores."

"Sure." Chris agreed. She followed Ash out to the backyard and the small fire pit she had out there.

Chris reached for the logs and put them on, along with a starter. She'd done this so many times that she didn't even think about it, but when Rhubie wrinkled her nose and gave her an odd look, Chris realized belatedly that they didn't know how often she'd been at the house.

Right.

Chris needed to hold herself back a bit. Ash stepped next to her and ran a hand down her arm, tangling their fingers together. "It's going to take us all a bit to get used to it. Be patient."

"Patience isn't something I'm good at."

"Sure it is." Ash smirked. "Just not with yourself."

Chris huffed. Ash was getting too good at figuring her out. "Want me to continue?"

"Yes, please."

It didn't take too much longer for Chris to have the fire

going. She sat in the camping chair and talked with Rhubie for a bit while Ash was inside dealing with Avonlee.

When they came out, Ash had skewers in her hand and Avonlee was right with her. Avonlee kept sending Chris sidelong looks. Chris wished she knew what Avonlee was thinking, but it was so hard to tell with her sometimes. Instead of asking questions, she chose to observe. This was Avonlee's house, this was her family, and Chris would respect every moment of it.

"I didn't think she would be dating you," Avonlee finally said when Ash had gone back inside.

"You and me both," Chris answered. "I wouldn't have guessed this one either."

"So is this year going to be weird? Are you going to treat me differently?"

Chris shook her head slowly. "As much as I can treat you the same, I will. But I imagine I'll be seeing a lot more of you outside of school. In which case, yes, I will treat you differently."

"Why?" Avonlee glared.

"Because you're my girlfriend's daughter, and that's different than if you were just my student." Chris couldn't have been more honest. "But I'm not your parent, and I'm not going to try to be. Okay?"

Avonlee nodded. "Good."

"Nothing to worry about with that part, okay, kid?" Chris held out her hand, hoping that Avonlee would take it. When she did, Chris gave it a good squeeze and grinned. "So...do you eat your s'mores burned, bronzed, or lukewarm?"

"What?" Avonlee looked at her confused.

"How do you eat your s'mores?" Chris pressed.

Avonlee glanced toward the fire. "Burned to a crisp."

"Perfect. Me too." Chris grabbed her own skewer and started to cook her marshmallow. "Oh, I brought other things to try too, like *Reeses* and *Rollos* and some unicorn chocolate bar."

The girls went wild for the different kinds of chocolate, having to try every single one. By the end of it, Ash was begging them not to eat anymore in case they made themselves sick. Chris laughed when Rhubie snuck another one. The night had gotten more relaxed as it went on, and that was exactly what Chris had needed.

When she was ready to go, Ash stopped her at the door. "Thanks for tonight. I promise it'll get easier."

"I know," Chris answered. She squeezed Ash's fingers. "I'll see you in a few days."

"Yeah, but I'll text you tonight."

Chris' cheeks heated, because with Ash's tone, she was pretty sure she knew what that meant.

"Oh, yeah, exactly that." Ash leaned in and pressed their mouths together in a smooth kiss. "And next time you come over and the girls are here, don't hold back when you want to touch me or kiss me. They need to see that you love me."

"I'll try," Chris murmured. "It takes practice."

"One day at a time," Ash answered. "And before you know it, we'll be in our future. And we'll be kissing and touching all the time, and the girls will be grown up."

"And you'll be a best selling author again?" Chris cupped Ash's cheek, and she knew that Ash wouldn't answer that question. When Ash sputtered, Chris shook her head with a light laugh. "You're adorable, but yes, it will get easier with time."

"Of course it will. When have I ever been wrong?"

"Well, you were wrong about me bullying you."

"Shut up." Ash laughed. But she sobered almost instantly. Leaning in, Ash kissed Chris again, this time lingering in it. "But I do hope that someday the girls will get used to this. That they'll learn to love you just like I have."

"Keep on hoping, Ashton. Maybe someday it'll happen."

Thank you!

There is no way I would continue writing and publishing without wonderful readers like you. That's just a fact at this point. Your support of small indie authors like me is immeasurable and astounding. I can't thank you enough.

I never intended to write this book. That seems to be the case with a lot of my books. But so many people wanted to know more about Chris. When I was meeting the principal at my son's school when he was in kindergarten and I found out that she was almost my high school English teacher (ALMOST! She wasn't!), I knew it was the perfect plot for a story.

And the perfect complication for Chris.

Maybe Someday was born for those struggling with addiction, those who haven't quite gotten sober yet, and those who have. Those who have been affected by it. Addiction is no small matter, and it affects and infiltrates every aspect of our lives.

If you are struggling with addiction, I strongly encourage you to reach out and find support. Getting sober is hard, but it's not impossible. One day at a time.

Thank you again for reading this book.

About the Author

Adrian J. Smith has been publishing since 2013 but has been writing nearly her entire life. With a focus on women loving women fiction, AJ jumps genres from action-packed police procedurals to the seedier life of vampires and witches to sweet romances with a May-December twist. She loves writing and reading about women in the midst of the ordinariness of life.

AJ currently lives in Cheyenne, WY, although she moves often and has lived all over the United States. She loves to travel to different countries and places. She currently plays the roles of author, wife, and mother to two rambunctious youngsters, occasional handy-woman. Connect with her on Facebook, Instagram, Twitter, or TikTok.

f facebook.com/adrianjsmithbooks

🐦 twitter.com/adrianajsmith

📷 instagram.com/adrianjsmithbooks

a amazon.com/author/adrianjsmith

♪ tiktok.com/@sapphicbookmaker

Also by Adrian J. Smith

Romance

Memoir in the Making

OBlique

Love Burns

About Time

Admissible Affair

Daring Truth

Indigo: Blues (Indigo B&B #1)

Indigo: Nights (Indigo B&B #2)

Indigo: Three (Indigo B&B #3)

Indigo: Storm (Indigo B&B #4)

Indigo: Law (Indigo B&B #5)

When the Past Finds You

Don't Quit Your Daydream

Love Me At My Worst

Inside These Halls

Crime/Mystery/Thriller

For by Grace (Spirit of Grace #1)

Fallen from Grace (Spirit of Grace #2)

Grace through Redemption (Spirit of Grace #3)

Lost & Forsaken (Missing Persons #1)

Broken & Weary (Missing Persons #2)

Young & Old (Missing Persons #3)

Alone & Lonely (Missing Persons #4)

Stone's Mistake (Agent Morgan Stone #1)

Stone's Homefront (Agent Morgan Stone #2)

Urban Fantasy/Science Fiction

Forever Burn (James Matthews #1)

Dying Embers (James Matthews #2)

Ashes Fall (James Matthews #3)

Unbound (Quarter Life #1)

De-Termination (Quarter Life #2)

Release (Quarter Life #3)

Beware (Quarter Life #4)

Dead Women Don't Tell Tales (Tales of the Undead & Depraved #.5)

Thieving Women Always Lose (Tales of the Undead & Depraved #1)

Scheming Women Seek Revenge (Tales of the Undead & Depraved #2)

Broken Women Fight Back (Tales of the Undead & Depraved #3)